LETHAL CURE

KURT POPKE

Printed in Canada

For information address:
Durban House Publishing Company, Inc.
7502 Greenville Avenue, Suite 500, Dallas, Texas 75231
214.890.4050

Library of Congress Cataloging-in-Publication Data
Kurt Popke, 1962

Lethal Cure / by Kurt Popke

Library of Congress Catalog Card Number: 00-2002115647

p. cm.

ISBN 1-930754-34-5

First Edition

10 9 8 7 6 5 4 3 2 1

Visit our Web site at
http://www.durbanhouse.com

Book design by:
Strasbourg-MOOF, GmBH

Dedicated to Corinne, Catalina & Magdalena,
My dearest treasures—My reason for being

&

To my grandfather,
Theo Otto

You filled my childhood with wonder.
Our time together was far too brief.

ACKNOWLEDGMENTS

Corinne, your encouragement kept me going. Thank you for your love and support, and for all of your excellent suggestions during the creation of this book.

Thanks to Diane Vessey, Genell Csik and Fred Popke for their thoughtful critiques of the early drafts. Your efforts helped mold the story.

Thanks to John Lewis at Durban House for his guidance, and to Bob Middlemiss and Kay Garrett for their excellent editorial help.

My deepest thanks to my parents, Gus and Ingrid, for the sacrifices they made to provide a joyful and secure home. Their love and values continue to guide me.

LETHAL
CURE

Prologue

Winston Quince sat in room five of the Roanoke Community Hospital ICU, staring quietly at the mosaic of liver spots on the backs of his hands. His breathing was in sync with the sound from his wife's respirator, but he was no longer aware of it. His eyes dragged up to the monitor screen. No change. The end was taking much longer than he'd anticipated.

After a month of increasing pain and delirium, Gwen had mercifully slipped into a coma. Once the cancer had spread to her brain, her deterioration had been so rapid that Winston had assumed she would be gone within hours of losing consciousness. But three days had passed, and it seemed that she hadn't gotten any worse.

As he watched the mechanical rise and fall of her chest, Winston found himself searching for any recognizable fragment of the radiant woman he'd been married to for 36 years. The months of chemotherapy and steroids had transformed her into a puffy, unfamiliar androgyne.

Winston knew the doctors would soon be after him to remove life-support. The realization that he was hoping she would die, just so he wouldn't have to make that decision, made him feel dirty and small.

He knew he was a weak person—hell, he'd known that for years. He also knew he was responsible for Gwen's cancer, but he kept that buried in the back of his mind. Down deep, he understood that if he allowed himself to face that terrible fact, the horror of all the other deaths he was responsible for would come welling up like a pit of vipers.

As his thoughts skirted these unbearable issues, the steady beat of the cardiac monitor suddenly became erratic. Then it changed to a continuous buzz.

Winston jumped from the chair, took a half step toward Gwen, and then stopped. He looked from the flat tracing on the monitor to Gwen's bloated face, no different than it had been a few moments ago. He slowly sat down and covered his eyes, his fingertips trembling against his forehead. Two nurses rushed in, but Winston didn't look up. After a few minutes, one of them left Gwen's side. She laid a hand on his shoulder and told him that Gwen's suffering was over.

As silent tears rolled down his face, Winston knew that he would now make one last trip to the office. He would finally do what he'd been too afraid to do. Then he would go home and wait for Fowler's goons.

Winston went to Gwen's side. Through his tears, he was able to see her beauty again. He kissed her on the cheek and whispered, "For you, my love. For you."

1

The drone of a bee browsing clover woke Sara Prescott from her nap. She rolled to her side and saw that she was alone on the picnic blanket. Propping herself on an elbow, she brushed a strand of black hair from her face and scanned the empty orchard. After a few seconds, Kelly's laugh drifted up from the meadow.

Sara looked across the field to where Jake and Kelly were exploring a creek. Kelly suddenly shrieked and ran upstream, then called for her father. Jake crouched by her side as she pointed to something in the water. It was too far to make out the words, but Sara could hear the excitement in her daughter's voice. When Jake leaned forward, he rested his hand on Kelly's shoulder. It was a familiar mannerism, indicating he was giving Kelly his full attention. It brought a warm flush to Sara. Jake was such a good father. Even after one of his 36 hour shifts, he always read Kelly to sleep before getting himself to bed.

As Sara crossed the meadow, her eyes lingered on the auburn highlights in Jake's hair and the way his shirt stretched taught across the muscles in his back. The warm flush intensified, spreading lower, and Sara was glad they had arranged for a sitter to watch Kelly that night. It had been over three weeks since she and Jake had spent an evening alone together.

Jake smiled as Sara approached.

"Good nap?" he murmured.

"Mmm-hmmm." She pressed her body against his. "Apple Hill was a great idea, but why don't we head back? Maybe Amy can pick Kelly up a little sooner than…"

Strident beeping suddenly pierced the calm.

Sara tightened her grip on Jake, but he pulled back and reached for his pager.

She watched as he studied the screen, reading the bad news in his eyes. She turned away before he could speak.

The familiar fear blended with her resentment; another sleepless night alone. They lived in an area of south Sacramento called The Pocket, located between Interstate 5 and a bend in the river. The neighborhood was relatively safe, but Sara still dreaded Jake's night shifts. Two years earlier she had started taking tae kwon do. She was already a brown belt, and it helped some. At least she wasn't paging Jake every half hour when he was working.

"It's the hospital," Jake said. He came up behind her and massaged her shoulders. "I'm sorry, Sara. You know I don't have a choice. I have to go in."

She stepped away and glared at him. Kelly had come up behind them, her eyes darting from one to the other.

"Come on, Kelly," Sara said, brushing past Jake. "We have to go."

Engines roaring, the Life Flight helicopter cut through the night sky as the pilot made a fast, low approach over the hospital parking lot. Dr. Jake Prescott slammed his car door and jogged to the helipad. The flight crew was unloading the patient, the strobe landing lights distorting their movements. Grit thrown by the blade-wash peppered Jake's face as he joined the team. An ER technician was on his knees on top of the gurney, straddling the patient's waist and performing chest compressions.

"What do you got, Dr. Agon?" Jake asked, slinging his backpack over one shoulder.

"Rollover MVA with a forty minute extrication," Diane gasped, glancing at Jake as she worked the ambu-bag. Blood was spattered across her face and racquetball goggles. "I did the airway with him still in the car. It was pretty hairy, but I got it."

"Way to go. I knew you'd kick butt."

Diane smiled.

"What's the rhythm?" Jake asked.

"We lost the pulse during transport. I think he's got a belly full of blood. We've got two IV's running wide open, but no dice."

Jake laid a hand on the patient's abdomen. It was distended and tense. The portable monitor revealed a rapid cardiac tracing. Pulseless electrical activity is a common terminal rhythm when a patient has bled out rapidly. The heart is still contracting, but there isn't enough blood left in the vascular system to generate a pulse.

"Good job, Diane. You've covered all the bases. Arneal's on tonight, I bet he cracks the chest." He slowed to a walk, and the team raced ahead.

As Jake rounded the corner to the ER, he saw ambulances backed up two deep in the bays, paramedics wheeling gurneys in and out. Shaking his head, he walked through the doors—another Friday night in the city.

The ER at Sacramento General is structured around a U-shaped hall. The arms and cross bar of the U have double doorways in the center of their outside walls. These doorways open into separate rooms called Areas 1, 2 and 3. Area 1 is off the limb of the hallway closest to the ambulance bay and, except for the CPR and critical trauma patients, that is where the sickest people go. Area 2, off the cross bar of the U, is where uncomplicated cases such as twisted ankles or simple lacerations are triaged to. Area 3 is for intermediate problems, like broken bones and abdominal pain.

The resuscitation room is located in the interior of the U. A leaded curtain divides the room in half, with a gurney on either side. An intimidating collection of monitors and equipment surrounds each gurney.

The decor of the Sac Gen ER is strictly utilitarian. The walls and linoleum floor are eggshell white. Both surfaces show wear from repeated disinfecting and scrubbing.

Jake stopped in the small changing room to stow his backpack and change into scrubs. On his way out, he looked in the mirror by the door. After staring into the reflection for a few seconds, he muttered, "Here we go," and exited the locker room to find Tony.

Tony Castaic was the ER resident who had covered the day shift. By the look of things, he would be eager to turn his patients over to Jake and head home. The third year ER resident's chief responsibility was Area 1—if Tony wasn't helping with Diane's MVA, that's where he would most likely be.

Jake stuck his head through the doors to the resuscitation room. He scanned the crowd milling around Diane's patient, but Tony wasn't there. Steve Arneal was the trauma surgery resident on duty and was running the code. He had two interns working at the patient's ankles with scalpels, cutting down to the saphenous veins in order to place large bore IV lines. Arneal was elbow deep into the patient's chest. As he worked to isolate the descending aorta, Diane was squeezing the patient's heart between her hands. When she glanced at Jake, he raised his eyebrows, nodding at her patient. She shook her head.

Jake stepped out of the resuscitation room, letting the doors close behind him. He headed across the hall into Area 1. Stopping at the horseshoe shaped desk in the center of the room, he scanned the curtained-off patient treatment areas surrounding it.

Tony was hunched over the head of the gurney in room G, working on a facial laceration. He was wearing a plastic face shield, a portable light glaring over his shoulder. His blue scrubs were spattered with Rorschach patterns of dried charcoal. Used in treating overdoses, charcoal particles bind to ingested toxins in a patient's gastrointestinal tract, preventing further absorption. It tastes terrible and tends to induce projectile vomiting in the patient. Usually when you're standing right in the line of fire. As Jake approached, he could see it crusted in Tony's hair.

"Hey, bub." Jake laughed and flaked a piece of charcoal from Tony's sleeve. "It's poor form to get douched this late in your training. That's strictly intern-level stuff."

Tony looked up from his suturing and shrugged. "It's been a ball-breaker today. I guess I'm not as light on my feet as I used to be." He paused for a second and finished tying a knot. "What are you doing here anyway, cuz? Did Hatch call in sick again?"

"Yeah. Another weekend shift, too. Imagine that."

"Man, that guy's weak," Tony said. "I'm glad you're here though. They're really shaking the box tonight."

Jake was familiar with Tony's box theory—that the violence they were seeing in the ER was the direct result of urban overcrowding. The first time he'd heard Tony speak of it was back in their intern year. He and Tony belonged to the same gym and hit the weights together whenever they both had some time off. In the shower after their first workout, Jake had asked Tony about the deeply puckered scar on the right side of his back. Tony had hesitated for several seconds before explaining that he'd been shot when he was a teenager in Los Angeles.

Pointing to a tattoo on his chest, Tony had gone on to describe how he had joined a gang at the age of twelve. The tattoo consisted of the letters E L A and an offset number 13 over the word DUKES. Jake could still remember the sudden L.A.-Chicano inflection in Tony's voice and the guarded pride that had burned in his face as he talked about his gang.

When Tony was sixteen there had been trouble with a rival gang and he had caught one during a drive-by shooting. Tony's tough accent had dropped away as he told Jake that getting shot was the best thing that ever happened to him.

It had been during his stay in the pediatric ward at USC General that his life had turned around. His roommate was a thirteen-year-old boy with terminal lymphoma. Tony had maintained his hard exterior for the first several days, ignoring the kid and giving the nurses attitude. Even when the kid's doctor had come to the room with the hard news that the chemotherapy wasn't working, Tony had been able to snort at the mother's wailing.

But he had been struck by the kid's attempts to console his parents that day. It wasn't until that night when Tony heard him crying that he'd talked to him for the first time. After that, he'd kept the kid distracted during the day, playing Nintendo and harassing the nursing staff. But the nights had been rough. Their midnight talks about death made Tony realize he had been wasting his own life.

The day the kid died had been the turning point for Tony. In his young mind, he believed that if he could make something of his life, it would somehow balance out the kid's death.

The strength of that conviction had carried Tony through the difficult transition of leaving the Dukes behind, going back to high school and then on to college. During his premed years, he had taken introductory psychology and been introduced to B. F. Skinner's work.

Tony had discussed Skinner's theories in some detail while he and Jake were getting dressed that day in the gym. Skinner had shown that if you crowd enough rats into a box and apply negative stimuli, they start tearing each other apart. Tony admitted that he leaned on that concept to ease his guilt over some of the things he'd done growing up in the *Barrio*.

Over the years, Tony had referred to Skinner's theory whenever the carnage in the ER was running at a particularly high tide—like it was that night, Jake reflected as he looked around at the patients in Area 1.

"I'm telling you man, the fur's been really flying today," Tony said, turning back to his work. "Let me finish this cut while I tell you about the gems you'll be picking up. This is Glenda." He pointed his hemostat at the sterile drape covering the woman's face. The hole in the drape revealed a nasty laceration on her forehead. "Glenda, this is Dr. Prescott. He'll be taking over your case tonight."

Glenda welcomed Jake with a loud belch. The smell of stale alcohol wafted over him.

Tony smiled behind his face shield. "Glenda's tox-screen was positive for crank and booze, and she was a little uncooperative when she got here. Acute vitamin H deficiency—it took fifteen milligrams of Haldol to calm her down enough to get her into the scanner. Her head CT is normal and, except for this cut, she seems to be okay. She came in tonight on the family plan with her husband and their eight-month-old daughter."

Tony pointed at her wrist, which was handcuffed to the gurney. "When she wakes up, she goes directly to jail. Do not pass go. Seems she and her husband were debating who should get the last of the crank they got by pimping her to their dealer. Glenda was holding one of her kids at the time, and things got a little heated. She used the kid as a shield when hubby went at her with a frying pan."

Tony looked at Jake with an expression that belied his flippant speech. "The baby deflected quite a few blows before he landed this shot to win the debate. The neurosurgeons took the girl to the OR, but looking at the CAT scan I'd say she's had it."

Tony returned to his suturing. "Dad was shooting up the last of the crank when the cops got there and found Glenda and the girl on the floor. He's only got a few scrapes and bruises. We're just waiting for the cops to haul him off."

By the time Tony had told Jake about the rest of his patients, he had finished suturing the laceration. "So, what's the plan?" he asked, pulling the drape from Glenda's face. He tilted his face shield up. Jake could see that there was even a little charcoal caked in his mustache. "Are you going to stick around here next year, or take the job in Colorado?"

"Colorado. We decided last week. Fort Collins seems like a nice town."

Jake didn't mention that Sara had been the one eager to leave Sacramento. Having grown up in a small, exclusive suburb of San Jose, she didn't want to raise their daughter in the city. She had been lobbying for Jake to turn down the faculty position he'd been offered at Sac Gen.

"Wow. You're not actually leaving this place, are you cuz?" Tony joked, gesturing at the crowded room. "How can you abandon all of these unfortunate souls?"

"Yeah, right. Look who's talking," Jake smiled. "You're the one going to Beverly Hills. Emergency doctor to the stars. You'll be bored stiff down there. The only chest trauma you're going to see will be ruptured implants."

"Right. Twenty-eight more days up in the SICU, and then it'll be nothing but prom night pimples and sunlamp burns for me." Tony laughed. Truth was, Tony had accepted a position at USC back in East L.A. It would be like working in a war zone, but returning to work in the *Barrio* was why he had become a doctor in the first place.

"It's hard to believe we're almost done," Tony said. He pulled the face shield from his head. "But we're not going anywhere until we finish our research projects. I finally collected all of my data. Now I've just got to crunch the numbers and write it up. How about you? Have you proven that water's wet yet?"

Jake let the dig slide. Tony had been giving him a hard time about his research project ever since he found out that Jake was simply cataloguing the health risks of smoking.

"I've completed the meta-analysis of all the relevant journal articles, and I finally got an e-mail response from one of the tobacco companies' research departments. It took forever to download, so it must be more than just the standard blow-off letter. I brought my laptop in, hoping I'd get a chance to work on it tonight." He looked around the crowded room. "But that doesn't seem likely."

"Nope." Tony smiled, handing the trauma code pager to Jake. "I'm outta here. Have fun." He dropped the face shield in the bedside trashcan and headed for the door, removing his gloves. After a few steps, he half-turned and looped the wadded-up rubber gloves over his head with a perfect hook shot into the can. He signaled two points and walked out.

Jake went to the main hall to find the triage nurse. Carol was at her post just outside the resuscitation room, taking a telephone report from an inbound ambulance crew. About forty-five years old, she had a new hairdo almost every week. The current one was a tight, metallic fuchsia perm. She wore her scrub pants backwards, so the pockets—which were always stuffed with colored pens— were in the front. Shouldering the phone to her ear, she jotted notes on the dry-erase board covering the wall; 16 Y/O M, SW TO R ARM, VSS.

After hanging up, Carol stepped back to look at the rest of the board. The spaces representing beds in the three different areas of the ER were filled with patient names. They were written in a garish combination of colors. No one else understood her color code, but she was the most efficient triage nurse on staff.

"Where am I going to put this guy with the stab wound to the arm?" she asked, glancing at Jake. "Area One is full. We're doubled up in Two." She glanced at the empty wheelchair next to her station. "I guess I'll watch him here until the hot appendix in 3E goes up to the OR."

She turned her attention back to the board. "The medicine teams are really dragging their cans tonight. They've got six patients taking up beds down here that are just waiting for admission orders." She pointed to names on the board with green X's in the admit column, her tight curls dancing angrily. "How are we supposed to move patients if we're tying up nurses with…"

The ambulance phone rang.

Pulling the black pen from her pocket, she grabbed the phone. "Sac General. What'cha got?"

Jake read along as Carol wrote; 54 Y/O F, HEAD LAC, +ETOH, VSS.

"We'll see you in five."

"Anything serious on the way?" Jake asked. "Or should I start at the top of the stack?"

"Just the stab wound and a drunk with a scalp laceration." She gestured at the charts on the counter in front of her.

They were for patients who had been put into rooms, but were still waiting for a physician to evaluate them. "Be my guest."

Taking the top chart from the stack, Jake read the name and chief complaint. B. GRIST. LEFT SHOULDER PAIN. He glanced at the board, wrote his initials behind Grist's name and headed down the hall.

Jake had just finished reducing Mr. Grist's dislocated shoulder when his code pager went off. The LED display read 911-5, which meant a critical trauma would be arriving in five minutes. Jake hurried back to Carol's station. She had written the pertinent information on the board; 35 Y/O M, GSW TO HEAD, CPR.

Jake entered the resuscitation room and was donning his protective gear when Steve Arneal arrived. Steve stopped to get the full report from Carol before entering the room to address the group of residents, nurses and ER techs. "We've got a gunshot wound to the head coming in. According to the wife, this guy heard a noise on his porch, went out to investigate and found some punks ripping off his son's bike. When he grabbed the bike, one of them pulled out a gun and shot him point-blank. He was pulseless and apneic when the medics arrived. They would've pronounced him at the scene, but his wife and kids were right there."

Steve glanced at Jake. "Why don't you just confirm tube placement. If the tube's good and he's asystolic, we'll call it."

When the paramedics wheeled the patient in, Steve told them to hold CPR as he felt for a carotid pulse. Shaking his head, he checked the monitor. Flat-line. He looked at Jake.

Using the laryngoscope, Jake saw that the endotracheal tube the medics had placed passed between the vocal cords. He paused for a few seconds. The trivial appearance of small caliber bullet wounds still amazed him. This victim was only a few years older than he was. The small blue wound at his left temple looked insignificant. It shouldn't have been able to kill him. There was no blood, no TV gore. Somehow it would be easier to comprehend if there had been. Death too, should imitate art. A woman was widowed and children made fatherless by nothing more than a dusky spot on the side of this man's head.

"Jake?" Steve asked.

"Yeah. Tube's good."

"All right," Steve said, glancing at the clock. "Pronounced at 21:18."

A sense of foreboding weighed on Jake as he removed his gloves. The first code of the night often set the tone for the rest of the shift.

Jake had just stepped up to the cash register line with his food when his pager went off. The display read 911-2.

"Crap," he muttered, setting his tray down on a counter. As he dashed from the cafeteria, he glanced at the clock. It was 1:50. The cafeteria closed at 2:00 am. He wouldn't be eating tonight, not unless it was another DOA.

Running up the stairs to the ER, Jake joined the rest of the team in the resuscitation room. Bright lights glared off stainless steel Mayo stands and instruments. Stark white sheets were stretched taut over the two gurneys. As the trauma team put on their protective gear, Carol hung up the phone and approached the group.

"Well gang," Carol said, "we've got a double-header coming in. They should be at our back door any second. It's a home invasion. There's one male in his early thirties with chest trauma, open right tibia fracture and a facial laceration. He's short of breath, but vital signs are otherwise stable. The medics are starting a second IV." Carol glanced at her note pad. "The other one's a female, mid-to-late twenties, with a gunshot wound to the abdomen. Pulse one-thirty, blood pressure of eighty by palpation. She's intubated. Medics are working on an IV."

Jake glanced at Arneal as they heard the beeping of the first rig backing up in the ambulance bay. "What do you say, *Jefe*? How do you want to run this?"

"You take the guy with the chest, I'll take the GSW." Steve grabbed the thoracotomy pack and ripped it open. "Sounds like she'll need the OR."

Steve Arneal turned to the rest of the team. He pointed at two of the surgery interns. "Carlos and Sheri, you help Jake. The rest of you are with me. Carol, call upstairs and get six units of O-negative down here STAT. Jim, Scott—we're going to need bilateral cut-downs on this lady."

Jake, Carlos and Sheri joined the two nurses on the other side of the curtain setting up for the code. Jake opened the airway box. It contained multiple endotracheal tubes, laryngoscopes and drugs used for crash intubations. He checked the laryngoscope light and removed a pre-loaded syringe of Succinylcholine and one of Versed, dropping them into the breast pocket of his scrubs. He looked at Sheri as he turned on the suction unit mounted on the wall at the head of the bed. "I know Carlos has done at least three chest tubes," he said. "How about you?"

"I helped with one last night," she said, hanging an IV bag on one of the hooks dangling from the ceiling. "I've only been on trauma for a week."

"Well, batter up," Jake said. "This guy's probably going to need one." He looked at Carlos, who had put a tourniquet, a 20 cc syringe and a set of blood specimen tubes on the small Mayo stand next to the gurney. "Carlos, why don't you strip him and stick him. Let's draw the full rainbow and get routine trauma labs for now."

"You got it." Carlos pulled his trauma scissors from the waistband of his scrubs, spun them by their handle around his finger and jammed them back behind his waistband.

Sheri was opening the chest tube pack as the paramedics wheeled the patient in. One of the medics was lying across the struggling patient's chest, pinning him to the gurney. Carol directed them toward Jake's team.

"What do you got?" Jake asked, as the medics lifted the backboard the patient was strapped to and transferred him to the hospital gurney. The patient lunged against his restraints, knocking the oxygen mask from his face as he tried to sit up. His left eye was wild and white with fear, his face covered with blood. A deep cut ran down his cheek from the ragged hole where his right eye used to be, splitting his lips. As he struggled, his breath came out in rasping sprays of blood. When they moved him onto the bed, the medic jumped back on his chest, forcing him down.

"This guy went ape-shit just as we were pulling up to your door," the medic gasped, turning his face away from the spattering blood. "The lady he attacked kicked the shit out of him. Knocked him off a second floor landing…"

"What?" Jake exclaimed, a vague anxiety grabbing at his gut.

"Yeah, she busted his leg and a bunch of ribs. We'd just started his IV when he lost his breath sounds on the right. As we were getting ready to needle his chest, he went ballistic."

Jake lowered his face shield and stuck his gloved finger through the hole in the front of the stiff collar that immobilized the patient's neck. The skin was slippery with blood as he felt for the trachea. His attention suddenly focused entirely on his patient. The trachea was displaced to the left.

One of the fractured ribs must have pierced the right lung. With each breath the patient took, air was forced out of the hole in the lung, entering the pleural space between the lung and the chest wall. As air collected in the pleural space, the pressure compressed his right lung, pushing the chest contents toward the left. Jake knew it was only a matter of seconds before the large veins that returned blood to the heart would collapse.

"He's got a tension pneumothorax. Let's put him down." Jake repositioned the oxygen mask over the patient's face and glanced at the medic. "As soon as he's paralyzed, jump off and pull his right arm over his head."

Jake looked at Sheri. She was standing next to the open thoracostomy tray, her gloved hands held up in front of her chest. Her eyes were jerking back and forth from the patient to her tray.

"Okay, Sheri. As soon as we get the arm out of the way, vent his chest." Sheri nodded, picking up the scalpel.

Jake pulled the syringes from his pocket and handed them to one of the nurses. "Okay, Grant. Sedate him with four milligrams of Versed, then push the hundred and twenty of Succinylcholine."

Jake grabbed an endotracheal tube and the laryngoscope.

Carlos had already cut away the patient's pants and was sticking a needle into his left groin, drawing blood from the large femoral vein. The patient's right leg was grossly deformed at mid-shin level, a jagged fragment of bone protruding from the skin.

The other nurse, Vicky, finished hooking the patient up to the monitors and began to call out his vital signs. "Pulse is one twenty-six and thready. Blood pressure is ninety over forty-five. Respirations, thirty-six." She taped the pulse oximetery probe to the patient's finger. It measured the degree of oxygen saturation of the blood in the capillaries of the fingertip. The LED display on the monitor read 88%. Vicky moved to the head of the bed and increased the oxygen flow. The oxygen saturation climbed to the mid-nineties as Grant finished injecting the Succinylcholine.

Jake looked at Sheri. She was still holding the scalpel, but now had a syringe in her other hand.

"Skip the lidocaine," Jake said, pointing at the syringe. "Cut him as soon as he stops thrashing around. You've got to get into the chest before we bag him." Once they started forcing air into the patient's lungs with the ambu-bag, the pressure in his pleural space would increase dramatically.

From the other side of the curtain, Arneal was barking out orders to his team. A few seconds later, the Succinylcholine took effect and Jake's patient stopped struggling. Jake pulled the oxygen mask from the patient's face and stuck the laryngoscope into his mouth. At the same time, the paramedic got off the patient's chest and pulled the right arm away from his body.

Carlos was ready with his scissors. With one long cut, he split the blood soaked T-shirt. Sheri poured Betadine over the chest and felt for a rib.

Jake searched for the vocal cords with the laryngoscope, but blood obscured his view. He grabbed the suction catheter and stuck it into the patient's mouth. Even when the blood was finally cleared from the throat, he still couldn't identify the vocal cords. The anatomy was too distorted.

You've got time, Jake told himself. Although it seemed much longer, he knew only a few seconds had passed since the patient had stopped breathing. He had at least another twenty seconds to get the tube in. He wondered if the other team members could see his hand shake as he forced the patient's jaw open wider with the laryngoscope.

Vicky glanced at the monitor. "His saturation's ninety-six percent," she said reassuringly. She put her fingers through the hole in the front of the cervical collar. "I'll try moving the trachea a little. Does that help?"

Jake repositioned the laryngoscope even further to the left and finally saw the vocal cords. "Yeah. Thanks."

Although he could now see the cords, he was having trouble directing the tip of the tube to the left and down. The angle was too sharp. The seconds raced by as he struggled to position the tube so it would slide between the cords. Just as he was about to pull out and give the patient a couple of breaths with the ambu-bag, he heard a loud rush of air and a startled gasp from Sheri. Suddenly the trachea was midline, and the tube slid between the cords.

Vicky connected the tube to the ambu-bag. She administered a few breaths with the bag as Jake leaned over the patient, using his stethoscope to listen for breath sounds. He heard air movement on both sides of the chest. He nodded to Vicky, "Sounds good. Go ahead and put him on the ventilator."

Vicky disconnected the ambu-bag and hooked the tubing from the ventilator to the endotracheal tube. "Standard settings?"

"Yeah. Let's give him a hundred percent O2 for now." Jake cleared his throat, trying to rid his voice of the adrenalin tremor. He looked at Sheri as he finished taping the endo-tracheal tube in place. "You saved my butt. Thanks."

He could barely make out her smile behind the blood spattered face shield. When she cut through into the pleural space, the trapped air had rushed out, spraying her with blood. Sheri kept the incision open with her finger as air hissed out with each ventilator breath. When the blood had drained from the chest, she inserted the Silastic chest tube through the hole, guiding it between the expanded lung and the inside of the chest wall. She quickly sutured the skin around the tube and wrapped it with Vaseline gauze, creating an airtight seal.

Vicky connected the free end of the chest tube to the pliable tubing of the Pleuro-Vac unit and turned on the suction. A steady rise of bubbles in the water seal indicated continued removal of air from the patient's chest. As the air leaked out of the hole in his lung, the chest tube was removing it from the pleural space.

Vicky then repeated the patient's vital signs, calling them out for Grant to record on the flow sheet. "Pulse is one-oh-five and strong. Blood pressure, one twenty-five over eighty. Oxygen saturation, ninety-nine percent." She glanced at the setting on the ventilator. "Ventilating at twenty breaths per minute."

"So," Jake asked the paramedic as he started his secondary survey of the patient. "What was that you said about the woman knocking him off the stairs?"

"Yeah," the medic said. He was leaning over a Mayo stand at the foot of the bed, filling out his run sheet. "And she's a tiny thing, too. The cops were responding to a 911 call about an intruder. When they got there, this guy was trying to drag his ass out the front door. Inside, they found where he had landed after crashing through the railing at the top of the stairs. They found the woman on the upstairs landing." The medic nodded at the lead curtain. "She'd been shot in the gut and was unconscious, but still holding a big hunting knife. They figure she slashed his face and knocked him through the railing. It's a good thing the 911 operator heard the gunshot and dispatched us directly to the scene. She was in shock when we got there."

Jake stared at the lead curtain. He tried to shake off the irrational dread the medic's story had caused. He had to focus on his own patient.

"Well, the only other obvious injuries on this guy are the right leg and the eye," Jake said, as he completed his exam. "I'll call ophtho and ortho. Grant, why don't you go ahead and order X-rays of the spine, chest, pelvis and right tib/fib. We'll keep him paralyzed with Vecuronium for now. Five milligrams."

"You bet." Grant placed the call and then began cataloging the patient's clothes and other belongings.

Jake wrote a quick note on the chart, which had been labeled Zachary Doe. He heard Steve Arneal yelling for more O-negative blood, and knew things weren't going well for his patient. He turned to join the other team working on the woman, but just then the orthopedic resident returned his call. After discussing the fracture with him, Jake looked at Grant.

"It's going to be a while before ortho can get a room in the OR. He wants us to go ahead and start antibiotics, so let's hang two grams of Ancef. We should probably give him a tetanus booster, too."

"He already got the tetanus. I'll call for the Ancef," Grant said. "Look at this, though." He handed Jake an envelope full of money. "This guy had fifteen hundred bucks in his pocket. Why would he be robbing somebody if he had that kind of cash?"

Jake didn't answer. He was staring at the address written on the back of the envelope. 4408 Rivercrest Drive. It took him several slow seconds to comprehend the fact that the address was his own.

"Hey, Doc. Are you feeling all right?"

"Sara!" Jake gasped, dropping the envelope. He ran to the other side of the room, pushing the heavy curtain out of the way.

2

Sara Prescott awoke with a start, sitting upright in bed. She wasn't sure what had awoken her, and after a few minutes she forced herself to lie back down. Rolling onto her side, her fear dissolved into irritation for being so damn jumpy. She glanced at her daughter sleeping next to her. Kelly's mouth was open slightly, the thumb of her right hand a few inches away on her Lion King blanket. Her dark hair was spread across her face, nasal congestion from a cold causing her to snore softly.

Suddenly, there was a loud crash from downstairs, followed by a muffled male voice.

A tight fear shot through Sara. After a fraction of a second, she rolled off the bed, grabbed the phone from the nightstand and dialed 911. She was wearing one of Jake's old U.C. Santa Cruz T-shirts; the one with the banana slug mascot curved around the letters on the front.

"This is Sara Prescott," she breathed into the phone when the operator picked up. "I live at 4408 Rivercrest Drive. Someone's in our home!"

"All right, Sara. We're sending a police cruiser right over. It will be there in a few minutes," the operator said. "Sara, my name is Madeline. Is anyone else home with you?"

"Yes. Kelly, my four-year-old daughter."

"Where in the house are you at right now?"

"In the bedroom," Sara whispered. She switched the receiver to her left ear and reached between the mattress and box springs, feeling for the hunting knife she kept there. "We're both in the master bedroom."

"Good, Sara. I want you to stay right there and stay on the line with me. Where is your bedroom located? I want to tell the police officers where you are."

"Upstairs. At the head of the stairs." Sara cradled the phone to her ear with her left shoulder and pulled the scabbard from the five-inch blade.

"Does your bedroom door have a lock?"

"Yes. I always lock it before I go to bed."

"Good. I want you to go to the door and make sure it's locked, then come back and tell me. Can you do that?"

"Yes."

Sara set the receiver on the bed, glancing at Kelly who was still asleep. She moved to the door in a crouch, holding the knife slightly away from her body. As she checked the door, she heard a creak from the staircase. She rushed back to the bed and grabbed the phone.

"He's coming up the stairs," she gasped.

"All right Sara. The police are almost there. Is your door locked?"

Sara saw the door handle slowly turn down, pause for a second and then turn back up.

"Sara? Is the door locked?"

Sara held her breath, nodding into the phone.

"Okay Sara, keep quiet for now. He'll move on and start looking for valuables. The police will be there in just a few minutes. Stay where you..."

A panel in the door suddenly shattered inward with a loud splintering sound. A man's boot was briefly visible before it was pulled back from the jagged hole.

Kelly sat up and looked around sleepily. "Mommy?"

Sara dropped the phone and grabbed Kelly's arm. "Get under the bed," she whispered, pulling her to the floor. She pushed her under the bed. "Stay there until I tell..."

The door crashed open, and a man in dark clothes staggered into the room. Taking a quick half step, he regained his balance after the kick. He held a long flashlight, the light reflecting briefly off the pistol in his right hand.

Kelly screamed.

The man shifted the flashlight beam onto Sara.

"Well, hey there, sweet thing," he said. He ran the beam of light up and down her body. "Peek-a-boo," he chortled, pausing between each syllable.

He quickly swung the light across the room, then back onto Sara. "Isn't the doctor in?" he sneered. "Hey, Chance," he shouted over his shoulder. "I don't think Dr. Prescott is home, but I found the missus. Pretty little thing, too. She could probably go for a little lovin' right now, seeing as she's going to be a widow soon. Afterward, I bet she'll tell us where her hubby's..."

Sara's growling scream drowned out his voice as she rushed him, delivering a jarring straight leg kick to the abdomen. His gun exploded a shot into the floor as he doubled over. Sara twisted right, driving her heel into his neck.

The man dropped his gun as he was thrown to his knees. Sara moved in. Holding the knife backhand, she flexed her arm up in front of her chest and coiled left.

As the man turned to locate her, Sara snapped right, driving the knife into his face. She felt the crunch of bone as the blade drove through the thin wall of his eye socket. She slashed it down his face as he fell to his side, screaming.

Sara stayed in close. Her mind was clear and sharp. No thoughts. Letting her body do what the years of martial arts practice had ingrained in her. She waited, poised above the man writhing on the floor. He was pressing his hand against his eye, blood streaming between his fingers. After a few seconds, he lunged to his feet. "You stinking bitch…"

Sara spun counterclockwise, driving her heel into the man's chest with a roundhouse kick. She felt his ribs crack as he staggered back into the hall. She drove two quick snap kicks to his face, knocking him across the landing to the banister.

Putting the full strength of her legs and torso into it, she drove the heel of her hand up into his chin. He crashed back through the railing.

Just as the man fell, Sara felt a blow spin her around. She didn't understand how the man could have delivered such a powerful kick as he was falling. It didn't make any sense. You just can't get that kind of force when you're off balance. She should have at least *seen* it.

Turning back to the bedroom, Sara felt a flush of nausea, confusing her even further. She'd been kicked while sparring before, but had never felt this sudden weakness. She took a step toward the shattered bedroom door and stumbled to her knees.

"Kelly?" she called weakly.

A dull pressure was building in her abdomen now, and her thoughts seemed detached and sluggish. She saw a dark figure moving down the hall toward her.

Tightening her grip on the knife, she tried to lunge to her feet, but collapsed.

She must have blacked out for a second, because suddenly a man was standing over her, his pale eyes watching her impassively for a long moment. He was wearing a dark sports coat, tan slacks and a tie. His arm hung loosely at his side, the long barrel of a pistol reaching down to his knee. A silencer.

The man took a step toward the broken railing of the landing and glanced over the edge. "Half-wit," he muttered. His blond hair was pulled back and tied in a small ponytail.

As Sara watched, he cocked his head and listened. The pain in her abdomen was so severe that it made it hard to concentrate, but then she heard it, too.

Sirens.

The man stepped over to Sara, shallow eyes studying her. He squatted by her side and cupped her chin in his hand, lifting her face toward his.

The sirens were still a long way off, but getting louder.

He cleared his throat, almost politely. "I apologize for my associate's behavior, Mrs. Prescott. It's hard to find good help these days—especially on short notice."

Sara's vision began to blur. She felt the man shake her jaw and she struggled to refocus her eyes.

"Mrs. Prescott. I do not have much time. You need to tell me where your husband…"

"Mommy," Kelly called from the bedroom.

The man looked into the bedroom for a moment, then over his shoulder in the direction of the sirens. He stood, facing the bedroom.

"No," Sara whispered. "Please. No." She tried to get up, but couldn't move. The man stepped over her and into the bedroom as Sara faded into unconsciousness, the sirens still so far away.

3

As soon as Jake pushed the curtain aside and saw the rumpled T-shirt on the ground, he knew. The yellow U.C. Santa Cruz slug was visible in the blood-splattered folds, and in a gut-dropping horror, he knew. He clung to the lead curtain as his world slipped out from under him.

The hollow sounds of Dr. Arneal's team working on the patient tortured his ears. The nurses were preparing for the short trip to the OR, loading the monitors onto the gurney. The interns transferred three units of blood from the ceiling to portable IV stands mounted on wheeled platforms.

Sara was obviously in trouble. In addition to the units of blood that were infusing, five empty bags hung from the ceiling hooks—and she was still in shock. Her blood pressure displayed on the monitor at fifty-two over twenty-six. Dr. Arneal had opened the left side of her chest and was working to isolate the descending aorta. The bullet must have clipped a major artery in her abdomen, and Arneal had to stop the bleeding as quickly as possible by blocking the flow of blood to the abdominal aorta.

Dr. Arneal grabbed a large hemostat and cross-clamped the thoracic aorta. "All right," he yelled. "Let's move! The OR team's waiting."

As they rolled the patient from the room, Jake crowded his way to the head of the gurney. Squeezing between a couple of the ER techs, he was able to see Sara's face. Her skin had the wet-clay look of hemorrhagic shock. A band of tape secured the endotracheal tube protruding from her mouth. A nasogastric tube passed into her right nostril. Strips of clear tape held her eyelids closed. The left side of her chest gapped open morbidly, her lung inflating and collapsing as the respiratory therapist breathed for her with the ambu-bag. The silver handle of the large clamp was visible beneath the lung. Her abdomen was grossly distended, the skin taut.

"Oh my God, *Sara*," Jake gasped, his knees suddenly weak. He was barely able to keep up with the gurney as they raced down the hall.

One of the ER volunteers was at the elevator, holding the door open as they approached. As the team crowded into the small space, Arneal glanced up and saw Jake trying to squeeze in behind them.

"Thanks, Jake," Steve said, holding up a bloody hand. "But we've got it."

Jake pushed his way in, knocking an IV pole over. One of the techs caught the pole and steadied the unit of blood swinging on the hook.

"Jake," Steve exclaimed. "What in the hell is wrong with...?"

"That's *Sara*," Jake said hoarsely. He pushed his way to the side of the gurney, laying a hand on her head. "This is my wife!"

Steve looked at Jake for a few seconds, then back at his patient.

It was suddenly quiet in the cramped space. The only sounds were the beeping of the cardiac monitor and the rhythmic rush of air from the ambu-bag.

It seemed to take an eternity for the elevator to climb to the second floor. As the doors crept open, the team poured out into the stark white surgical unit. They rushed toward the surgical team waiting in the hall.

"Francis Doe," Dr. Arneal said. "Isolated abdominal gunshot wound in hemorrhagic shock. She's getting her eighth unit of 0-negative blood." They transferred the gurney across the red line on the floor that separated the anteroom from the surgical area. "The aorta's been cross clamped for two minutes," he called out as the surgical team whisked her away.

As Jake started to follow them down the hall, Steve grabbed his arm. He turned, trying to pull free from Steve's grip.

"Hold on, Jake," Steve said. "You can't go in that way. Sterile precautions. Come on, we have to go through here."

"Oh Jesus, Steve. Sara."

"Come on. Through here." Steve led him into the surgeon's changing room. He grabbed two sets of scrubs and handed a pair to Jake. "Put these on," he said, removing the scrub top he was wearing.

Jake changed mechanically, his mind a blank. They pulled booties over their shoes and put surgical caps on. As they headed across the dressing room to the door marked OR, Jake's fingers fumbled with the straps of his surgical mask. They entered the surgery hall from a side door and rushed to room eight.

Sara was already inside, and Jake watched through the window as he joined Steve at the scrub sink. They had moved her onto the operating table and were quickly prepping her for surgery.

"That's Dr. Watney," Steve nodded through the glass at a tall African-American man. His gloved hands were folded in front of his chest as he waited next to a surgical tray. While the scrub nurses finished draping Sara's abdomen, Dr. Watney watched her vital signs on the anesthesiologist's monitor. The portion of his short beard visible between his mask and surgical cap was frosted with gray.

"He's one of our top trauma attendings," Steve continued, rinsing the antiseptic soap from his hands. "He can be a little rough on the staff, but for this kind of surgery you couldn't get anyone better." Steve turned the water off with the foot pedal. "All right. Let's go."

Jake took a shaky breath and followed Steve inside. He'd been in an OR many times, but suddenly it all seemed alien.

Stainless steel carts were pushed up against all available wall space. Their wire basket shelves were filled with plastic suction canisters, bags of various IV solutions and a confusion of other equipment. Three bulbous lights were suspended from the ceiling on articulated arms, glaring down on the operative field. Trays of surgical instruments and an electro-cautery unit crowded the operating table.

As they prepared for emergency surgery, the eight member OR team milled about in a bewildering choreography. One of the nurses appeared at Jake's side with a surgical gown and pulled it on over his arms. Moving behind him, she tied his gown as another nurse helped him into a pair of sterile gloves.

Steve was already gowned and gloved, and had moved up to the table. Jake finally forced himself to look at Sara. The harsh surgical lights eliminated all shadows and subtle shadings. Only the front of her bared torso was visible. It was stained yellowish-brown from the Betadine scrub and isolated by blue drapes. At Sara's shoulder level, a drape hung between two IV poles. The anesthesiologist worked quietly behind this screen, adjusting IV fluids and medications.

Jake stepped woodenly to the foot of the table as Dr. Watney held out his hand. The nurse slapped a scalpel into his palm. Dr. Watney paused briefly, the blade poised over Sara's body.

"A chance to cut is a chance to cure," he murmured. Jake flinched as, in one deft sweep, Watney made an incision from just below Sara's sternum to her pelvis. Dark blood welled from the incision, and the nursing staff quickly placed suction catheters into the wound.

Jake felt a sudden nausea. Among the confusion of thoughts and emotions racing through his mind, a small, detached portion wondered at his reaction. The sight of blood had never bothered him. It was the medium in which he worked. But this was Sara. She shouldn't be lying on a cold operating table. She should be on a picnic blanket in an apple orchard, laughing as bees browsed the blossoms overhead.

Dr. Watney looked across the table at Steve as he waited for the suction to clear the surgical field. "You brought me another hell of a mess, Dr. Arneal." He tilted his head in Jake's direction. "Who's this tag-along? You know I don't allow any damn lookiloos in my OR." He turned back to the incision and began to retract Sara's bowels from the wound, trying to expose the source of the bleeding. "Especially ones that look like they're going to faint on me."

"This is Jake Prescott, one of the ER residents," Steve said softly. Moving a loop of intestine out of the way, he nodded at Sara's torso. *"This is his wife."*

Dr. Watney glanced at Jake, then resumed exploring the abdomen. The rest of the surgical team stared at Jake for several seconds, one of the nurses resting a gloved hand on his arm. A low rushing sound buzzed in his ears, and his legs felt weak again. He reached out to support himself on one of the Mayo stands, but misjudged the movement. Surgical instruments clattered loudly to the floor. One of the OR techs grabbed him from behind, holding him up under his arms.

Dr. Watney glared at him for a second, then softened. "It looks like the bullet caught the root of her superior mesenteric artery and several loops of bowel. I'm going to need the full support of my team to take care of your wife." He looked at the technician supporting Jake and gestured at the door with his head. "Why don't you step outside? We'll be able to do our jobs better."

Jake let the OR tech lead him from the room, and sat on the bench beside the scrub sink. Resting his forearms on his knees, he let his head hang down and concentrated on breathing slowly. As he stared at the floor, Jake felt the shock fade. It retreated from a gathering, consuming rage that took him deep inside. It crystallized a hard clarity in his mind—gave him a single, driving purpose.

A bullet had ripped through Sara and their lives. A bullet fired from the gun of a stranger who had violated their home. A man whose life he had just saved. Jake lurched to his feet as the OR tech stuck his head through the doorway.

"Watney repaired the artery," the tech said. "They've taken the clamp off the aorta and it's holding. Hey," he called out, as Jake brushed past him. "They've got the bleeding stopped."

Jake tore off the cap, mask and gown as he strode down the hall. He dropped them into a trashcan by the elevators, and headed down the adjoining stairs.

Entering the ER hallway, he walked directly to the resuscitation room. Carol was busy updating the far side of the triage board as he entered the room. A medicine team was performing CPR on an elderly male in the room where Sara had been a few minutes ago. Jake walked past them to the other side of the curtain.

Except for his wife's attacker, that half of the room was empty. Jake noticed his wrist was now handcuffed to the guardrail of the gurney. A steady bubbling sound came from the Pleuro-Vac unit. A quick glance at the monitors showed that the patient's vital signs were stable.

Jake looked down at the man. A metal shield covered his right eye and his facial laceration had been sutured. Removing the tape holding the patient's other eye closed, Jake lifted the lid. He stared into the eye for several cold seconds, but saw no response. The paralytic drugs were still working. Moving to the monitors by the head of the bed, he pushed a button on the pulse oximetery unit and the display flashed: *AUDIO ALARM SUSPENDED—10 MINUTES*. He also disabled the alarms on the cardiac monitor and ventilator.

Jake slid the pliable tubing connecting the patient's chest tube to the Pleuro-Vac unit next to one of the wheels of the gurney. He hesitated for a second, but the image of Sara's violated body on the operating table flooded his mind. Kicking off the wheel lock, he held the tubing in place with his foot and rolled the gurney on top of it. The wheel compressed the tube, and Jake levered the lock back on. He glanced at the Pleuro-Vac. It was silent. The bubbles had stopped.

Without looking at his wife's assailant, he walked from the room.

Carol was on the telephone just outside the door. She hung up and ran a few steps to catch up with Jake, laying a hand on his arm.

"My goodness. They told me that was your *wife* they took upstairs," she said, her eyes wide with concern. "How is she doing?"

"They've got the bleeding stopped," Jake said, his voice surprisingly steady. He was aware that tears were running down his face, but it didn't feel like he was crying. He turned back toward the elevator.

"Jake," Carol said, squeezing his arm. "The police are here. They need to talk to you right away."

"Later," Jake said, starting to move down the hall.

He felt Carol's nails dig into his arm. Her lips were pressed tight against her teeth.

"What?"

"They couldn't find your daughter."

Jake stopped, searching Carol's face.

"Your wife told the 911 operator that Kelly was in the bedroom with her, but they couldn't find her."

"They couldn't find her?" Jake grabbed Carol's arms. "What do you *mean*, they couldn't find her?" He shook her, his brain clawing to comprehend what his heart refused to grasp. "Where are they?"

"Area 1. They were calling the OR looking for you."

As Jake ran back down the hall, Carol massaged her arms where his fingers had dug into her flesh.

Two uniformed officers and a middle-aged man in a charcoal gray suit were standing by the nurse's station. The man in the suit was hanging up the telephone as Jake rushed up to them. He was a little shorter than Jake and thick across the chest. His dark hair was close-cropped. The brown skin of his face was clean-shaven, without a trace of stubble. He studied Jake with eyes so dark it was hard to distinguish pupils from irises.

"Where's Kelly?" Jake demanded. "Did you find my daughter?"

"Dr. Prescott," one of the officers said. "Why don't you have a seat and…?"

"Did you find her!" Jake stared at the man in the suit.

The man shook his head and leaned against the desk. "I was just speaking with dispatch." His voice was soft, with a hint of an accent that Jake couldn't place. "The men at the scene have searched your house thoroughly and can not find your daughter. I am Detective Nunes, Dr. Prescott. Let me tell you what we know."

He shook Jake's hand, his eyes unwaveringly on Jake's.

"We believe that at least two people were involved in the break-in. The officers at the scene found a Sig Sauer P228 on the floor in the bedroom. The lab will be checking it for prints, but we believe that it belonged to the man here," Nunes said, nodding his chin in the direction of the resuscitation room. "There was a bullet in the floor by the gun, and only one empty cartridge. We found your wife on the upstairs landing, where it looks like she was shot by a second man."

"Second man?" Jake tried to follow what the detective was saying. He was having trouble concentrating, unable to accept that Kelly was missing.

"Two shots were fired. One into the bedroom floor, and the one that hit your wife. I spoke with a nurse involved in your wife's resuscitation. He said the X-rays showed the bullet lodged in the muscles of her back." Detective Nunes held up fingers to illustrate his point. "Two bullets. One gun, with only one empty cartridge. That means that there must have been a second gun—a second man."

Jake nodded, trying to focus. The detective's steady gaze and straightforward manner were somehow reassuring.

"We assume that the second man took your daughter," Detective Nunes continued. "We are searching the neighborhood right…"

"*Why?*" Jake asked. "Why would a thief take Kelly?"

Detective Nunes shrugged. "We're not even certain this was a burglary. Not unless the fifteen hundred dollars the suspect had on him was yours."

"What? No, we don't keep that kind of money in the house."

"Well, nothing else seems to be missing. That argues against robbery as a motive."

"Then what did they want?"

The detective paused as a nurse hastened by, clutching a clipboard. "We don't know, Dr. Prescott. We definitely have several unanswered questions. Fortunately, the nurse told us the suspect is doing well and should recover. When he regains consciousness, he should be able to tell us why they were there and where the other man may have taken your daughter…"

"What?" Detective Nunes interrupted himself, studying Jake's face. "What's wrong, Dr. Prescott?"

Jake stared at Detective Nunes for a second, then turned and ran from the room. He rushed past the team that was still working to stabilize the CPR patient. When he pushed past the curtain, he saw that he was probably too late. The man's skin was mottled, his hands a dusky blue. The Pleuro-Vac sat quietly on the floor. A heart rate of 160 was displayed on the monitor. The red light on the pulse-oximetry monitor was flashing silently, the LED display blinking: *PULSE NOT DETECTED*. The pressure within the patient's chest must have already increased to the point that the large veins returning blood to the heart were collapsing. The patient was in shock.

Jake quickly unlocked the gurney's wheels as he felt for the patient's carotid artery. He could feel a thready pulse. As he rolled the gurney off the tubing, he heard a loud, bubbling explosion of air in the Pleuro-Vac unit.

Glancing at the display on the ventilator, he saw that the patient's airway pressure was off the scale. As the trapped air rushed out through the Pleuro-Vac, the pressure decreased. The bubbles gradually slowed, and Jake could feel the carotid pulse getting stronger.

He punched the button to start the blood pressure cuff and watched the monitors. The patient's heart rate was down to 135, and the pulse-oximeter was now getting a reading. It was only 74%, but climbing steadily. The blood pressure cuff finished its cycle, the display reading 88/50. Jake moved the handcuff out of the way, feeling for a pulse in the patient's wrist. It was easy to find.

The mottling of the man's skin was starting to resolve. Jake turned to reactivate the blood pressure cuff. His hand paused for a second when he saw that Detective Nunes was standing behind him, watching.

Jake pushed the button, then stood facing the monitor, waiting for Nunes to say something. The numbers on the screen shot up as the cuff inflated, and then trended downward.

The monitor displayed the blood pressure at 114/82. Jake looked at the numbers for a long time before turning to face the detective. Nunes was standing quietly with his feet apart, his weight back on his heels. His index finger moved back and forth across his lower lip. Jake no longer found his stare reassuring.

After a long silence, Detective Nunes apparently made a decision. He pointed at the Pleuro-Vac tubing.

"It certainly was fortunate that you came back to check on your patient. It appears that he had taken an unexpected turn for the worse." Detective Nunes held Jake's gaze. "Come on," he said, turning to walk out of the resuscitation room. "Let's see if we can't find your daughter. From what the nurse told me it will be at least a day or two before we can question this guy."

4

It was seven-thirty in the morning, and Billy Ray Chance was sitting on a bed as lumpy as the porridge at Holman Pen. He was eating the meal he'd picked up from the Burger King down the street. His tie was loosened, and his coat was hanging from the suspension bar just past the bathroom. The piece of shit TV bolted to the motel wall was tuned to some local morning show, the volume cranked up to overcome outside traffic noise. His gun was on the battered nightstand, resting on a folded towel. If he had to grab for it, it wouldn't slide. Water spots stained the ceiling; the carpet was threadbare. Renuzit air fresheners were stuck to the walls to fight the musty funk that comes with rooms rented by the hour.

As far as Chance was concerned, the accommodations were perfect.

The room was located at the rear of the motel, its only window covered by dark green curtains. It faced a high cinder block wall that bordered Highway 80 as it ran through West Sacramento. The motel was on the seedier end of West Capitol Boulevard. Its occupancy rate had to be less than forty percent. Several of the rooms—including the one adjacent to Chance's—were permanently vacant, with windows broken out, or doors off their hinges. Graffiti covered the stucco walls. The crankhead manager had been easily intimidated, and Chance didn't anticipate any eavesdropping maids or unexpected visitors.

As he reached for another French fry, Chance glanced at the girl. She was lying on her side, facing away from him; her wrists bound behind her back and tied to her ankles. The gag was still in place around her head. The muffled sobs had stopped twenty minutes ago, and she wasn't thrashing around anymore—she was handling it all pretty well. Chance knew that kids were pretty tough. When he was her age, his mother had kept him in a six-foot square storage closet in their basement. He had spent the first nine years of his life in that hole before he'd been taken away and dumped into the foster care system—and he had turned out just fine.

He had a lucrative career, owned an expensive car, wore tailored clothing and was rolling in dough. Hell, they should make an after-school TV movie about his life. He was living proof that any kid, as long as they're not soft, can still make something of themselves—no matter what kind of shit life dishes out. Chance smiled at the girl. Of course, *she* wasn't going to get a chance for any of that. Fowler's instructions had been very clear. Absolute containment.

Chance finished the burger and pulled his insulin kit from the drawer in the nightstand. He removed the small, spring activated needle-plunger and one of the test strips. Placing the plunger against the tip of his ring finger, he activated it, the bite of the needle drawing a small speck of blood. Squeezing his fingertip between thumb and middle finger, he milked a drop of blood onto the test strip. At the same time, he punched the timer button on the Glucometer. When the alarm sounded, he wiped off the blood and examined the strip. The blue color was fairly dark. Chance said "two-thirty" out loud, before inserting the strip into the Glucometer.

It was a little game he played with himself—guessing his blood sugar based on the intensity of blue. Hell, after fifteen years of this shit, he'd gotten pretty good at it. Probably didn't even need the damn machine anymore. When the unit beeped, he checked the display. It read 244. He tended to run a little high whenever he was on the road.

After doing a little calculation in his head, Chance removed a disposable syringe and a vial of insulin from the kit. He drew up the appropriate dose and injected it into the skin of his abdomen. Putting the vial back in the kit, he returned it to the nightstand. He got up and tossed the syringe into the cardboard box in the corner of the room that served as a wastebasket. Chance turned down the sound on the TV, then sat on the bed. He grabbed the phone and punched in Arthur Fowler's number at Harrison.

"Fowler," the bland voice said.

"Hey Arty," Chance said. "It's Billy Ray. Things didn't go quite as well as we'd hoped."

Silence spun down the wire.

"First of all, the information I got was bogus. Prescott wasn't even home tonight." He crumpled the Burger King bag and lobbed it into the trash. "And the local talent y'all had set up for me was a joke. This clown Metzger knocked a plant off the counter right after we got inside. Then he tried to get friendly with Prescott's wife, and she beat the living shit out of him. I had to pop her before we had a chance to chat, so I couldn't find out whether or not Prescott has talked." Chance took a loud sip from the straw in his soda. "She must have called the cops as soon as Metzger dumped the plant. I had to bail before I could find the computer, so I don't know where Quince's e-mail is."

Mr. Fowler still didn't have anything to say. Chance smiled to himself. He could imagine him sitting at his desk, his lips going white as he tried to control the anger Chance's bad news must be causing. It had long been a personal challenge for Chance to elicit some kind of an emotional response from Fowler, but so far he had been unsuccessful. Chance enjoyed goading him, but he knew he had to be careful. A large portion of Chance's income came from eliminating people who had gotten on Fowler's bad side.

"The only stroke of luck we had is that I managed to grab Prescott's daughter before the cops got there. We should be able to use her to squeeze Prescott." Chance reached over to the other side of the bed and picked up the family portrait he had taken from the nightstand in the Prescott's bedroom. He studied Jake Prescott's face again as he added, "When things calm down a bit, I'll contact him to set up a meeting."

"Where is Metzger now?" Fowler asked.

"I had to leave him. The cops were crawling up my ass."

"So Metzger is now in police custody?"

"I don't think Metzger will be talking to anyone soon," Chance said. He dropped the portrait back onto the bedspread. "Prescott's wife knocked him off the upstairs landing before I shot her. And I'm pretty sure she's not going to make it. I'm going to have to find out what hospital they…"

"Let me understand this, Mr. Chance," Fowler interrupted. "What you are saying is that not only did you fail to retrieve the file, you also left two people alive who can identify you. That with the police on the way, you left a man at the scene who can tie you to our corporation. Is that what you are telling me, Mr. Chance?"

Billy Ray Chance felt a cold nausea slice his stomach. "Yes sir. I suppose that's true. I've secured the girl in a safe place, and I was headed to the hospital to tie up the loose ends as soon as I gave you a report."

"I hope that you had better results with Quince before you left Roanoke," Fowler said after an uncomfortable silence. "*He* didn't give you too much trouble, did he?"

"He didn't give me any trouble at all. It was almost like the little twitch was expecting me." Chance decided to dwell on the favorable report for a bit.

"The only thing that flustered him was when I told him I was heading out here to clean up the mess he'd made. I guess he hadn't thought that you'd be able to trace his e-mail to Prescott. Turns out he had a low pain threshold. It took only a few minutes before he told me where he kept his gun, so setting it up as a suicide was…"

"Listen to me," Fowler interrupted. "The urgency of the situation has increased significantly. Quince was more dangerous than we had initially thought. The documents he took, the ones he scanned for his e-mail file, are missing."

"I thought your boys had recovered them from his…"

"Apparently the documents locked in his file cabinet at work were copies," Fowler said. "We searched his home and office, but we've been unable to locate the originals. He must have sent them to Prescott."

"Shit."

"'Shit' indeed, Mr. Chance. Those documents would be admissible in court and could cause considerable damage. Although retrieval of the e-mail is critical, locating the original documents is of paramount importance.

"Let me be very clear about something," Fowler continued. "The information contained in those documents is extremely sensitive. Top management is very concerned and is watching our progress closely. We can't afford any more errors. Do you understand my meaning, Mr. Chance?"

"Yes, sir. Yes, Mr. Fowler."

"If you cannot control the situation, I will be forced to send someone else to deal with the problem. And with you."

The line went dead.

Chance fumbled the receiver as he replaced it in the cradle. His mouth was dry, and he was disgusted to realize that there were beads of sweat on his forehead.

Yes, sir. Yes, Mr. Fowler, sir.

How pathetic.

He never sucked ass like that. Not even when he was a kid and his foster parents routinely beat the crap out of him. Billy Ray had never shown fear to anybody. He had even kept his nerve with that rat bastard guard who'd raped him during his first stay at Juvie. He hadn't shown that fat prick any fear, not even when he'd gone back to settle the score a few weeks after he had been released.

Chance had been just sixteen at the time, and he'd had to steal a car so he could follow the guard home. Although Chance had only killed a few cats and a dog prior to that, he never let that fat bastard know how scared he was as he slashed his throat for him. He had kept the hollow nausea under control, even managing a laugh as he cut that pig's pecker off and crammed it in his mouth before he died.

And now here he was practically pissing his pants because of a threat made by some dried up old fart over the phone. But, even as Chance chastised himself, he understood that his reaction was based on his knowledge of Arthur Fowler. He was the most lethal person Chance had ever met. He was cold and methodical about his duties as head of security for Harrison. In the years Chance had worked for him, Fowler had never shown a second's hesitation in eliminating any threat to the corporation's security. Chance would have to get things fixed, and quick. He stared at the girl on the bed, thinking it through.

Making a move on Metzger or Mrs. Prescott so soon would be too dangerous—shit, the cops would be crawling out of the woodwork at this point. But he could at least find out what hospital they had been taken to. And if they were still alive. If he was careful, he might even be able to case the place.

It was still dark outside as Detective Nunes eased his Ford Taurus out of the hospital parking lot. He headed north on the short stretch of Stockton Boulevard to the eastbound Interstate-80 onramp. The traffic was light in the early morning hours. Only a few cars passed them as Detective Nunes stayed in the center lane, the speedometer at exactly 55 mph.

"We think we've located the car the suspect in the ER was driving," Nunes said to Jake, his eyes fixed on the road. "It was parked on the street a few houses down from your place. The officers already questioned your neighbors, and no one recognized it. The woman who lives in the house where it was parked said it wasn't there at midnight when she let her cat in."

As they approached the I-5 interchange, Nunes moved into the right-hand lane. "When I spoke with Detective Case at the scene, they had called in the plates and were just about to gain access to the vehicle. Hopefully they'll have identified the owner by the time we arrive, and we can put a name to the man in your ER."

As they drove past Southside Park, Jake looked at the Chinese pistache trees bordering the pond. It was too dark to make out their color, but he had enjoyed their rich, jade hue on his way to work just a few hours ago. He found himself searching their shadowy forms for a small sense of familiarity—for some sort of connection to a world that had become alien to him. Jake tried to pay attention to what Detective Nunes was saying, but his mind kept hunting for places that Kelly might be hiding.

"Apparently, there was another car parked behind the vehicle they are searching," Nunes continued. "Detective Case found where the water in the gutter had flowed around another set of tires. We assume the second man had his own car at the scene. Unfortunately, no one in the neighborhood was awake to see it."

"Maybe she's out in the back yard," Jake said abruptly, turning to face Nunes. "Did they look out back?"

"It's standard procedure to search the surrounding area." Nunes slowed the sedan as they merged onto the southbound I-5 interchange. They remained in the right-hand lane for the short stretch on Interstate-5 until they exited at 43rd Avenue. The street was deserted and they caught all of the green lights to Rivercrest Drive.

Jake's hand moved to the door handle as they approached his home. There was a dark sedan in his driveway, and a couple of black and whites were parked on the street in front of his house. Otherwise, the neighborhood looked as peaceful as always.

As Nunes was setting the hand brake, Jake jumped out and ran up the front steps. An officer stepped in his way as Jake burst through the door, placing a firm hand on Jake's chest.

"Hold it," the officer said. "We're investigating a…"

He glanced past Jake and saw Detective Nunes.

"Oh, Dr. Prescott. Come on in," the officer said, as Jake pushed past. "Just try to stay out of CSI's way."

"Kelly," Jake yelled, as he rushed up the stairs. He ran past two men crouched on the floor outside the master bedroom, and into Kelly's room. Her closet door was open,

the hangers crowded with clothes. A red sweater, several socks and a pair of underwear lay on the floor next to a jumble of shoes. Jake glanced around quickly, looking for possible hiding places. The room felt barren. The platform bed was empty, the covers pulled up tight with Kelly's collection of stuffed toys on top.

Jake yelled for her again as he left her room. He slowed as he approached the shattered door to the master bedroom. The men working around a small dark stain on the carpet were wearing rubber gloves and taking samples with swabs. Another man was dusting a fine white powder on the broken railing. Detective Nunes was standing at the head of the stairs.

Inside the master bedroom, the walk-in closet was open and the clothes had been pulled from the oversized hamper next to Sara's shoe rack. Jake glanced inside the empty hamper, then pushed several of Sara's long dresses and overcoats aside. Nothing.

"We've searched the house thoroughly," Nunes said from the closet doorway. "I'm afraid Kelly is not here."

Jake stepped past him back into the bedroom. The large cabinet in the lower part of the television armoire was open, the box of videotapes and portable CD player pushed to one side. The bed was unmade. Jake walked over and pulled back the covers. Empty.

Kneeling next to the bed, he looked underneath. His heart skipped a beat when he saw a dark form, but even as he reached for it, he knew it was too small. He grabbed the soft material and pulled it from under the bed.

It was Kelly's blanket. Jake slowly sat down, staring at the images of Mufasa and Sarabi with young Simba.

She was gone.

He felt sick and numb as he looked around. This room, where he and Sara had slept and made love for the past two and a half years, was suddenly foreign to him. This was where Sara had battled with an intruder just a few hours ago. Where she had been shot trying to protect Kelly. This was where his terrified daughter had been dragged from under the bed and taken away.

Rage stalked him as he struggled to understand why his family had been attacked. He suddenly realized that Detective Nunes was squatting next to him, resting a hand on his shoulder.

Jake searched his face.

"Someone took her," Jake said. "She never goes anywhere without this blanket."

Nunes helped Jake up. "Let's see what we can do to find her."

They went back downstairs and into the kitchen. A man in gray slacks was sitting at the table. He had made a fresh pot of coffee, and there were three steaming mugs on the table.

Nunes sat down and picked up Jake's Star Trek mug. His brother-in-law had given it to him for Christmas. The mug featured heat sensitive images of Captain Kirk, Dr. McCoy and Spock on a transporter pad. Since the mug was full of hot coffee, the transporter pad was empty. The away team had beamed out.

Nunes gestured with the mug at the other man. "Jake, this is Detective Case. He's been working the scene since we got the call. I asked him to fill you in on what he's discovered so far."

"Well, I'm afraid it's not much," Detective Case said. When he spoke, his thin lips moved like he was a bad actor in a silent movie. He was younger than Detective Nunes—Jake placed him in his mid-thirties. He had sandy hair and a wispy mustache. His clothes fit him loosely, and his narrow nose was crooked.

Jake sat down, holding Kelly's blanket in his lap. He stared at it as Case continued.

"As far as we can tell, at least two guys were involved. They probably arrived in separate cars. We've identified the car down the street as belonging to a Robert Metzger. Does that name mean anything to you?"

Jake thought for a few seconds, then shook his head without looking up. She loved this blanket.

"He's had several arrests for B and E's, drug charges and one rape that never went to trial. Used to be an independent operator, but our boys downtown think that he must have made some contacts during his last stint in prison. Since he got out, he's been suspected of being involved in more organized criminal activities. His description fits the man you took care of in the ER. Did he look familiar to you?"

Jake shook his head again.

"This may have been a simple burglary that went sour, but we don't think so. As far as we can tell, nothing of any value was taken."

Jake glared at Case.

"Sorry. What I mean is, that except for your *daughter*, nothing else seems to have been taken." Case picked up his mug and took a sip. "At this point we have to assume that kidnapping your daughter was the reason for the break-in. Has anybody made any threats against you or your family? Is there anyone you can think of who would take your girl?"

"No."

Detective Case looked at Detective Nunes. Jake waited.

"Pardon us," Nunes said, "but we are unfamiliar with your social situation." He set his coffee down. Kirk, Bones and Spock had partially rematerialized. "The majority of child abductions are committed by estranged parents or someone that is known by the family. We need to rule out the possibility that somebody else might feel that Kelly belongs with them."

"I'm sorry. I'm not sure what..."

"Is Sara Kelly's natural mother?" Detective Case asked. "Is there another woman with a biological connection to your daughter?"

"Kelly is our daughter. Sara's and mine."

"Can you think of anyone else who might want to harm your wife and take your daughter?" Detective Case asked. "A jilted lover of yours perhaps? You know, a *Fatal Attraction* thing?"

"Are you *serious*?" Jake exclaimed, thrusting forward in his chair. "Why are you wasting time asking me this kind of crap? We should be *doing* something. My wife's been shot. My daughter's been kidnapped. And we're sitting around having a damn *tea party*!"

The room was quiet as Jake glared at Case. A faint smile flickered across the detective's lips. Jake's face reddened as he realized that Case was pleased to have caused his outburst.

"Jake," Detective Nunes said quietly, "we don't mean to be insensitive, but experience has taught us that this type of crime frequently has a domestic motive. It makes sense for us to rule that out first. Okay?"

Jake kept staring at Case.

"I suppose. But there's nothing like that going on. We lead ordinary, boring lives. I can't think of anyone who would have any reason to hurt us. Nobody has made any threats or even...Wait a second," Jake said, looking at Detective Nunes. "There *was* a prisoner from Folsom that I saw in the ER about two months ago who said he was going to kill me. He was pissed when I sent him back to jail."

Nunes' eyebrows went up.

"We see these guys every once in a while who fake an injury in order to spend some time in the hospital—I guess it beats prison. Well, this guy was brought in when the guards found him on the floor in his cell. He claimed to be paralyzed after falling off his bunk. Even after X-rays and an MRI showed no injury, he still said he couldn't feel his legs, and wouldn't move them. I finally had one of our cuter nurses go talk to him, and while he was distracted, I pricked his toe with a needle. He yelled and jerked his foot back. I told him he had made a miraculous recovery and could go back to Folsom. He went ballistic, screaming how he was going to kill me, but he's supposed to have another five or ten years to serve."

"Do you recall his name?" Case asked. He pulled a pen and a small note pad from his breast pocket. "We should check him out to see if he has any connection to Metzger. Maybe they did time together or something."

"No, but I'm pretty sure he came in sometime in early March."

"All right." Case made a note on his pad. "Folsom should be able to tell us who they sent to the hospital in March. Can you think of anyone else?"

Jake leaned back in his chair and gripped Kelly's blanket. He was suddenly tired. He wanted to get out of his scrubs and into a hot shower. "No."

"Well, we should be able to get more information from Metzger as soon as he's able to talk," Nunes said. He drained the last of his coffee. The Star Trek crew had returned safely from their mission. "Why don't you take another look around to see if anything is missing that we might have overlooked? Then we should head to the station and look up Metzger's file. Check his KA's."

"Known associates," Nunes responded to Jake's puzzled look. "See if you recognize any of them."

5

It only took a phone call to the emergency services dispatcher for Billy Ray Chance to find out that Sacramento General was the regional trauma center. Then he shaved and showered, and put on his gray Edmonds suit. Before leaving for the hospital, he let the kid use the can, tied her back up and turned the television up loud.

Once he arrived at Sacramento General, finding out what rooms Metzger and Sara Prescott were in was a breeze. The old bat working the information desk told him that both patients were in the SICU on the sixth floor. Chance took the elevator up, but the unit was closed to general visitors. He hung around in the waiting area outside the security doors. Staff members got in by using the magnetic strip on their name badges to trip the lock. Visitors had to use the intercom to identify themselves and which patient they were there to see.

One group announced that they wanted to visit a patient named Farno. When they came out, one of the ladies kept blubbering that the doctors were wrong; that they didn't know how much of a fighter her husband was. She assured the rest of the group that he would be coming out of his coma any time now.

Chance waited a while, then pushed the button on the intercom and said that he was Mr. Farno's cousin. The voice over the intercom told him to come in, and the door buzzed, signaling that the lock had been released.

The entrance to the SICU was at the top of a wide, L-shaped hallway. A white Formica desk ran the length of the inside of the L. The outside walls of the hallway were floor to ceiling glass, partitioned into several rooms. Billy Ray went to the nurse's station and glanced at the dry-erase board on the wall behind the desk. Eight rows were on the board labeled A through H, one for each room. The patients' names were listed in the first column, followed by the names of the nurse and doctor caring for each patient, and then several columns of information that Chance did not understand. He noted that Sara Prescott was in room E, and that Z. Doe/Metzger was written in the space for room H. The clerk behind the desk turned away from her computer screen to inform him that Mr. Farno was in room F. She pointed to the first room past the corner of the L. Chance thanked her and walked down the hall.

As he entered room F, Chance saw two cops sitting outside the door at the end of the hall. That would be Metzger's room. A nurse was at the head of Farno's bed fiddling with a plastic tube that was running into his mouth. His head was heavily bandaged and dark bruises surrounded both eyes. Chance positioned himself at the patient's bedside so he could look through the glass wall into the adjoining room where Sara Prescott was.

He spoke to the nurse briefly, feigning interest in the patient's condition as he studied the layout of the ward. After a few minutes, he left the SICU. He took the elevator back to the ground floor and was exiting through the main lobby when a young man entering the front door caught his attention. He was slightly less than six feet tall, had wavy, auburn hair and a stubble of beard. He was wearing a pair of Levi's and a T-shirt. He looked a hell of a lot like the man in the Prescott family photo.

Leaning against a brick pillar, Chance pretended to examine the flowers in a planter. The man nodded at the volunteer at the information desk, then walked toward Chance, heading for the elevators.

Chance waited as the man helped some old coot in a wheelchair get off the elevator before he made his move. The doors started closing as Chance approached, but the man pushed a button, opening the doors.

When they reached the sixth floor, Chance exited the elevator and walked down the hall slowly enough for the man to pass him. As the man reached the doors to the SICU, Chance sat in the same chair he had waited in before. He was close enough to hear the man speak into the intercom.

"Jake Prescott to see my wife."

Chance leaned back in his chair and smiled. He took a slow, deep breath as Jake entered the SICU.

It was almost ten o'clock when Detective Nunes dropped Jake off at the main entrance to the hospital. He entered the lobby and nodded at the volunteer at the information desk as he walked to the main elevator. The doors were just closing when a man in a well-tailored suit approached the elevator. Jake hit the button to open the doors.

"Thank you kindly, sir," the man said as he stepped in. He studied Jake's face with yellowish brown eyes that were as flat as agar in a Petri dish.

Jake made a dismissive gesture with his hand. The man turned away and faced the doors as they closed. His blond hair was pulled back into a small ponytail that hung down to his collar. He pushed the button for the sixth floor. A wide gold band with a rectangular jade stone was on his little finger.

When the elevator arrived on the sixth floor, Jake entered the SICU, pausing just inside the door. He had spent a month on an SICU rotation during his intern year, and again during the early part of the third year. He knew what to expect during the immediate post-op period of a critical trauma case. This was not going to be easy.

Monitors, IV pumps and a ventilator crowded Sara's bed. She was unconscious and intubated. An arterial line in her left wrist was connected to the monitor hanging from the wall over the head of her bed. Her blood pressure was 126/82. A central line was in her left subclavian artery, piercing the skin just below the collarbone. The nasogastric tube that snaked from Sara's nostril was attached to the vacuum port in the wall below the monitor. The only sounds in the room were the mechanical hiss of the ventilator and the steady beep from the cardiac monitor. A bag half-filled with urine hung from the foot of the bed, its tubing disappearing under the sheets. On a stand next to the bed, an IV pump was carefully regulating a dopamine drip to fine tune Sara's blood pressure. Jake glanced at the LED display on the unit and saw that it was set at a low dose.

It was a scene Jake had thought he was comfortable with. Intellectually, he knew her numbers all looked good—great, in fact—for someone who had just been through major surgery. Emotionally, however, seeing Sara so dependent on life-support overwhelmed him. The rushing dizziness he'd felt in the OR returned. He dragged one of the chairs next to her bed and sat down, reaching between the IV lines and monitors to lay his hand on hers. He leaned forward and whispered in Sara's ear for a few moments, then rested his forehead lightly against the side of her head. He sat with his eyes closed for several minutes, and then felt a touch on his shoulder.

A nurse was standing at his side. He straightened in his chair, wiping his eyes. He recognized her from his last rotation through the SICU, but didn't recall her name.

"Dr. Prescott," she said, squeezing his shoulder. "Sara is doing great. We've titrated the dopamine down, and are about ready to shut it off completely. Dr. Watney was here about half an hour ago, and he's very pleased with how she's doing." The nurse smiled warmly. "He asked me to call him when you got here so he could talk to you. He's on his way up."

Jake nodded.

When Dr. Watney arrived, he and Jake went out to the nurse's station. He was still in surgical scrubs and cap, his facemask pulled down and hanging loosely under his beard. Deep wrinkles creased his forehead. He poured himself a cup of coffee and held the pot up at Jake. Jake shook his head, and Dr. Watney put it back on the hot pad.

"Jake, your wife is doing remarkably well." He opened a packet of sugar and dumped it into his Styrofoam cup. "She lost quite a bit of blood, but we were able to get the bleeding controlled quickly, and her aorta was only cross-clamped for twenty minutes or so. Her urine output is normal and her serum creatinine is fine, so there doesn't appear to be any kidney damage from the interruption of blood flow." He took a tongue blade from a cup and stirred his coffee.

"As you know, preserved kidney function is usually a good indication that the blood flow wasn't interrupted long enough to damage the spinal cord." He tapped the tongue blade on the rim of his cup before flipping it into the waste can. "We'll see how she does when she wakes up."

Dr. Watney sat on the edge of the desktop and went over the surgery and Sara's prognosis in full detail. As Jake listened, he noticed that two police officers were down the hall, sitting in a couple of chairs in front of room H. He glanced at the patient board on the wall behind Dr. Watney and saw that Z. DOE/METZGER was in that room.

"Sara's had a bad injury, Jake. You know that," Dr. Watney continued. "But all indications point to a full recovery. She's young and in excellent physical condition—I'm confident she'll do well."

After Dr. Watney left, Jake went to the rack of patient charts and removed Metzger's.

He flipped to the nursing flow sheet, where the patient's vital signs and critical parameters were logged. Jake knew that with a traumatic pneumothorax, the time it took for the hole in the lung to seal was the key. That was the determining factor in how long it would be before the patient could be extubated—before Metzger could talk, and tell them who had taken Kelly. According to the notes, Metzger's air leak was rapidly decreasing and his other vital signs were stable. Jake estimated the tube would be pulled in another three to four days.

He put Metzger's chart back in the rack, pulled Sara's out, and headed back to her room.

When Chance left the hospital, he drove to the Prescott home. Since Jake was visiting his wife, their home would probably be empty. Chance parked in the shade of a huge sycamore several houses down the street and sat in his car. It had been over ten hours since the cops had arrived, and he was pretty sure they would have finished jerking off in there hours ago. He was eager to get at Prescott's computer, but it never hurt to play it safe. Chance watched the street for a while.

It was pretty quiet—just some old spook in a yard across the street, watering a weedy looking flowerbed.

Half of an hour dragged past. The only action was when a small dog trotted around the corner and crapped on someone's lawn. The old man continued to spray a lazy arc of water over the weeds. When Chance couldn't take it anymore, he started his car and drove past the Prescott house. He turned at the corner, parking where the street dead-ended into the levee that ran behind the homes on Prescott's side of the street. He got out and pulled the Smith and Wesson from the bag in the trunk. Stuffing the gun behind his belt, he climbed the railroad tie steps to the top of the levee. Chance walked along the levee's jogging trail until he was behind Prescott's. He pretended to enjoy the view of the river until he was certain nobody was around.

There were a few young trees planted in Prescott's small, fenceless back yard. A plastic table and chair set and a small barbecue were on the slab of cement that served as a patio. Several toys were scattered around. Chance shuffled down the slope, frowning at the dirt on his shoes before moving to the back door. He pulled on his gloves. The door was locked, but one of the small panels of glass broke easily under the tap of his gun butt.

Chance paused inside the door, listening. The air was still. After a few seconds, he knew nobody else was there. Putting his gun away, he moved through the rooms downstairs, but found nothing. He went upstairs, taking two steps at a time. He glanced through the shattered door into the master bedroom before heading down the hall. The next room was the bathroom, and after that, the little girl's room. Across the hall was what appeared to be a guest room. It was crowded with boxes of junk, but no computer.

Chance went back out to the hall and stared at the dark stain in the carpet. The computer geeks at Harrison's security division had tracked Quince's e-mail to Jake Prescott at this address. Chance looked up and down the hall. Fowler's geeks were very good at their job. It had to be here. He began a more thorough search.

A small roll-top desk in the corner of the master bedroom had a computer docking station on it. A phone line and power cable ran down through a hole in the back of the desktop. A mouse and printer were connected to the docking station, but there wasn't an external monitor or hard drive. Several floppy disks were stacked next to the printer.

Chance closed his eyes. "Laptop," he muttered. "Sonovabitch has a laptop."

6

The yellow and blue box kite was over 500 feet up, dancing on the breeze of a perfect fall day. Brilliant cascades of leaves were falling onto the expanse of grass at William Land Park. Sara was sitting at Jake's side as they watched Kelly fly the kite. She was squealing with delight as she ran back and forth, making the kite bob and soar. Jake's pager went off, and he checked the message. When he looked up, the sky was dark with clouds, a gale whipping the bare branches of the trees. Kelly was halfway across the park, the runaway kite dragging her over the hard ground. Jake was paralyzed by confusion and shock. He knew he should get up and run after her, but he couldn't move. Sara screamed, shaking his shoulder violently, but he couldn't move...

Jake jerked awake, half rising from his chair. He was next to Sara's bed in the SICU. A nurse was shaking his shoulder, calling his name.

Harsh light slanted in through the window. There were several new bouquets of flowers in the room. "How long have I been asleep?" he asked.

"A few hours." The nurse smiled. "I'd heard that residents do sleep from time to time, but I'd never actually seen it."

Jake stretched, shedding his nightmare. He glanced at Sara's monitor. "How's she doing?"

"She's fine. We're backing off on the sedation a bit. She'll probably be more alert in a little while. I woke you because there's a call for you." She stepped over to one of the IV pumps and checked on the flow rate. "It's a policeman. He said that he needed to talk to you about your daughter."

Jake jumped up. "Which phone?"

"At the desk," the nurse called after him. "Line two."

Jake picked up the phone and punched the flashing button. "Hello, Detective Nunes? Have you found Kelly?"

"Sorry, Jake," a voice said. "This isn't Detective Nunes. But I do know where your kid is."

"Who is this?" Jake's hand tightened on the receiver.

"Who I am isn't important. What is important is that I have your little girl," the voice said. "By the way, how's the missus doing? She wasn't looking too good, last I saw her." A nasty laugh crackled across the line. "Sorry about that, but she was kicking the shit out of my partner. I had to do *something*."

"Where is Kelly?" Jake's voice was tight.

"You want her back?"

"Yes!"

"Well, I've got something you want and you've got something I want. Maybe we can work something out."

"What do you want?"

"You must be a bright fella, Jake, being a doctor and all. I'm sure that if you put your mind to it, you'll be able to figure out what we're after."

"Money? Is that it? How much?"

"Let's not get cute, son." A hard edge crept into the voice. "You know damned well what this is about. If you don't quit screwing around, I'm going to start carving on your little girl."

"I'm not screwing around! I have no idea what you're talking about." Jake looked up, realizing that several of the nurses were staring at him. Tony Castaic was sitting at the lab computer, looking at Jake. For a fleeting second, Jake wondered what Tony was doing up in the unit, then he remembered that he was supposed to have started his SICU rotation that day. Jake lowered his voice and turned around. "Just tell me what you want."

The line was silent for several seconds.

"What do you *want* from me?"

There was no response.

"Hello? Are you there?" Jake yelled into the receiver, panic in his voice. "Tell me what you want!"

After a few more seconds of silence, Jake heard a soft click, followed by a dial tone.

"Some bitch," Chance said to himself after he hung up. "Poor bastard doesn't even know what he's got."

Chance was back in the hotel room. The sharp stench of piss, mixed with the musk of the room, greeted him when he had walked in the door. The orange and green bedspread the girl was lying on was wet with urine. He knew it was his fault—that he had been gone too long—but he still slapped her around a little before he sent her into the bathroom to clean up.

Chance stripped the bed down to the bare mattress and covered the urine stain with one of the coarse bath towels. When the kid came out of the bathroom, her bloodied lip had already started to swell. She hardly struggled when he tied her back up before making his phone call.

Now Chance watched her lying quietly on the mattress as he considered his conversation with Prescott. He obviously hadn't received Quince's documents or read the e-mail.

Chance couldn't believe his luck. What a godsend. It made the containment issue a snap. Once the e-mail and documents had been recovered and the Prescotts were dead, the risk of exposure would be eliminated. The only tricky thing would be getting Prescott to give up the file without tipping him off to its importance.

Chance had to think. The longer he waited before calling back, the more suspicious Prescott would get. He sat on the edge of his bed, tapping a pencil against the telephone. The figure of a marijuana leaf had been scratched into the veneer of the nightstand. Next to that, somebody had volunteered his endorsement of Brandi, a hooker who apparently had elevated blowjobs to an art form.

The cadence of the pencil tapping slowed for several beats, then stopped. Of course. It would be best to go with what Prescott himself had suggested. He would just call him back and demand some money in exchange for the kid. He'd pick an isolated spot for the exchange, and when Prescott showed up, it would be a simple matter to force him to hand over his laptop.

Chance quickly came up with a figure of $20,000 to demand as ransom. He had studied the background file on the Prescotts on the flight out, and knew they had only slightly over two grand in their checking and savings accounts, combined. Chance doubted Prescott could produce that kind of money, but to ask for less would arouse suspicion.

Chance dialed the number to the hospital.

Prescott picked up on the first ring. "What the hell is going on?"

Chance laughed. "I was just messing with you. Sorry. I should have realized that with your wife shot and your sweet little girl in the clutches of a maniac you might be a little touchy."

"What do you *want* from me," Prescott pleaded. "Anything, just don't hurt Kelly."

"I appreciate your cooperative attitude, son. I truly do. And I feel a little bad about shooting your wife, so I'll give you a break. Even though you're a rich doctor, I'm willing to trade one snot-nosed little girl for a mere twenty-K."

"Twenty thousand? I don't have that kind of money. I'm just a *resident*. In a few months I'll be earning more, but right now we're barely making it from paycheck to paycheck."

"Well, it's not that I doubt your integrity, Doc, but an IOU just isn't going to cut it. It'll have to be cash, I'm afraid." Chance's flat eyes gleamed. "But I'll tell you what I'll do. If twenty thousand would be too much of a burden, I could just slice her throat for you right now, and it won't cost you a cent." Chance smiled when the girl drew her head down into her shoulders.

"No. I'll get it somehow," Prescott said rapidly. "It may take a little while, but I'll get it. I'll get it."

"That's the spirit, son. I'll call you back at this number tomorrow at noon to tell you where to bring the money." Chance paused briefly. "And Jake, no cops. I've got a connection on the police force, and I'll know it if you bring the cops in on this. If I even suspect they're involved, your girl dies. Capeesh?"

"Yes, I understand. No police. But how do I even know that Kelly is still alive? Let me talk to her."

Chance laughed. "You watch way too much television, son."

"Let me talk to her," Jake screamed, but the line was dead.

Jake tried to get his breathing under control. The unit was unnaturally quiet, and he felt the nurses' eyes on him. He turned abruptly and went back into Sara's room, walking directly to the window.

Sacramento is known as the City of Trees, and Jake had always enjoyed the view from the Tower rooms. Except for a few high-rises downtown, very few buildings were visible beneath the canopy of trees. It looked more like a forest than a city. The man could be hiding Kelly anywhere out there.

There was a rap of knuckles on glass behind him. He turned around as Tony Castaic entered the room. Tony was wearing green scrubs under his white coat, a stethoscope around his neck.

"They told me what happened. I'm sorry, man," Tony said. "It looks like Sara's going to be all right though."

"Thanks Tony. She's going to be fine. She's pretty tough."

"I'll say." Tony put a hand on Jake's shoulder. He jerked his head in the direction of Metzger's room. "She really kicked that *cabrón's* ass."

Jake nodded.

"What was all that on the phone?"

"The guys that broke into my house last night took Kelly. They…" Jake's voice cut out. He felt Tony's grip tighten on his shoulder.

Tony glared across the unit at Metzger's room, cursing under his breath in Spanish. "Who's got her? What do they want?"

"I don't know. I just spoke with the man who has her. He wants twenty thousand dollars by tomorrow." Jake shook his head. "Where am I going to come up with…?"

"I've got about forty-five hundred. It's yours, cuz."

"That's not what I meant, but thanks." Jake looked at Tony, reading the strength in his face. "I don't know what to say, Tony. That's a lot of money…"

"*De nada*. When do we meet this scum?"

"No way, Tony," Jake shook his head. "These guys are dangerous. I can't ask you to get involved in this."

Tony's hand shot out and grabbed Jake's wrist. A fierce intensity burned in his hard, black eyes. "We are brothers," he hissed. "Asking has nothing to do with it. When you need me, you don't even have to think about it."

The raw power of Tony's loyalty was palpable. Jake had a glimpse of what it must have been like for Tony growing up in L.A. The bond that held gang members together was probably the one thing in their lives that had any meaning, and the willingness to risk everything for that bond was a given.

"Thanks, Tony," Jake said. "But the money is more than enough. With what Sara and I have saved, that would make about six or seven thousand. I just need to think of a way to scrape the rest of it together before noon tomorrow."

"How about your parents? I'm sure they'd be able to help out."

"Of course." Jake's face brightened immediately. "They could wire me some cash."

They went back out to the nurse's station, and Jake placed a call to his parents in San Diego. They had left on a trip to Europe several weeks ago and were due back soon, but Jake couldn't remember when, exactly. After several rings, he got their answering machine. It was the type that beeps once for every message already recorded on the tape before it allows a caller to record a new message. Jake counted fourteen beeps before he hung up.

He looked at Tony and shook his head. "They're not home. Still on vacation."

He picked up the phone again and dialed information for Fort Lauderdale, Florida. Jake asked the operator for the number for William and Barbara Haas, and placed the call.

He covered the mouthpiece as the call was going through and said to Tony, "Sara's parents." He closed his eyes for a few seconds and shook his head. "Oh, man. I can't believe I haven't called yet to tell them what happened. How am I supposed to tell them their daughter…?" He moved his hand from the receiver. "Hello, William. It's Jake." He paused. "I've got some bad news…"

Tony patted him on the back and walked away.

After assuring Mr. Haas that Sara was doing well, Jake told him about Kelly's kidnapping and the ransom demand. Mr. Haas said he would wire the money to Jake and Sara's account right away and that they would be on the first flight out. After an emotional goodbye, Jake hung up.

When he returned to Sara's room, the nurse was at the bedside. Jake noticed that Sara's heart rate had increased to 105. He glanced at the blood pressure on the monitor and saw that it had increased a few points as well. The nurse caught his look and reminded him that they were easing back on the sedatives. She explained that Dr. Watney needed to assess Sara's neurological status to determine if there was any damage to the spinal cord.

Sweat glistened on Sara's forehead, and her hand was clammy when Jake picked it up. Her eyes were open, but it took her several seconds to focus on his face. The intense expression of relief that filled her eyes surprised him. She squeezed his hand and tried to sit up. Jake put his hand on her shoulder.

"Lie still, honey." He struggled to keep his voice steady. "You're going to be fine. Do you remember what happened?"

Sara nodded and closed her eyes, a tear squeezing between the lids. She tightened her grip on his hand.

"They took Kelly." Jake buried his face in her black hair. "They took our little girl."

Jake felt her head nod. He waited, steadying his nerves. Sara didn't need to have him falling apart on her.

"I spoke to the man who has her. As soon as I get the money together, I'll meet him and get her back. I called your parents a few minutes ago, and they…"

Sara had let go of Jake's hand and was pushing against his chest. He sat up, and Sara began to shake her head, the tape that held the endotracheal tube in place pulling at her lip. Her red-rimmed eyes burned fiercely. The heart monitor was beeping more rapidly, and Jake glanced at the screen. Her pulse had jumped to 124.

"It'll be okay, Sara. I'll get the money to this bastard and we'll get Kelly back," Jake said. "He's going to call tomorrow to set up the exchange, and I'll…"

Sara shook her head more violently. The pressure alarm on the ventilator began to sound as she struggled to talk against the breaths the ventilator was trying to force into her lungs.

"Sara," Jake said, grabbing her hand from his chest. "Try to relax. She's going to be all right. I promise. I'll get her back."

Sara continued to struggle, and the monitor above the head of her bed began to alarm as well—her blood pressure was climbing. She pulled her hand away from Jake's grasp and began to gesture wildly, her hand waving back and forth in a repetitive motion.

The nurse moved to the other side of the bed and put a hand on Sara's shoulder. "You've got to lie still, dear. You just had surgery. Try to calm down." She glanced at Jake and then looked down at Sara's legs.

Jake followed her gaze. His breath caught as he saw that, although Sara's upper body was moving, her legs were morbidly still.

67

The nurse tried to help calm Sara for a few more seconds, then went to the medication cart in the hall. She returned with two syringes and began infusing the first medicine through the IV port. "I'm giving you some medication to help you relax, dear." She turned to Jake and added, "Versed and Vecuronium."

Jake nodded. Sara wasn't letting the ventilator breathe for her, and the repair on her mesenteric artery was too fresh to risk blood pressure this high. Sedation and paralysis were indicated.

Sara thrashed even more violently as she watched the nurse start to administer the Versed. Then, with visible effort, she forced herself to lie still. She looked straight into Jake's eyes, desperate to communicate with him. Keeping her eyelids opened wide, she looked down at her own hand. With slow, deliberate movements, she began to move her hand, miming the act of writing.

Jake grabbed a pen and the nurse's clipboard from the bedside table, flipped to a blank page and handed the pen to Sara. He held the clipboard for her so she could write.

The ventilator alarm had stopped, but her blood pressure alarm was still sounding. The nurse finished pushing the Versed and switched syringes to give the Vecuronium. Sara began to write as Jake watched.

"'Looking for you', is that what it says?"

Sara nodded.

"You were looking for me?" The guilt Jake felt for not having been there to protect his family overwhelmed him. "I know, Sara. I'm sorry I wasn't there, that I had to go to work last…"

Sara shook her head, her eyelids beginning to droop. The large dose of Versed had already started to work. She scrawled BAD GUYS in front of her first message, and then below that line she wrote another YOU in large letters. She was underlining the second "you" when the pen slipped from her fingers.

Jake pulled the clipboard from under her limp hand and read the note.

"They were looking for *me*?" He searched Sara's face, but her eyes were closed. He thought he detected a small nod, but then she was still. The only movement of her body was the rise and fall of her chest as the ventilator cycled. "Why would they be looking for me?"

He slumped into the chair. It didn't make any sense, but it explained the kidnapper's odd behavior during the first call. It seemed that he wanted something besides money.

Jake wracked his brain, but couldn't figure why these men were after him. Showing up for the ransom exchange would only be playing into the kidnapper's hands. The more he thought about it, the more anxious he became. If they grabbed him, he wouldn't be able to save Kelly.

But he had to do something to get her back. The thought of Kelly with this psychopath was unbearable. He made a conscious effort to avoid thinking about what he might be doing to her. Dwelling on that would drive him to act recklessly—to make mistakes. He had to think this through, consider all of the angles.

He had no experience with this sort of thing—no algorithm to follow to solve the problem. If only this were like medicine, where if he had a problem he wasn't trained to manage, he could always consult a specialist.

Jake sat up and grabbed the armrests of the chair. "Luther," he exclaimed, jumping to his feet. "Terry Luther."

7

Terry Luther was a patient of Jake's during his Life Flight rotation the previous year. He had been shot in the chest and abdomen, and the first medics on the scene called for helicopter transport. During the flight back to the hospital, Luther's blood pressure bottomed out and the crew had been unable to start an IV in the collapsed veins in his arms. Jake placed a large line in his jugular vein, and they were able to push enough saline to maintain perfusion until the helicopter landed. The crash thoracotomy in the ER revealed that a bullet had nicked the right atrium of Luther's heart. Sticking his finger into the hole, Jake stemmed the blood flow long enough to get Luther to the OR.

It was one of the most dramatic saves Jake had been involved in, and he had visited Luther several times in the SICU during his recovery. The last thing Luther could remember from that night was Jake working on his neck in the helicopter. Luther told Jake that he was a private investigator and gave him one of his cards. He had urged Jake to call if he ever needed any help.

As Jake left Sara's room, he felt a rush of excitement, a first hope. Luther would know what to do.

Ten minutes later, Jake nosed the Citation into a parking space a few shops down the street from Luther's office in Old Town Sacramento. He hurried along the boardwalk, passing a studio where tourists could dress in gold rush era clothing and pose for photos. He almost collided with the door to Luther's office when it failed to swing open. A FOR LEASE sign was taped to the inside of the glass.

Jake knocked loudly, trying to suppress the desperation rising in his chest. When there was no answer, he rattled the door for a second, then walked back to the photography studio.

As he entered the shop, a little bell on the door chimed, and a man came out from the back. He was dressed like Sheriff Coffee on *Bonanza*, complete with a star pinned to his open vest. His potbelly hung over his belt. He was holding a half-eaten burger and a soda.

"Howdy pardner," he said to Jake. "Ready to picture yourself in the Wild West?" He waved the burger at a rack of costumes.

"No thank you. Not today," Jake replied. "I'm looking for the private investigator next door."

The man took a bite of burger and chewed for a while.

"Terry Luther? The private investigator next door?" Jake pointed to the wall separating the two suites.

"Yeah, sure. I know that wise-ass. Went belly-up about five months ago." He wiped some sauce from his mouth with his shirtsleeve. "I guess getting shot took the starch out of him. I always knew he wasn't as big a hard ass as he made out."

"Went belly-up?"

"You ask me, he turned yellow."

"Do you know how I can get in touch with him? I need to talk to him."

"You could try that art place down the street. The co-op. He has some of his crap on display down there." He snorted out a laugh. "I don't think he's sold anything, though."

Jake left the studio and walked a few blocks down the plank boardwalk. He waited for a horse-drawn carriage to pass, then crossed the cobblestone street to enter the Artist's Co-Op.

Sandalwood drifted in the air, and some New-Age music played softly. The floor space was crowded with tables covered with artwork. There were bowls, vases, lamp stands, cutting boards and animal carvings. A collection of sheet-metal sculptures spun in the breeze of a large fan.

A woman in her mid forties was behind the counter. She had waist-long gray hair and was wearing overalls. A ceramic dragon sat on the counter, a trail of fragrant smoke rising from its nostrils.

"May I help you?" she asked, smiling at Jake.

"I hope so. Do you know how I can get in touch with Terry Luther? I believe he's one of the artists in your group."

She nodded, pointing over Jake's shoulder. "That's his lathe work on the table next to the game boards."

Jake glanced at the wooden bowls and plates. "Do you have his phone number? I went to his office down the street, but it's closed."

"I'm afraid I can't give out his number." She frowned sympathetically. "Tell you what, why don't you give me your name, and I'll see if I can't reach him for you."

"That would be great. It's Jake Prescott." He paused, wondering if Luther would remember his name from a year ago. "I met him when he was in the hospital."

The woman picked up the phone. "Why don't you browse around while I try and track him down?"

Jake examined Luther's work. There were several sets of salad bowls and dinner plates, as well as a few oversized fruit bowls. The variety of wood was written on the bottom of each piece, along with a date and Luther's name.

"Terry says he'd love to talk to you, Doctor Prescott," the woman said, putting a slight emphasis on the title. She held the phone out to him.

"Hello, Mr. Luther?"

"Hey, Doc. Where the hell you been? You promised you'd stop by," the voice boomed over the phone.

"I meant to. Sorry. How have you been?"

"Oh, hell's bells, Doc. I'm right as rain in May. Listen, I'm glad you called though. Ever since I left the hospital, I keep getting these sharp pains in my chest. You didn't lose your car keys that night, did you?" He laughed so loud Jake had to hold the receiver away from his ear.

"No," Jake said, "but I remember they came up one scalpel short."

Luther laughed again. "Well Doc, what can I do for you?"

Jake turned away from the counter and dropped his voice. "I need to talk to you, Mr. Luther. Can I meet you somewhere?"

"Absolutely, Doc. Why don't you come on over to my place. I'll be working out in the garage all day, so..."

"Great. I'll come right over."

Jake wrote down Luther's directions and headed back to the Citation.

Jake cruised slowly down Beechwood Court, checking the numbers on the houses. He was in an older area of northern Sacramento that had been developed when housing tracts were designed with winding streets and no sidewalks. Modesto Ash lined the street, providing shade for the parked cars. The school Jake had passed on the corner of Beechwood and Rising had just let out, and children were walking home along the street.

Jake was passing a knot of boys tossing a basketball around when he spotted Terry Luther's address. It was a two-story gray clapboard house with white trim and a shake roof. A silk tree spread its canopy over the front lawn and flowerbeds. The flowerbeds were crowded with gladiolas, snapdragons and ranunculi.

When Jake got out of his car, he heard a mechanical whir coming from the open garage door. It had been a year since he had last seen Terry Luther, but even with his back turned, Jake recognized his red flattop and broad shoulders. Luther was wearing chinos, a work shirt and boots.

Jake stopped just outside the door. A white paper mask was over Luther's mouth and nose, and a pair of safety glasses protected his eyes. Reddish sawdust covered the front of his body. A dry, nutty odor permeated the garage. Jake noticed the bulge under Luther's shirt above his left hip and wondered why he would be wearing his gun at home. Maybe the man in the photography studio had been right.

Luther was holding what looked like an oversized screwdriver against his right hip. As he guided its tip across the tool rest on the lathe, ribbons of red shavings peeled off the spinning piece of wood. The rough shape of a bowl developed as Luther worked.

When he reached for a different tool, he saw Jake. He grinned behind his facemask, flipped a switch on the lathe and the noise faded.

"Well, shit fire and save matches," he boomed, wrapping a hand over Jake's shoulder. "If it ain't the man who saved my bacon. How's every little thing, Doc?"

"It's good to see you again, Mr. Luther," Jake managed a smile. "Thanks for letting me come over on such short notice."

"Hell's bells, I've got nothing but time," he laughed. "And what's this 'Mister Luther' crap? For somebody who pawed around inside my chest, you're pretty formal."

His grip on Jake's shoulder tightened. "It's *Luther*, Doc. People I count as friends call me Luther."

He held onto Jake's shoulder for a second longer, then brushed the shavings from his shirt. The nutty odor intensified. "Padauk is a handsome wood, but this red sawdust is murder. Listen, let me clean up a bit, then we'll have a *cerveza* and catch up."

Luther slapped the dust from his clothes before he and Jake went into the kitchen. He pulled a couple of bottles of Bohemia out of the refrigerator.

"I've got to water the porcelain. Then we'll go out back."

Jake nodded, opening his beer. He looked into the living room. A mission style couch and loveseat set faced a large fireplace. The mantel was made of old used brick, heat stained from heavy use. Two skylights in the vaulted ceiling filled the room with light.

A hallway exited the other end of the room, and Jake could hear water running in a sink. The water shut off, and a tuneless whistling served as a prelude to the sound of Luther urinating.

Jake took a step back into the kitchen. "Hey Luther," he called into the living room, "I'll be out back, okay?"

"You better not, Doc," Luther yelled back. "Not until I introduce you to Gus. He'll rip you a new one if you go out there by yourself.

"I'll be out in two shakes," he added, his laughter overriding the sound of the toilet flushing.

"Come on," Luther said when he came back into the kitchen. Sunlight streamed through a pair of French doors into the dining room. Luther walked around the trestle table to a sideboard. He opened a flat, lacquered box.

"Gar?" he asked, sliding the humidor around so Jake could see inside.

"What? Oh, no thanks." Jake shook his head.

"Yeah, I can't blame you. Nasty habit." Luther put a cigar in his mouth and closed the humidor. He dropped a Zippo lighter into his shirt pocket. "Expensive, too. I used to smoke Cubans, but things have been lean lately." He took the cigar from his lips and rolled it between his thumb and fingertips. "But the Royal Jamaican is a damn fine smoke. And a shit-load cheaper."

Luther opened the French doors. Jake followed him out, but paused, nervous around dogs.

"Gus," Luther called, stretching out the vowel. He followed it with a staccato of five short "Gusses," and then made a sound through his nose like a bicycle horn. Almost immediately, a honk returned from around the corner of the house, and a huge brown and white goose waddled out.

"What the shit?" Jake exclaimed, taking a step back. "I thought you were talking about a dog."

The goose heard Jake's voice and lowered its head to just a few inches above the ground. It advanced toward him, honking. Its black beak had a large knob on top.

Luther scooped him into his arms. "Gus, you grouch," he laughed, stroking the back of its neck. The goose continued honking at Jake, its head and neck quivering. "This old bird is a better watchdog than any hound I've ever met. Hell, the Krauts used them to patrol the Berlin Wall.

"Don't get me wrong, I like dogs. A buddy of mine has a border collie he enters in sheep trials. With just a few hand motions and whistles, old Sam will pen a sheep for you, shear it and knit you a sweater. But as a home security system, old Gus can't be beat."

Luther removed the cigar from his mouth and kissed the top of Gus' black knob. "You want to take a bath?" he murmured as he carried the goose to a plastic wadding pool in the middle of the lawn. He dropped him into the water, and the goose splashed around with his wings.

Luther pointed at a pair of Adirondack chairs in the shade of a huge catalpa. Clusters of white, trumpet-shaped flowers topped the tree's large, heart-shaped leaves. "Take a load off, Jake, and tell me what's wrong. You look tighter than a tick." He lit his cigar, its smell overwhelming the catalpa blooms.

"I'm in trouble, Luther. I hate to call in an old promise, but I need help, and I don't know where else to turn." Jake sat down. "Are you still working as an investigator? The guy in the photo shop next to your office said you're...um, pursuing other interests now."

Luther nodded. "I'd be surprised if Febiger put it that delicately, but he's right. I haven't taken on any new cases since I got out of the hospital. It's not as if I made a conscious decision, it's just that after…"

Jake held up a hand. "You don't have to explain yourself to me. Shit, you almost died. I know I'd quit if that happened to me. I was just hoping you could refer me to…"

A pained expression crossed Luther's face. His green eyes burned into Jake's for a few seconds, then he studied a small grove of Japanese maples in a corner of the yard.

Gus finished his bath and began to preen.

"You're right, of course," Luther said finally. "I suppose it's time I admit to myself that part of why I haven't taken on any new cases is out of a…" Luther rubbed at the back of his neck as he searched for the words. "Well, out of a heightened awareness of my own mortality. But the real reason I'm not working is even more pathetic.

"While I was in the hospital I promised myself that I wouldn't start any other cases until I'd cleared the one I'd botched so badly. My client was a young woman whose ex-husband was stalking her.

"The only way to work a situation like that is nearly continuous, close-proximity guarding. She was a beautiful woman, and I made the mistake of allowing a relationship to develop." Luther paused. "It was because of that mistake that she died. Her ex went ballistic when he discovered that we were together. The phone calls became more threatening and frequent, then they stopped." He flicked ash from the cigar.

"Two days later, he killed her."

Luther's knee began jerking up and down. "Katherine and I had just made love—he must have been watching and slipped in as soon as I left the room. I was just getting in the shower when I heard the shot. He was sitting on the bed in a pool of blood, her head cradled in his lap when I ran in. He never said a word; just pointed the gun and fired."

"Oh, man, Luther. I didn't know."

"Afterward, when the cops were questioning me in the hospital, they told me the ex had disappeared. The whole time I was in the ICU, I focused on getting better so I could track him down." Luther abruptly stopped bouncing his leg. "Only I haven't been able to bring myself to get started. Thinking about Katherine is too painful."

He pulled on the cigar, but it had gone out. "It's high time I got back in the game, Doc. Helping you may be just the thing to get me moving again. Sort of an enema for the soul." He fished the Zippo from his pocket. "Why don't you tell me what's going on."

"It's my little girl. Kelly." Jake forced the words out. "She's been kidnapped. Somebody broke into my house last night. They shot my wife and took Kelly."

Luther's hand stopped, the lighter a few inches from the cigar.

"Sara is hurt pretty badly. She regained consciousness for a little while this morning, and the only thing she could think of was to warn me that I was the one they were after."

Luther watched him intently, then lit his cigar.

"Do you think Sara's right? That they were really after you?"

"I know Sara thought so. And when the bastard called me today, he said he wanted to exchange something for Kelly. He seemed to expect me to know what they were after, and got mad when I offered to pay a ransom—like he thought I was jerking him around or something." Jake shrugged. "When he realized I didn't know what he was talking about, he hung up. A few minutes later he called back and tried to play it off as a joke—that he really wanted money after all. But I don't think so."

"What do you think he wants?"

"I don't know. I've been trying to figure it out, but I can't come up with anything." Jake finished his beer. "They already broke into our house. Why not just take whatever it was?"

Gus launched himself out of the pool, droplets glistening as he roused his feathers. Luther thought for several minutes before responding.

"Well, let's assume for the moment that this is not a straightforward kidnapping. Maybe Sara was right. Maybe what they were after wasn't home last night." Luther pointed at Jake with the tip of his cigar. "Can you think of anybody that's got a personal beef with you?"

"No. Not that I can think of. I mean, there was this prisoner that I took care of in the ER who threatened me, but the police are already looking into that. I can't think of anybody else." Jake's knuckles whitened around the chair arm. "I've gone over and over this, and it just doesn't make any sense."

Gus moved next to Luther's chair, his knobby beak worrying the grass for bugs.

"Let's try a different angle then. Start with the basics. How many people were involved, stuff like that."

"Well, two guys broke into our house, but now there's just one. Metzger's out of the picture."

"Metzger?"

"That's the guy that's in the hospital. The one that Sara knocked off the upstairs landing. He's the one that I…"

"Hold on a second. You've already identified one of the men involved?" Luther interrupted. "Why don't you start from the beginning and go through the whole thing in sequence. Take your time and focus. Don't leave anything out, no matter how trivial it seems."

Jake rubbed his hands over his face, then went over the events, starting when Sara and Metzger had arrived in the ER. As he talked, he peeled strips of gold foil off the beer label and dropped them into the bottle. He covered everything in as much detail as he could remember. The only thing he left out was how he had almost killed Metzger.

"Okay," Luther said. "I think I've got the gist of it. Just a question or two." He flicked some ash from the cigar. "As I understand it, the police ID'd Metzger from the car that was at the scene. Are we certain that this guy is, in fact, Metzger? Maybe the car wasn't his."

"No, it's Metzger. I saw his photo in the police file. It's the same guy. They checked his prints too."

"Okay. Good. Now, how much cash did you say was in the envelope that Metzger had in his pocket?"

"Fifteen hundred dollars."

"And I take it that he must have had that on him before he broke in; that you don't have that kind of cabbage stashed somewhere in your house?"

"We don't have that kind of money in the *bank*."

"You said your address was written on the envelope, right?"

Jake nodded.

"And this other guy is now asking for twenty thousand to get Kelly back?"

"That's right."

"So, eighteen five profit, and that's without figuring for other expenses. Hardly seems worth the effort."

He pushed the cigar butt into his empty bottle.

"Seems like something else is going on besides a kidnapping. And you're the one this guy wants to get his hooks into."

Jake waited.

"It's a fair bet that when you meet him tomorrow, things won't go as advertised," Luther said. "What time is this payoff supposed to happen?"

"I don't know. He's going to call me tomorrow at noon."

"Okay."

Luther paused. "Jake, I want to make it clear that I'll play it any way you want to, but the smart thing is go to the cops. I know Nunes. He's a good man. Believe me, this kidnapper was just blowing smoke when he warned you about the police…"

Jake shook his head, anxiety mounting. "No, Luther. He said he'd kill Kelly if I involve the police. He claims to have connections in the department, that he'll know if I even talk to them."

"Of course he's going to tell you something like…"

"Luther, I just can't take the chance. If it were your daughter, would you?"

"I guess not. But I've got to tell you, Doc, not knowing what this guy is after puts us at a big disadvantage. I'll try to track down some of Metzger's running buddies—see if they know what he was up to. You should speak with Nunes again and find out if they've made any headway."

"Okay."

"What we do know is that he's got your daughter and he's going to use her to get whatever it is he wants from you. If it turns out he actually is after a simple ransom, fine. You give him the money, get Kelly back and case closed. But we should be ready for this thing to go bad. If you just saunter up to him with the twenty K, it may be the last stroll you ever take."

"What else can we do? I have to get Kelly back! I don't see what choice we…" Jake suddenly snapped his fingers. "Wait a second. I could wear a bulletproof vest."

"It'll be pretty close quarters, Jake. He'd probably just put one into your head at that range." Luther's eyes darted at Jake. "But," he added quickly, "wearing a vest wouldn't be a bad idea. I even have an old one."

He glanced at Jake's torso. "It'll be a little big, but you should be okay. We could also use some of my surveillance equipment. I've got these slick little transmitter-receiver units that fit in your ear. I'll be able to speak to you and hear what you're saying without this guy knowing it. If things go south, I can jump in."

Luther straightened in the chair, his shirt stretching over the bulge above his left hip.

"Do you have an extra gun?" Jake asked, pointing at Luther's side.

"What?" Luther's hand moved to the lump above his hip.

"Shit fire, Doc. I don't think you'd want this kind of weaponry." Luther lifted his shirttail, revealing a bag partially filled with a thick brown fluid. "But a fully loaded colostomy bag *can* make a formidable weapon."

Luther erupted into laughter and let the shirt drop.

"Oh, man," Jake said. "Sorry."

Luther wiped the tears from his eyes. "Hell's bells, son, your face is as red as a baboon's ass. Don't worry about it. I've gotten pretty used to this thing. In fact, it'll probably come in handy on long stake outs."

Luther's smile faded. "But unless you've had some practice with a handgun, I think it would be a mistake for you to be carrying one tomorrow. I'd imagine this guy's had quite a bit of experience with guns. You'd hesitate, he wouldn't."

"Believe me, I wouldn't hesitate."

"Why don't you just concentrate on getting Kelly back, and let me worry about the firepower? If we play things right, it won't come to that anyway. Hopefully, all he wants is money."

"Yeah," Jake said doubtfully. Gus waddled to the base of the catalpa and tucked his head behind a wing.

"All right," Luther said, standing. "I'll throw together some sandwiches while we discuss strategy."

8

The Lexus Billy Ray Chance had rented at the airport was a nice ride. It was bright red and handled well. He found himself cruising above the speed limit several times that morning while looking for a place to set up the meeting with Prescott. A sports center called Arco Arena just outside town caught his eye. Billy Ray spent an hour driving around the huge complex, checking it out. The setup was almost ideal. The arena was surrounded by desolate fields sitting in the crotch of the I-5/I-80 interchange northwest of Sacramento. Several streets traversed the fields to the east, south and west, providing easy access to both freeways.

While the parking lots and access streets were probably congested during sporting events, there was very little activity that morning. Only half a dozen cars had driven through the area while he was there. Billy Ray was pleased. He had checked the box office window; no events were scheduled for the day. A Sunday afternoon should be quiet enough so that his meeting with Prescott wouldn't be interrupted.

The only downside that Billy Ray could see was a couple of security guards hanging around. He had spotted two white pickup trucks with ARCO ARENA SECURITY written on the door panels. They were parked next to each other in the main lot, facing opposite directions so the two slobs inside could shoot the shit without having to get off their asses. Although Billy Ray drove past them several times, they never moved. He wasn't too concerned. He knew that private security agencies usually didn't allow their guards to carry guns.

After checking on the girl in the hotel room, Chance decided to lunch at Paragary's, a restaurant downtown that received a favorable review in the morning paper. He was seated at one of the outside tables. After ordering, he watched the young women in spring dresses promenade along 28th Street. He glanced at his Rolex. It was already past noon—Prescott would be expecting his call. He used his cell phone to call the SICU and told Prescott to meet him in parking lot C at Arco Arena at two o'clock.

The carafe of California wine the waitress had recommended went well with the gourmet pizza. The dessert menu was tempting, but Chance refrained. Leaving a generous tip, he left the restaurant.

As he approached the Del Paso Road exit on northbound I-5, he switched off the cruise control and coasted down the off-ramp. He turned south at Relentless Drive and followed it for about a mile as it wound through the empty fields. Then he cut across to Sports Parkway on one of the connecting streets. Sports Parkway skirted the greenbelt bordering the arena parking lots. He glanced at his watch as he rolled past the cement archway at the entrance to parking lot C. It was 1:40, twenty minutes before Prescott was due to arrive. He'd have plenty of time to locate the security guards and scout around for any cops hiding in the bushes.

The two security trucks were now parked at the rear of the complex, in the shade of a cluster of pines. They were parked door to door again, with only an inch or two between them.

The complex was quiet. A few kids were jumping their bikes off a dirt mound in a field, their dust drifting in the gentle breeze. Otherwise, the only activity was a car parked in lot D, next to the greenbelt separating it from lot C. It was a white economy-job, and Chance felt a moment of irritation when he realized he couldn't tell what make it was.

At that distance, it shouldn't have been a problem, but his vision was starting to blur. It always happened when he was on the road. Eating out really screwed with his diabetes. After a few days of high blood sugar, the glucose would start to crystallize in the lenses of his eyes, and his vision would go to hell. It always cleared after he got his sugar back under control, but you never know with diabetes. He'd really have to start watching his diet from now on. A blind assassin wouldn't do anybody any good. Except maybe the target, of course. He grinned at his own joke.

Squinting as he drove closer, Chance studied the old geezer on the grass in front of the white car. He was wearing sneakers and overalls, his gray hair sticking out from under a red baseball cap. He was tossing a ball for a black and white dog.

Chance made a couple of loops around the complex, but didn't see anybody else. He pulled up next to the entrance to lot E, parking the Lexus so he could watch the approaching streets.

He reclined his seat a few clicks and lowered the window. This was going to be a snap. When Prescott saw that the kid wasn't there, he'd bust a nut. Getting him into the Lexus by promising to take him to his daughter would be like decoying with live ducks. And then, a little demonstration on the low pain threshold of four-year-old girls, and Prescott would be falling all over himself to hand over his laptop. After that, Chance just had to tidy up a few loose ends and he would be on the next eastbound plane.

Chance smiled to himself and tuned in a country station. Shania Twain's voice tripped sensually over lyrics about unrequited love. On the other side of the street, the kids were messing around on their bikes. Chance laughed when one of them hit the jump too fast and flew ass over elbows into the dirt. The other two kids raced up to him and stood straddling their bikes as he rolled around on the ground for a while. He eventually sat up, holding his head in his hands.

Across the parking lots, the old man was playing geriatric fetch with his dog. He'd throw the ball about ten feet. The dog would grab it, race around him in erratic loops and eventually drop the ball. It would then take him an eternity to shuffle over and pick up the ball. After watching for a few throws, Chance was ready to shoot the old fart to put him out of his misery.

The kid finally got up and wiped his face. He started to torque the handlebars of his bike back into position when Chance spotted a brown car approaching on Relentless Drive. It slowed to take the connecting street to Sports Parkway, and then pulled through the archway into lot C.

Prescott.

"Come to Papa." Pulling the Smith and Wesson semi-auto from its holster, Chance knocked off the safety and slipped it back under his coat.

Jake's bowels felt like water as he pulled his car into the parking lot. Luther's disguise panicked him for a few seconds as he drove across the empty parking lot. He was certain the fragile senior couldn't be Terry Luther, but then a voice crackled in his earpiece.

"You hear me? You should be in range."

"Yes," Jake answered loudly. "Yes, I can hear you." The flesh colored transmitter/receiver, about the size and shape of a kidney bean, fit snugly in his ear canal.

"Fine. That's fine. Just use your normal voice. These things are pretty sensitive," Luther's voice said in the earpiece. "Go ahead and stop there, Jake. If you get much closer, we'll tip our hand. I need to be part of the background."

"All right," Jake said, stopping the Citation.

"Now remember, Jake, you're in charge. Just take control, and don't get out of the car. Our man is parked on the street behind me in that red Lexus. He should be coming over any time. Just play it loose—I'm right here if things don't go well."

"Okay." Jake watched Luther through the passenger door window. The strength in his voice was an odd contrast with his frail movements as he played with the dog.

"Now remember, Jake, the first thing to do when he pulls up is to read his license plate to me. Then let me know where Kelly is in the car. Make him come to you. Just stay in your car with the motor running and the transmission in drive. If he pulls a gun or something, beat it out of there."

"What if he won't give me Kelly unless I...?"

"Okay, Jake," Luther's voice cut in. "Here he comes. Remember, I won't be able to hear what he says. You're going to have to keep me up to speed without letting him know you're talking to me. And don't look at me."

Jake licked the sweat from his upper lip as he watched the red car slowly pull into the parking lot. The heavy vest under his windbreaker was stifling. As the Lexus approached, he read the plate number out loud, his mouth suddenly very dry.

"I don't see Kelly," Jake said. "I don't see Kelly anywhere!"

"Okay Jake, stay cool. Just sit tight, and let's see what he does. Find out what he wants."

The Lexus pulled to a stop about twenty feet in front of Jake's car. The driver remained seated for several long minutes, hands resting on top of the steering wheel as he stared at Jake. His blond hair was pulled straight back from his impassive face. Jake placed him in his mid-to-late thirties. A hint of recognition nagged at his memory.

It wasn't until Jake had averted his gaze for an instant that the man moved. A smile crept across his lips as he stepped out of the car. There was something lethal in the way he moved.

As the man turned to close the car door, Jake noticed a short ponytail hanging just above the collar of his sport coat. He was suddenly certain he had seen this man before, and fairly recently. The man's yellowish eyes swept the parking lot before he walked up to Jake's car door.

Jake looked straight ahead through the front windshield, certain that if he faced him, the man would notice the device in his right ear. His face grew hot as he fought to control his breathing. A trickle of sweat rolled down between his shoulder blades. The man rapped a knuckle against the window. Jake cut his eyes at him, and the man made a winding motion with his hand. Jake cracked the window a half-inch and focused on the man's tie.

"Let's go, sport." The man waved the fingertips of his right hand toward his chest. "Out of the car."

"Where's Kelly?" Jake's voice rasped. "You said you'd bring Kelly."

"Change of plans. I left her in a safe place. Get out of the car. You're coming with me." The man gestured with his fingers again and took a step back. "I'll take you to her."

"No." Jake forced his eyes up to the man's face, but quickly dropped them back to the tiepin.

"What's going on, Jake?" Luther's voice rustled in his ear.

"No," Jake added. "You didn't bring Kelly, and I'm not going anywhere with you to get her."

"You'll do as I say, chief, or your daughter pays the price." He reached forward quickly and jerked on the locked door handle.

Jake recoiled from the window, his foot slipping from the brake pedal. The Citation rolled a few feet, and then shot forward as Jake's foot accidentally punched the accelerator. Jake quickly corrected and found the brake pedal, the Citation screeching to a halt a few yards short of T-boning the Lexus.

"Gun?" Luther's voice rang in his ear.

"No. No, I'm fine."

Jake looked in his rearview mirror and saw the man was crouched slightly, his right hand inside his coat. After a few seconds, he straightened up and walked after Jake's car. He shook his head slowly as he approached the window.

"Shit, son. You're about as jumpy as a gator in a boot factory. Now come on out of there and let's talk this over. You want your girl back, don't you?"

Jake suddenly went cold, remembering where he had seen this man before. He looked at the man's right hand and saw the gold pinky ring with the large jade stone.

"You're the guy in the elevator."

"That's right, slick." The man winked as he pointed at Jake and dropped his thumb on the base of his extended index finger.

"What were you doing there?"

"Checking in on your old lady," he said, smiling. "Security at that place is about as tight as the poop-shoot on a ninety-year-old faggot. I could pay her a visit any time I like." His smile stiffened. "Unless you get out of your car and come with me right now, not only does your kid die, your wife will take a sudden turn for the worse."

"Damn it!" Jake said, ramming the transmission into park. He jumped out of the car and stopped with his face only a few inches from the man's. His fists clenched tightly at his side as he ignored Luther's frantic commands to get back in the car. "What do you want from me? What did I do to make you come after my family like this?"

"Whoa. Easy now." The man took a step back and held both palms out in front of him, smiling broadly. "Let's just get in my car and go get your girl. Y'all will have a big sloppy reunion. It'll be a freakin' Kodak moment."

"Bullshit. I'm not getting in your car. Not until I know what's really going on—what you're really after. You haven't even asked to see the money yet. And I'll be damned if I'm going to…"

"Shut your hole, you little shit stain." He glanced past Jake's shoulder. "Where's the money? It's time to get moving."

"In the back seat." Jake gestured with his head at the Citation.

"Jake," Luther's voice said in his earpiece as the man stepped past him. "I've been having Sam drop the ball between you and me, and I'm within a hundred yards. Get him facing the other way. And no matter what he says or does, do *not* get in his car. I won't be able to help you if you do."

Jake took a few steps away from the Citation and turned to face the man who was reaching through the open driver's door to unlock the back. As the man opened the door and reached for the briefcase on the back seat, Jake glanced past him at Luther. He was about eighty yards away and scuffling toward a bright red ball on the edge of the greenbelt. Sam was dancing and jumping in tight circles around his feet. When the man turned and stepped away from the Citation, Jake moved back to keep him facing away from Luther.

"Look," Jake said, desperate with the certainty that the man did not intend to release Kelly. "Why don't you count the money now, make sure it's all there. Then you go get Kelly while I wait here with the money." He was winging it, trying to keep the man fixed on him, not Luther.

"What the hell are you talking about, Einstein?" The man snorted, holding the briefcase up in his left hand. "I've already got the money. Now I'm not going to tell you again; get in the damn car and let's go."

"No," Jake said, reaching for the briefcase. "There's no way I'm going to let you…"

The man's right arm moved so quickly that Jake didn't realize what was happening until the barrel of a gun jammed into his throat.

"Get in the car," the man hissed icily, "or I blow your face off."

"Oh, God. Gun." Jake pulled his head back. "Gun. Gun," he said again, praying Luther could still hear him.

"That's right, chief," the man sneered. "You catch on fast. Now let's move it."

"I'm coming, Jake," Luther's voice said in his earpiece at the same time. "Just stay right where you are."

"Oh, God," Jake said repeatedly, fighting to keep his knees from buckling. He kept his head tilted back, eyes wide with fear. A jet on final approach to Sacramento International Airport angled down to the west. The sky was amazingly blue.

"I don't have time to listen to your damn Hail Marys," the man said. Jake clenched his eyes shut as the man cocked the hammer. "I'm giving you to the count of five to get your panties out of a bunch and get in my car…"

The barrel jerked slightly as the man suddenly stopped talking.

"All right," Luther said quietly, his voice audible in both of Jake's ears. "Let's all stay nice and calm."

Luther was behind the man, pressing his gun against the base of his skull.

The man's eyes widened for a moment, then narrowed again as he turned his head a fraction to the left, trying to get a look at Luther. "Old fart with the dog?"

"You got it."

"Cop?"

"Nope. A friend of Jake's. I used to be a PI."

The man looked like he had just discovered half a cockroach in his salad. "Blind sided by a burned-out private dick. I must be slipping."

"Don't feel too bad. I used to be pretty good before I went into retirement. You okay, Jake?"

"I guess," Jake said through his clenched jaw.

The three remained perfectly still as seconds ticked by.

"Well," the man asked. "Now what?"

"I was thinking you drop your gun and tell us where Kelly is," Luther suggested.

"Not a chance," the man snorted. "How about I blow the good doctor's face off, and then deal with you."

"You'll be dead the second you squeeze the trigger. Why don't you tell us where Kelly is, and we let you walk? No cops."

"Sure thing," the man said lightly. "She's in the penthouse suite of the downtown Hilton. Am I free to go now?"

"I don't think so," Luther said. "Maybe if we knew what you really want, we could work something out."

"Sorry. That would fall under 'breach of contract.'"

"Who hired you?" Jake demanded. "What do they want from me?"

"That's for me to know and you to find out."

Luther made a disapproving sound. "That's not the kind of attitude that's going to lead to a resolution of this standoff."

"Standoff?" The man laughed. "You boys may *think* you've got me by the short hairs, but as I see it, I'm the one holding trump." His smile was tight. "You don't know where I've stashed the girl."

Jake looked at Luther.

"That's right, fellas. Unless I walk away from this, you'll never know where she is, and she'll die a slow, miserable death.

"Here's the deal," he continued. "As a show of good faith, I'm willing to be the first one to put his gun away. All you have to do is let me get in my car and drive away. I'll get in touch with you at the hospital tomorrow, and we can set this whole thing up again and do it right. No surprises."

"No way," Jake exploded. "There's no way we're letting you…"

"Now Jake," the man hissed, digging his gun deeper into Jake's neck. "I understand you're worried that I might take this little double-cross out on your daughter, but I'm a bigger man than that." The unctuous tone returned to his voice. "I'm willing to start over with a clean slate. No hard feelings. As long as you do what I say from here on out, she'll be fine."

The man turned his head, looking at Luther over his shoulder.

"What do you say, pop? We got a deal? And you better hurry up and decide, because that white truck coming down the road is what passes for security at this place." He gestured past Jake with his chin. "And with this three-strikes law, I simply can't afford any involvement with the law."

He paused for a second, but Luther didn't say anything.

"It's time to shit or get off the pot, fellas."

"All right," Luther said. "Leave the money, and you've got a deal."

"Fair enough." He dropped the briefcase on the pavement.

"No way, Luther," Jake protested. "We can't just let him waltz…"

"He's right, Jake. He's got the winning hand here. We've got to let him go."

"Listen to the man, son. You're beat." He cut his eyes back at Luther. "Okay, I'm going to put my gun away now, nice and slow. Then I'm getting in my car and driving away. Right?"

"Right."

The man gently lowered the hammer on the semi-auto and slipped it back under his coat. When Luther pulled the gun away from his head, he turned and studied Luther for a few seconds before walking to his car. Jake stood open-mouthed as the man got in and turned on the ignition. The man looked at Jake with his pale eyes. Then he winked and shot him another gunman's salute.

"Catch you later, sport." He gunned the engine and sped out of the parking lot.

"We just let him walk away," Jake said, his voice trembling. "We should have done something."

"I know, Jake." Luther stared after the Lexus as it raced northwest on Relentless Drive. "But in order to land a lunker, you sometimes have to loosen the drag and let him run. He would have started shooting if we hadn't let him go."

"But we're no closer to getting Kelly back than we were an hour ago," Jake said, his ashen color developing a hint of green. "What are we going to do now?"

The pavement began to roll under his feet as the adrenaline surge wore off. Luther led him by his elbow to the front of the Citation.

"Sit down for a second." Luther patted the hood.

Jake sat on the fender. He took deep, shaky breaths, waiting for the nausea to pass.

"Unfortunately, it didn't work out like we'd hoped," Luther continued. "But you're wrong about us not being any closer to getting Kelly back."

"How so?"

"We've got his license plate number now. And the Hertz sticker on his windshield means we won't even need to take the time to run his plates through the DMV. If we get lucky, he'll have used his real name when he rented it." Luther pulled the baseball cap and gray wig from his head and rubbed the red bristles of his flattop.

"Tracing him through the car may not be necessary though, seeing as he was gracious enough to leave us a nice set of fingerprints." Luther pointed at the briefcase. "That's going to give us a lot of mileage. He told us he's already had two felony convictions, so ID'ing his prints should be a snap. We've got several ways to run at this now."

"Yeah, I guess." Jake got off the fender. "And once we know who he is, we might be able to figure out what he wants. And who he's working for."

"That's right." Luther's eyebrows arched, a hint of mischief in his eyes. "And your strategy of getting out of the car paid off, too. Now we know he was hired to do something besides simply putting a bullet into you. You gave him the perfect opportunity, and he didn't take it. Very shrewd, Jake. Very shrewd."

He looked over at the edge of the greenbelt where Sam was lying and whistled a single blast. Sam grabbed the ball, jumped to his feet and raced across the asphalt. When the dog reached them, he immediately sat at Luther's left side.

Luther rested his hand on the dog's head for a moment before continuing. "While I was playing fetch with Sam here, waiting for you guys to show up, I realized we could come at this from an entirely different angle." Luther paused for a moment, smiling at Jake. "I can't believe I didn't think of it before."

"What?"

"Metzger." Luther held his open hand just below Sam's muzzle, and the dog dropped the ball into his palm.

"Metzger? What do you mean?"

"I'm sure he could clear things up for us."

"He's still intubated," Jake said. "It'll be days before he's able to talk."

"I thought Sara was still on the ventilator too," Luther's smile grew as he tossed the ball up and down a few times, "and she was able to warn you that these guys had a hidden agenda, wasn't she?"

"He can write," Jake said. "Of course, he can still write."

9

Chance was cursing, smacking the steering wheel with his hand, when he flew past the west bound I-80 interchange. He glanced at the speedometer and saw that he was going over ninety. Taking his foot off the accelerator, he forced himself to take slow, deep breaths.

He couldn't afford to get hauled in for something as stupid as speeding. Things were already fouled up enough. This assignment should have been a piece of cake—grab up some Poindexter doctor and force him to hand over the Quince file before offing him. No big deal. But here it was, two days into it, and things were getting messier by the minute.

Chance took the next off-ramp and parked on the shoulder of the Garden Highway overlooking Discovery Park. He sat in the car, fuming. Prescott had to get cute and hire a private detective. If it hadn't been for that prick, it would've all been over.

"I'll teach that shit to screw with me," he muttered, allowing himself to fantasize. He'd send Prescott the girl's thumb one day, a toe or an ear the next. His mind was hot with amputations and bloody packages. It was the kind of fantasy that always helped him calm down—gave him some release—and he was soon able to think about Prescott without flying into a rage.

It was obvious that Prescott and his damn bodyguard knew that he didn't give a shit about the twenty thousand. They still didn't have a clue as to what this was all about, but they definitely knew something was up. Something had tipped them off.

Metzger.

Metzger must have said something.

Chance flushed as he realized that Fowler would blame him. He'd already chewed him out for leaving Metzger alive at Prescott's. If he found out about Metzger talking, Chance's butt would really be in a crack.

But it looked like Metzger hadn't been specific when he started squealing, otherwise Prescott would have known about Quince. That meant he still had time to clean house, but he would have to act fast. Metzger wouldn't hold out long.

Chance smiled. He'd take care of Metzger, then square things with Prescott. Business before pleasure.

He started the Lexus, spun a U-turn, and got back on I-5 heading north. Doing Metzger with two bulls posted outside his room would take a little finesse, and Chance warmed to the challenge. It was like his old shop teacher at the Boy's Ranch said: it all comes down to choosing the right tool for the job.

He chewed on his lip for a few seconds as he thought about it. "Of course," he said. Sacramento was supposed to be the methamphetamine capital of the nation. "When in Rome..."

By the time he'd turned onto the I-80 interchange toward West Sacramento, Chance had roughed out a plan.

The Code Blue alert blasting on the hospital's overhead paging system jarred Jake. He was stressed and cramped at Sara's bedside when the alarm went off, signaling that one of the patients in the SICU was in cardiac arrest. Jake jumped from his chair, afraid that it might be Metzger. He was halfway out the door when he saw that the staff was running in the other direction. They all crowded into room B, where multiple alarms were sounding.

He suddenly realized that this was a stroke of luck, a diversion he could use to his advantage. Since it was doubtful that Metzger would volunteer where to find Kelly, Jake and Luther had come up with a strategy that might compel him to talk. Jake needed several uninterrupted minutes with Metzger to make it work, and in the closely monitored SICU that was going to be difficult.

They decided he should wait until the 6:00 a.m. shift change to sneak into Metzger's room. Hopefully the nurses would be too busy to notice him when they were signing over their patients to the incoming staff.

Jake had stopped by the ER that night on his way up to the SICU. He changed into scrubs and grabbed his white coat from the staff lounge. Next, Jake slipped into the ER resuscitation room and raided the airway box for a couple of pre-filled syringes: one containing Versed, the other Flumazenil. Jake frequently used Versed for sedation during painful procedures such as setting broken bones. Besides putting people out, it also has powerful amnestic properties. Even if a patient arouses briefly from the pain during the actual manipulation of bone fragments, he'll have no recall of the event afterward. This made it the ideal choice for

Jake's purposes; he didn't want Metzger to remember the interrogation. In addition, it was safe. If he did happen to give Metzger too much Versed, he could reverse its effects with Flumazenil.

Slipping the syringes into his coat pocket, Jake had headed upstairs to the SICU. After checking on Sara and talking with her nurse, he set his wristwatch alarm for 5:45 a.m. He settled in and forced himself to relax.

Now, as he glanced around the empty unit, he decided that he wouldn't get a better opportunity. Codes in the SICU often kept the staff busy for thirty to forty minutes. That should give him enough time to get what he needed from Metzger.

Jake buttoned his white coat and headed for Metzger's room. He nodded at the two guards who were watching the code at the other end of the unit. One of the guards smiled as Jake entered the room.

Closing the sliding glass door behind him, Jake moved to the bed and suspended the alarm systems on the various monitors in the room. He noticed the amount of air bubbling into the Pleuro-Vac unit had decreased significantly compared to when Metzger was in the ER. The hole in his lung was healing.

Jake went to the ventilator beside Metzger's bed and looked at the console. It was set at an SIMV of twelve, meaning the machine would usually wait until Metzger initiated a breath before it would kick in to deliver the oxygen mixture under positive pressure. If Metzger didn't initiate at least twelve breaths per minute, the ventilator wouldn't wait for him to start to inhale; it would deliver the preset number of breaths.

Jake looked at Metzger and saw he was sleeping comfortably, the metal shield still protecting his right eye. The red LED display on the ventilator indicated he was breathing sixteen breaths a minute. Jake turned the dial from SIMV to BLOW-BY.

While the ventilator continued to supply the 60% oxygen mixture, it stopped providing any assistance for Metzger's respirations. He would have to pull air into his lungs on his own.

Metzger began to move around on the bed, both wrists secured to the guardrails with leather restraints. His breaths became shallow and his respiratory rate quickly increased. After a few seconds, his eye opened.

"Rise and shine, you son of a bitch," Jake hissed.

Metzger's eye focused on him.

"Do you know who I am?"

Metzger shook his head.

Jake pulled his nametag from the breast pocket of his coat and held it up. Metzger's eye darted from Jake's face to the photo ID a few times before it opened wide.

"That's right. Jake Prescott. The guy you were supposed to kill." Jake's smile was ugly. "Well guess what, prick? Now you belong to me."

Metzger's eye scanned the room, then locked back on Jake.

"Just you and me." Jake pulled a pen and prescription pad from his coat pocket. "Now, I'm going to ask you some questions about who hired you and why, and you're going to write down the answers for me."

Metzger's face contorted, the fresh scar twisting grotesquely. With the endotracheal tube in his mouth, it was impossible to tell what Metzger was trying to say, but his intent was obvious.

"Let me explain the situation to you. The reason it feels like you're sucking a tomato through a garden hose is because I turned your ventilator off. You're breathing on your own now. And, while it would be fun to watch you slowly suffocate, I don't have that kind of time."

Jake pulled the syringe of Versed from his pocket.

"This, my friend, is Succinylcholine," he said, wagging the syringe in front of Metzger's eye. "It's a paralyzing drug. It blocks all muscle activity. Including," Jake added, poking the dressing over Metzger's fractured ribs with the capped needle, "those little guppy-breaths of yours."

Jake removed the cap and jabbed the needle into the rubber port in Metzger's IV, making sure that Metzger could see what he was doing. He pushed in one milligram of Versed—enough for Metzger to feel its effects, but not enough to make him too unresponsive to answer questions. He waited as Metzger thrashed violently for a few seconds.

"That was just a little taste to let you know I'm serious. You may feel a bit weak and drowsy, but it probably isn't enough to kill you."

Jake pulled the syringe from the IV port and slipped it into his mouth, holding the barrel sideways between his teeth. He held the pen next to Metzger's right hand.

"If you want to stop this, write down the name of your partner and where he's holding my daughter."

Metzger snapped his wrist in the restraint, knocking the pen to the floor.

Jake shook his head. "All right, if that's how you want to play it."

He squatted to retrieve the pen, taking the opportunity to glance through the glass door at the guards. They were out of their chairs and had moved a few steps down the hall, watching the activity at the other end of the unit.

"One more chance." Jake slid the needle into the port. "Once I inject the full dose, you'll have about a minute before you're unable to breathe. If you don't write down what I want to know, I walk out of here."

Jake leaned in close to Metzger's face. "You think my wife messed you up? Wait'll you see what I've got in store for you. You'll be here alone, unable to move. Helpless. You'll want to fight and scream for air. Beg for your life. Do anything just to be able to take one…more…breath." He made a show of pushing the rest of the Versed into the IV before recapping the syringe and dropping it into his breast pocket. "But in a few seconds, you won't be able to do anything. Your body will simply lie there like a slab of meat as you slowly suffocate."

He smiled and picked up the pad. "Now sure, I can understand your concern. What guarantee do you have that I'll turn the ventilator back on if you tell me what I want to know?"

Jake paused for effect. He estimated that he had a good two to three minutes before Metzger drifted to sleep.

"Well, I don't know what to tell you." He held the pen up to Metzger's hand again. "I guess you'll just have to trust my sense of ethics—you know, the Hippocratic oath and all that crap."

Just as Metzger took the pen, the overhead paging system announced: *Cancel Code Blue, SICU. Cancel Code Blue.*

Jake glanced over his shoulder and saw the staff filing out of room B. They were smiling. The patient must have done well.

"Shit," Jake said. He wouldn't have enough time to ask all the questions Luther had outlined for him. Within a few moments, the nurses would be checking the rest of their patients' telemetry monitors at the nursing station. Jake had little time before someone came to investigate Metzger's rapid respirations.

"Okay," Jake said hurriedly. His mind raced to select the most important questions. "Who hired you to break into my house last night?"

Jake watched as Metzger's hand began to strain against the restraint with agonizingly slow movements. He craned his neck to read as Metzger wrote HARRISON on the pad.

"What's his first name?"

Metzger shook his head at Jake.

"Don't screw with me now, prick."

Metzger shook his head again, but this time he started to write. His face was damp with sweat as he struggled against the pain to maintain his rapid, shallow breathing. He wrote BILLY RAY CHANCE on the pad.

"Quit screwing around. If Billy Ray Chance was your partner's name, who the hell is Harrison?"

Metzger started to write again. His handwriting was a little sloppier as he scrawled; AIR, and then PLEASE.

"You'll get it as soon as you quit jerking me around..." Jake suddenly realized that Metzger must have been trying to tell him that he had had *two* partners. Maybe the guy at Arco had left a man behind to guard Kelly.

"Okay, I got it. Billy Ray Chance. But what about the other guy? What is Harrison's first name?"

Metzger's respiratory rate began to slow. The sedation was starting to deepen, and Jake wouldn't have time to use the Flumazenil.

He looked through the glass door again. The nurses were now standing in a cluster near the telemetry monitors.

"What in the *hell* is Harrison's first name?"

Metzger began to scratch weakly on the pad behind HARRISON, but his hand went limp and the pen dropped to the floor.

Jake pulled the pad from Metzger's hand and stared at what he had just written; TOBAC... Jake's heart skipped a beat as understanding washed over him in a cold wave. He hurried to the door, his legs suddenly weak.

The guards were in their chairs and the nurses were chatting at the desk. Jake reached for the door and paused, aware of the silence in the room. Metzger's breathing had relaxed as the full effect of the Versed took hold. His brain was no longer responding to the urgent demands his body was making for oxygen.

Jake stood by the door and looked through the glass at Sara's room. He stared at the dark form of her bed for several hard seconds before turning around. He twisted the ventilator knob back to SIMV.

The ventilator began to cycle full breaths into Metzger's lungs as Jake walked from the room.

As he moved past the guards, he looked at the nurses behind the desk. Metzger's nurse glanced at him, turned to answer another nurse's question, and looked back at Jake. He felt her eyes on him as he walked back into Sara's room.

10

Jake sat on the edge of the chair in the semidarkness of Sara's room. The skin on the back of his neck was crawling with the awareness that the nurse was probably still staring at him. Any moment now, she would go check on Metzger. When she discovered that he was unresponsive, she would report her findings to the officers guarding the room. If he were arrested, there would be no hope of getting Kelly back.

When the guards hadn't burst in after several long minutes, Jake stole a glance over his shoulder. Metzger's nurse was pouring herself a cup of coffee, still chatting with the other nurses.

Jake exhaled and wiped his palms on his scrub pants. Angling the pad to catch the light, Jake stared at what Metzger had written.

HARRISON TOBAC
BILLY RAY CHANCE
AIR PLEASE

Harrison Tobacco was one of the companies he had contacted for his research project. The one, in fact, where

Winston Quince worked—and Quince had sent him the large e-mail file just a few days ago. The file that was on his laptop in his locker downstairs. If Harrison Tobacco was behind this...Jake's stomach churned.

He checked his wristwatch. 5:14 a.m. He kissed Sara on the forehead, then went downstairs. The ER was relatively quiet, the staff lounge empty except for one of the attending physicians napping on the couch. Jake opened his locker and removed his backpack. He was on his way back to the Tower elevator when he passed the cafeteria.

Jake hadn't eaten for over twelve hours. He wasn't hungry, but he hoped a little food might calm his stomach. He grabbed a tray and loaded it with a bowl of fruit, pancakes and a carton of milk. He found an empty table near the back wall and removed the laptop from his backpack. He poured syrup over the stack of pancakes and waited for the drive to boot. When the desktop appeared, he opened the e-mail folder. The Quince document had a small key-shaped icon next to it that Jake had never seen before. When he clicked on the document, the key flashed and then a small window appeared stating, VERIFYING RECIPIENT. After a few seconds, DECRYPTION AUTHORIZED flashed in the window. Jake frowned at the screen as the e-mail file opened.

A body of text filled the screen; the image of a paper clip on the right hand corner of the header indicated an attached document. Jake began to read:

Dr. Prescott,

Congratulations. Your pursuit for "inside information" (as you put it) on the tobacco industry has finally paid off. Your letters and e-mail requests have earned you the dubious honor of serving as

my Father Confessor. (Please pardon any melo-
drama on my part...I've had to consume nearly a
fifth of Jack Daniels in order to muster up enough
courage to go through with this.)

By way of introduction, I was recruited
by Harrison and Company immediately upon
completing my Ph.D. in biochemistry at Tulane
University. I have spent the last thirty-five years
in the Product Research and Marketing Division
at Harrison. My first project with the company,
back in the early sixties, dealt with efforts to
modify our merchandise in order to increase sales.
(The bulk of the data I am sending you is from
this "Enhanced Product Consumption" study, which
I piloted.) It was a resounding success, and I
enjoyed an early promotion to Head of Division.

After 1965, when the Surgeon General's office
issued its first warning about smoking, I became
involved in industry research that was designed to
prove that tobacco was, in fact, not addictive and
not as carcinogenic as the Surgeon General claimed.
As it turned out, I had a certain flair for designing
biased studies and fudging data, and I continued to
rise rapidly in the company.

I was also blessed with an aptitude for
believing my own fabrications. For many years I
sailed along with a clear conscience (truly con-
vinced that cigarettes were as safe as mother's
milk), enjoying the increasing salary and satis-
faction that I was doing my job well (I readily
accepted the idea that what we were doing was
no different than what a cereal company would
do to make their product taste better and increase
sales). I suppose, in retrospect, that my becoming
a chain smoker shortly after the Surgeon General
issued his first warning was a fairly transparent
attempt to quell any misgivings that may have

surfaced in my Psyche (I still burn through four
packs a day). Recently, however, a cataclysmic
event has led to the dissolution of my intricately
constructed facade.

I have just buried my wife of thirty-eight years.

Gwendolyn died of lung cancer last week. As
one of her doctors so enthusiastically pointed out
when he discovered where I worked, since Gwen
was never a smoker, her cancer was from second
hand exposure to my cigarette smoke. (He even
sent me journal articles, for God's sake.) While my
capacity for self-deception is prodigious, even it has
been insufficient to repel the onslaught of horrible
truths brought about by Gwen's illness. Having to
witness how my smoking led directly to Gwen's
tortured death has forced me to acknowledge that
my involvement in the tobacco industry's decades
of deception has led to the suffering and death of
untold numbers of consumers.

I can no longer divorce myself from the har-
rowing reality that I have been an active participant
in an ongoing genocide. By way of atonement for
my sins (although I realize that it is far too little
and far too late), I have sent you the original documents that most clearly demonstrate the tobacco
industry's intentional poisoning of humanity in the
name of profit. For your protection, I sent the documents via a circuitous route. While this will delay
the delivery of the documents, it should make it
impossible for Harrison to track. Do with them as
you see fit. (I'm e-mailing you these scanned copies
as a preview.)

Winston Quince

Jake had started on his pancakes, but as he finished Quince's letter, he pushed the plate aside. He moved the cursor onto the paper clip icon, pausing for a few seconds before double clicking on it.

Jake picked up his fork again as the document opened. He worked on the fruit bowl as he scanned the file. The presentation slides were in a PowerPoint format. The background was cobalt blue in the left upper corner, fading into a medium blue across the diagonal center of the screen and then back into the dark blue in the lower right corner. The text was concise and arranged in an outline format. Jake returned to the first slide, which was a table of contents listing four major topics:

INTER-DEPARTMENT MEMOS

ENHANCED PRODUCT CONSUMPTION STUDIES

BIOGENETIC MANIPULATION OF *N. TABACUM*

FIELD TESTS

Several numbered slides followed each of the headings, and Jake glanced at the last entry under FIELD TESTS. There were a total of forty-seven slides. Jake read through all of the entries in the table of contents as he finished his fruit. The last entry under INTER-DEPARTMENT MEMOS caught his eye. It was titled P R & M's FINAL REPORT ON ENHANCED PRODUCT CONSUMPTION STUDY—SLIDE 14.

It seemed like a good place to start.

HARRISON & COMPANY

Memo

To: Marshall Saunders, CEO

From: Winston Quince, PR&M

CC: R. Bickler, T. Schuh, D. Stave

Date: July 12, 1968

Re: Enhanced Product Consumption Study B—Final Report

Dear Mr. Saunders,

I am happy to report that the Enhanced Product Consumption study is complete. As you well know, we at Product Research and Marketing have been working on this project for slightly over a decade. We appreciate your support and patience, and we feel that you will be greatly pleased with the results. I am confident that you will find our full presentation at next week's board meeting quite exciting; however, per your request, I am providing you with a brief summary of our findings at this time.

The initial stage of this study in which sixteen different compounds in tobacco were isolated that elicited enhanced consumption behavior in the primate lab was instrumental in laying a strong foundation for the rest of our work. The second phase of the project carried out by the Plant Genetics Department in which *N. tabacum* was genetically engineered to increase the content of these compounds was a resounding success. In slightly over two years they had succeeded in developing twelve different strains of *N. tabacum* that contained increased quantities of one or more of the sixteen compounds originally isolated. We then created thirty-four different blends of these *N. tabacum* strains and went back to the primate lab. We identified five of the new-blend cigarettes that produced remarkably enhanced consumption behavior in the test subjects.

The last phase of our study in which these five blends were field-tested has just been completed, and the results are impressive. We distributed the five new blends to different regions of our market and then monitored their consumption parameters over the past four years. While blends number one and four did not demonstrate statistically significant increase in sales, the remaining three showed steadily increasing sales profiles. Blend number two performed the best with a 38% increase in sales over the study period. Even when the increased mortality rate that these enhanced blends demonstrated during the primate trials is factored into the long-term marketing projections, there is still a net increase of 20 to 25% in predicted profit margin over the next twenty-five years.

I look forward to presenting this data in more detail next week. Sincerely,

Winston Quince

Winston, Quince, PR&M

The pancakes felt like lead in Jake's stomach as he finished reading the screen.

He reread the last paragraph and glanced quickly around the cafeteria. The room was full of people and, although nobody seemed to be paying any attention to him, Jake suddenly felt very exposed. He returned to the table of contents and reviewed a few of the old studies, which revealed that the enhanced cigarettes clearly led to increased product consumption. He was appalled by their summations that, although the average "individual consumer longevity" was expected to decrease, the predicted net increase in overall sales warranted switching production to the genetically altered cigarettes. Jake found a follow-up study, done fifteen years after the switch had been made. It gloated over the accuracy of these predictions, highlighting the $45.8 billion profit gain the change had generated.

Jake closed the laptop. His hand trembled as he unzipped his backpack; then he slipped the computer out of sight. His breathing felt tight as he realized that the information on his computer could cost the tobacco industry billions of dollars.

Quince's papers made it clear that the more addictive cigarettes had been marketed in spite of known increased health risks. The amount of money that Harrison and Company stood to lose if Quince's documents were released was staggering. It was doubtful that the company, possibly even the entire industry, could survive the exposure.

Jake tasted bile in his throat. Since Sara had been shot and Kelly kidnapped, simply returning Quince's papers wouldn't end it. Harrison would have to cover up that violent attempt to recover the incriminating documents.

They had to kill him—and his family.

The air in the cafeteria became heavy and oppressive. He was aware that the tobacco company's assassin—Billy

Ray Chance, according to Metzger—knew where to find him. Jake grabbed his backpack and, with a quick look over his shoulder, forced himself to walk casually out of the cafeteria.

After ten minutes of sneaking around in the dark parking lot, Jake decided that his car wasn't being watched. He got in, putting his book bag under the dash on the passenger side. Just as he inserted his key into the ignition, a rapid, high-pitched beeping began to sound. Jake froze, certain he was about to be blown apart. After a second, he realized the sound was from his watch alarm. He tried taking a deep breath, but it didn't help. He lunged out of the car and threw up. After the violent contractions ended, he remained bent over and tried to choke back the tears.

Harrison was too powerful. He would never see Kelly again. If she wasn't already dead, the past few horror-filled days would be her last. And there wasn't anything he could do to help her.

He finally wiped the bile and slobber from his face and got back in the car. Driving the residential streets surrounding the hospital, he made certain he wasn't being followed before heading back to Luther's.

11

Jake was halfway down Luther's block before he realized that many of the houses on the street were still dark. Checking his watch, he saw that it was only a few minutes past six. Although he could see lights through Luther's front window, Jake decided to stop at a pay phone first to let him know he was coming. He drove to the Starbuck's on the corner of Watt and Marconi to make the call.

After speaking with Luther, Jake ordered a couple of mochas to go. He drove cautiously back to Luther's, checking his rearview mirror. As far as he could tell, nobody was following him.

Luther had opened his front door a few inches, but Jake paused on the stoop to depress the doorbell with his elbow. He was carrying the coffee, his backpack slung over one shoulder.

"C'mon in, Doc," Luther called from within the house.

Jake pushed through the door and shouldered it closed behind him. He could hear cutlery as he crossed the living room.

"Morning, Luther," Jake said, stepping into the kitchen. He held up the tray for a second before setting it on the counter. "I picked up some coffee on the way over."

Luther was standing at the counter between the sink and stove, chopping cilantro. He was wearing a pair of Nike running shoes, gray sweats and a white T-shirt. A dishtowel was tucked into the front of the sweats, serving as an apron. There were small piles of diced tomato, mushrooms and onions on the cutting board.

"Hey Jake," Luther greeted him with a smile. "How's Sara?"

"Pretty good, considering. They're already starting to wean her off the ventilator."

"That's great." Luther pointed at the mochas with his knife. "Thanks for the Java. I was going to start a pot as soon as I got the eggs on."

Jake nodded. He felt Luther's eyes studying him.

"Get any sleep?"

"Not much."

"You gotta sleep, Jake."

"I can't. He's got Kelly." Jake hesitated. "It doesn't go away."

"Yeah. I guess not." Luther pushed the cilantro to one side. "But we have a job to do. And you'll need to be sharp. Can you prescribe yourself a sleeping pill?"

Jake shook his head. "I'm staying away from that."

Luther took two strips of bacon from the pan and chopped them with quick movements of his knife. "Then at least eat a good breakfast."

He scraped the vegetables and bacon into a glass bowl containing several raw eggs.

"I had a little trouble sleeping, myself. I made some progress on the case yesterday, and I guess it got the old juices flowing again." Luther whipped the eggs. "I got the briefcase to a buddy of mine at the crime lab downtown and asked him to put a rush on it. Then I headed over to the airport and had a chat with the receptionist at the Hertz agency. She told me the guy that rented the Lexus was called David Brown. He had a Louisiana driver's license and Visa in that name, but it must be an alias. When I got back from the airport, my friend had left a message on my machine that he'd been able to lift several prints from the briefcase. He got an immediate hit on the computer. It seems our man has been convicted of two felony assault charges and was arrested, but never convicted, in an unsolved murder case in Maryland. And his name isn't David Brown."

He turned to the refrigerator and pulled out a carton of milk, pouring a splash into the eggs. "His name," Luther said, bobbing his eyebrows up and down, "is Billy Ray..."

"Chance," Jake finished for him.

Luther wiped his hands on the dishtowel. "Shit fire. Here I was, all proud of myself, and you've beaten me to the punch."

Jake handed Luther a mocha. There was an indefinable quality about the man that made Jake feel better—made him feel his trouble wasn't insurmountable after all. "Well, you found out his alias. If he used the same name to rent a hotel room or something, that'll help."

"I suppose you're right. Maybe my afternoon wasn't a complete waste." He started whipping the eggs again. "I like to think I'm contributing something to this investigation."

Jake rubbed his eyes with the heels of his hands, trying to rid them of the heavy, gritty feel. Images of Kelly and Sara crowded in.

"We'll get her back, Jake." Luther added some salt and pepper to the mix. "What did you find out from Metzger?"

"I didn't have as much time with him as I would've liked, but I think I know what this is all about." Jake sipped his mocha, trying to rid his mouth of the bile taste. "It's pretty bad."

Luther removed the rest of the bacon from the pan, folded the strips into a paper towel and poured the egg mixture into the pan. "What say we eat first before we get into it?"

"Sure. Not much for me, though."

"Do me a favor, Doc, get the juicer started." Luther used his spatula to point at a bulky white machine sitting on the edge of the sink. "My mind's about as nimble as a hog on ice until I get my morning fix."

There was a bowl of cut carrots, beets, kale and dandelion greens next to the juicer. Three small knuckles of a white-fleshed tuber that Jake didn't recognize were sitting on top.

Jake found the power switch and started feeding in the vegetables.

By the time Jake had finished, Luther was carrying a couple of plates loaded with the scramble mixture into the dining area. Jake followed with the pitcher of juice.

"Dig in," Luther said, starting on his eggs.

Jake tried a small bite, then put his fork down.

"Try, Jake."

He picked his fork up again and pushed the eggs around.

"Well, at least drink the juice." Luther filled the glasses. "What it lacks in appearance, it makes up for in foul taste."

Jake eyed the glass.

"Go ahead, man. It's pirate piss, but the ginseng will unfurl your sail with a snap. And the vegetables keep you going all day."

Jake managed to get a few sips down. It was awful.

Luther drank his in one swig. "Ahh," he said. "Now I'm good to go. Let's hear what you found out from our buddy, Metzger."

Jake reviewed his encounter with Metzger that morning. "So," he concluded, "although our discussion was cut short,

I was able to get Chance's name out of him. He also gave me another name. Harrison."

"Who's Harrison?"

Jake pulled out his prescription pad and tossed it onto the table so Luther could read it. "Harrison *Tobacco*," Jake said, going into the kitchen to get his backpack.

Luther frowned at the pad. "Harrison Tobacco? What's Harrison Tobacco got to do with this?"

Jake opened his laptop. "Let me show you."

He and Luther poured over the data in Quince's file for an hour. Luther leaned back in his chair and ran a beefy hand down his face. "Harrison knows you have this? Sweet Mary. No wonder they've come at you so hard."

Jake nodded.

"How in blue blazes did you get it?"

"I asked them for it." Jake shrugged. "We need to complete a research project before we can graduate from residency, and I decided to do a meta-analysis on all the known effects of tobacco on human health. I've had a personal interest in it for quite a while. So, to be complete, I contacted the major tobacco companies and asked them for any research they may have done within the industry. Who knew they'd actually send it to me? I was expecting some bogus claims about the safety of cigarette smoke, and this guy Quince drops *this* in my lap."

Jake clicked on the Word document icon, and Quince's introductory letter filled the screen.

Luther read the letter. "Shit fire. Quince certainly didn't do you any favors. Harrison must know Quince is sending you the original documents. He could've at least covered his tracks better."

"I know. And Sara and Kelly are paying the cost. Harrison must have found out as soon as he sent the e-mail. They were in my house within a day and a half."

"And they'll be pretty desperate to keep a lid on this. There's no way they can let it get out that they intentionally made cigarettes more addictive to increase their bottom line. Especially since they knew they were more carcinogenic. They're already on the ropes as it is." Luther gathered the dishes and carried them into the kitchen.

Jake pushed the laptop away and stared at his glass of juice as Luther rinsed the dishes.

"You know something, Doc?" Luther continued. "Until now, I had sympathized a little with the tobacco industry. I mean, they've been persecuted pretty mercilessly the last few years."

"What?"

"Well, it seems to me that the politicians who are gunning for Big Tobacco are doing so to serve their own agendas, not out of any concern for public health. It's pretty obvious that most of them are just trying to grab as much of the carcass as they can in what's become a feeding frenzy. The state governments claim the tobacco industry should reimburse them for health care costs caused by smoking, but only a small portion of the money that's been awarded has been used for that purpose. Most of it's been siphoned off for other things like sidewalk restoration and to pad budgets. It doesn't seem right."

"I don't know, Luther. I've seen the terror in the faces of too many patients gasping for their last breath for me to sit around and wonder if we're being fair to Big Tobacco." Jake shook his head. "I watch a lot of people die in my line of work. You'd think it would be hardest with the young, healthy people who were in a car wreck or something. But for me, it's always been the old COPD'ers who are the toughest."

"Who?" Luther came back into the dining room.

"Chronic obstructive pulmonary disease. Emphysema. I think it's because that's how my grandfather died when I was a teenager. The last few months he was too sick to live alone anymore, so he brought his oxygen tank and ashtrays and moved in with us—providing me with a front row seat to the final days of a lifelong smoker.

"So now when I think of him, I don't see the man who did things like buy a rabbit so that with a little sleight of hand he could show me how the Easter Bunny laid eggs. Instead, I remember the shriveled husk of a man with an ugly cough, his hair smelling like an ashtray and his few remaining teeth the color of slow death. I remember that at sixteen I found him to be a disgusting embarrassment— that I wouldn't bring my friends home anymore, and resented my parents for bringing such a freak into…" Jake paused for several seconds, "…for bringing that loving man into our home."

Jake raised his eyes to Luther's. "Most people I see in the ER are there for an acute problem. I've never met them before, and I usually never see them again. But COPD'ers are always coming in for some fine-tuning of the medications that are allowing them to hang on just a little bit longer. You get to know them."

Jake felt vulnerable under Luther's stare. He knew he should shut up, but couldn't.

"When there's finally nothing more you can do for them, you get to stand there with your hands in your pockets and watch them claw and fight as they suffocate in front of you."

Luther sat quietly for a few moments. He was about to say something when Jake continued, a tight, hard edge in his voice. "So you'll have to forgive me if I don't have much sympathy for Harrison Tobacco." He nodded at the laptop. "And, providing it doesn't get in the way of getting Kelly back, I'll hand this stuff over to the media, or do whatever I can to shut them down."

The low battery chime began to sound, and he turned the computer off.

"Sure, Jake. I can see how you'd feel that way." He laid a hand on Jake's shoulder. "Especially now that they've attacked your family. Why don't I try to track down Quince's package. Having those original documents would definitely be a strong bargaining chip for getting Kelly back. I'll also try to locate Billy Ray Chance. Calling all the hotels in town will take some time." Luther managed a small smile. "Perfect opportunity for you to get some sleep."

"I'll be okay."

"We need you sharp. Get some sleep. There's a bed in the guest room."

"Just be sure to get me as soon as you find him."

"Absolutely."

12

Tony Castaic's feet were killing him. His first night on the trauma service had been busy, a pile up on I-5 keeping him down in the ER resuscitation room for several hours. Then he spent the last two hours in the OR, holding retractors as the surgeons removed some guy's ruptured spleen. By the time they finished, it was 4:30 and Tony had to start pre-rounding on his patients before the 7 a.m. attending rounds. With the new admits, he had over twenty-five patients on his service.

After checking on the ward patients, he considered stopping at the cafeteria to put his feet up and slam a quick cup of coffee, but it was already quarter to six. He would have to hustle if he wanted to be up to speed on the ICU players. He hurried to the sixth floor and headed for the SICU. He was using his ID badge to unlock the door when it suddenly flew open. A man pushing one of the large housekeeping carts burst through the door, almost knocking Tony over.

"Hey," Tony exclaimed, jumping out of the way.

123

"Pardon me," the janitor said. He was tall and had blond hair, which he wore in a short ponytail. His coveralls were a few inches too short. He flashed an apologetic grin, but his straw colored eyes were cold.

The man jockeyed the cart through the door, and Tony entered the SICU. Grabbing the nursing charts for his patients, he sat next to the charge nurse, Becky.

"How's Sara?" He scanned the first chart's flow sheet. Sara had remained stable overnight, and Becky had been able to titrate the oxygen mixture on the ventilator down to sixty percent.

"Remarkably well, given her injuries," Becky said. "I've never seen anyone stabilize that quickly."

"She's tough. Don't forget, she's been married to Jake for five years. A bullet in the gut is a cake walk in comparison." Tony smiled, opening the next chart.

"Looks like Metzger's doing okay, too," he said, tracing his finger along the pulse oximetery line on the graph. "That small pulmonary contusion on yesterday's chest X-ray never blossomed?"

"No." Becky wrinkled her nose. "I kept a close watch on his fluid balance, and he's been stable as a rock. Until a few hours ago, he didn't give me a moment's rest. On the call button constantly. Wanting his pillow fluffed, his nose scratched, crap like that. And his hands," she added, rolling her eyes. "Even though he's in restraints, I'll bet I've got more bruises on my ass than a hemophiliac Chippendale's dancer."

She smiled at Tony. "He finally drifted off to sleep, and I've just been watching his vitals on the monitor. I didn't want to go in there and risk waking him up. I probably didn't need to worry, though. Housekeeping was just in there, and he never made a peep."

"Hopefully we can extubate him soon so the cops can get him…"

Tony was interrupted by an alarm from the monitor. They both leaned back in their chairs to look at the screen.

A red bell was flashing on the section of the screen that displayed vital signs for room H.

"*Now* what?" Becky exclaimed, wheeling her chair over to the monitor. The screen format consisted of eight horizontal sections, each area containing a miniature display of the ECG tracing and vital signs for the individual rooms, A through H. Several of Metzger's vital sign readings were flashing in sync with the auditory alarm. Becky touched the box surrounding the H, and the screen format changed; the top half of the screen now dedicated to a full representation of Metzger's vitals.

"What's that all about?" Tony rolled his chair next to Becky's.

Metzger's heart rate was 137, and his blood pressure had shot up to 243/132.

"Got me. Maybe he needs some more Demerol?" Becky suggested doubtfully—they both knew that such an abrupt jump in vital signs wouldn't be from inadequate pain control.

"I don't know. Look at the ECG. He's throwing a hell of a lot of PVC's."

In addition to the rapid heart rate, the rhythm strip also showed that the QRS complexes, which represent the electrical activity of the ventricles, were frequently too early and too large—Premature Ventricular Contractions. Although most people have occasional PVC's, the frequency of Metzger's was alarming. Something was irritating his heart, making the ventricles contract out of sequence.

"Crap. There's a couplet," Becky exclaimed, pointing at a paired set of the oversized complexes. "If he keeps this up, he's going to go into V-tach."

As if on cue, the monitor tracing showed a run of PVC's that lasted almost ten seconds.

"Shit," Tony blurted, as they both jumped to their feet. "*That* was nasty."

They ran past the guards, entering Metzger's room. A cacophony of electronic beeps filled the room. Every damn alarm was going off—the heart rate, blood pressure, ventilator, everything. After a few seconds of stunned hesitation, they hurried to the bedside.

Metzger was in obvious trouble, writhing around on the bed like a worm on hot pavement. His sheet was bunched over the lower half of his body; the exposed skin flushed and glistening with sweat.

"Calm down, Mr. Metzger," Tony said, although it was obvious that the patient was beyond all comprehension. "Calm down!" He pushed against Metzger's chest, trying to get him to lie still. His skin was unbelievably hot to the touch.

"*Santa Maria,*" he said, searching Becky's face. "He's on fire."

"No way. I just checked his temperature three hours ago, he's been afebrile all…" Becky stopped abruptly as she laid her hand on his forehead. "What in the hell is going on?"

"Shit if I know."

They donned gloves as they checked the monitor. Metzger's heart rate was 142, and the PVC's were even more frequent. The blood pressure reading hadn't changed, and Becky pushed the button on the monitor so the automated cuff would retake the pressure immediately. She also set it to cycle every two minutes. Glancing at the ventilator, she saw that the airway pressure was dangerously high.

"This guy's going to code any second. What do we do?"

Tony shook his head and gripped the guardrail on the bed, the latex gloves tight across his knuckles. The blood pressure cuff finished its cycle, 258/146 flashing on the screen. He could smell his own perspiration start to blend with the rank stench of Metzger's sweat-soaked body. Too many things were going wrong. He wasn't sure where to start, but they had to do *something*.

"All right, Becky, let's cover the basics. ABC's. Airway. Breathing. Circulation. First, airway. Is the ET tube in good position?"

Becky grabbed Metzger's head and tried to steady it against his wild thrashing. The endotracheal tube was still in position, but the tape that secured it to his face had pulled the lip laceration apart. Blood flowed freely from the wound, obscuring their view of the tube itself. Tony had started to suction the bloody froth from the patient's mouth when Becky suddenly cried out.

Metzger's body had stiffened grotesquely, his back arching up so high that only his heels and the back of his head were in contact with the bed. He hung there for several impossible seconds, then slammed back down—the terrible contractions of a grand mal seizure wracking his body with such force that the bed bucked on the floor.

Becky was frozen at the bedside, watching Metzger's horrible contortions. Her eyes were wide, panic stirring in their depths. "I'll get the crash-cart," she cried and ran from the room.

Tony lifted Metzger's left eyelid with his thumb and examined the pupil. It was maximally dilated.

Becky returned with the crash-cart and opened the top drawer.

"Ativan?"

"Yeah. Four milligrams, IV push." Tony turned to the monitor, studying the screen. "Where's the temp?"

"We were just checking it every four hours," Becky said, drawing the Ativan into a syringe.

"Better hook up the rectal probe." Although Metzger's convulsions were distorting the baseline of the ECG, Tony thought that in addition to the frequent PVC's, the QRS complexes of the underlying rhythm looked wide.

After injecting the Ativan, Becky grabbed the thermometer probe. Uncoiling the cable, she plugged it into the monitor. She moved to the side of the bed and pulled the soaked sheet from Metzger's body.

"Jeeze, look at *this*," she said, staring at the Foley catheter taped to Metzger's thigh. The urine in the tubing was a dark rust color.

"Great. Rhabdo. Just what we needed." Tony tried to help Becky as she struggled with the thermometer, but Metzger's convulsions were too violent to place the rectal probe.

"Go ahead and give him another two of Ativan," he said, letting go of Metzger's legs. "We've got to control his seizures. Better give him a couple amps of calcium chloride too."

"Calcium?" she asked. "For seizures?"

"He's got rhabdomyolysis." Castaic nodded at the Foley catheter. "His muscle cells are all breaking open, spilling their contents into his blood stream. In addition to the red myoglobin, there's a shit load of potassium being dumped into the circulation." He pointed to the ECG tracing on the monitor screen. "It's the high concentration of serum potassium that's screwing with his heart, making the QRS's so wide. And the calcium should…"

"And the calcium should help block the cardiac toxicity caused by the elevated potassium," Becky interrupted, nodding.

She pushed in the second dose of Ativan and then grabbed the ampules of calcium chloride. She was just popping the caps off with her thumbs when Metzger's seizure suddenly stopped. She started to breathe a sigh of relief, but immediately realized that Metzger was too still. There was no voluntary movement at all. She had just become aware of the continuous buzz from the cardiac monitor when Dr. Castaic barked that the patient was in V. fib.

"Defib at two hundred joules," he said sharply. He punched the code blue alarm on the wall at the head of the bed.

Becky turned to the defibrillator mounted on top of the crash cart. She flipped the power on and set the dial to 200. Grabbing the paddles from their holders, she held them poised over Metzger as she waited for the unit to charge.

When the unit beeped, she pressed the paddles against Metzger's chest. "Clear," she called out. She pushed the buttons on the paddles, jolting Metzger's body.

There was a large deflection of the ECG baseline, but then the tracing returned to the irregular oscillations of ventricular fibrillation.

Castaic nodded at Becky. "Again, at three hundred."

As she set the dial to 300 joules and waited for the unit to recharge, several nurses and techs ran into the room.

"Ann," Tony said to the first nurse, pointing at the vials Becky had dropped on the bed, "give him the calcium as soon as we start chest compressions. Then get some Epi ready."

"Clear," Becky called, and shocked the patient. Again, the tracing returned to ventricular fibrillation.

"Three sixty," Castaic said.

Becky placed the paddles back on Metzger's chest. She glanced around to make sure no one was in contact with the bed and yelled, "Clear."

Metzger's body jerked more forcefully than with the first two discharges, and when Tony checked the monitor, he saw that the patient had converted back to a sinus rhythm.

The QRS complexes were definitely widened. He dug his fingers into the patient's groin, feeling for the femoral artery.

"He's got a good pulse." He nodded at Ann. "Go ahead and give him the calcium before we lose him again." He turned to the other nurses crowding around the bed. "Check his pressure. And we need an ABG."

One of the nurses quickly felt for a pulse in the crook of the patient's left arm. Once she located the brachial artery, she drew blood for the arterial blood gas. Tony noted that it was bright red, indicating adequate oxygenation. He asked the nurse to make sure the lab ran a potassium level on the sample as she rushed from the room. He watched the monitor as they waited for the blood pressure cuff to complete its cycle. The frequency of the PVC's continued to increase, triggering a disquieting memory in Castaic's mind. The cardiac irritability, seizures, dilated pupils and rhabdomyolysis combined to create a clinical picture that was unpleasantly familiar.

Massive stimulant overdose.

182/133 began to flash on the monitor, interrupting Castaic's thoughts. That was pretty damn high for someone who had just been pulseless for a minute and a half. Severe hypertension was also part of the stimulant toxidrome, but it didn't make sense. How could an ICU patient, who was tied down and intubated, OD?

Tony looked across the bed and saw that Ann had administered both amps of calcium. "Hold the Epi. We've got good pulses. It's all those PVC's I'm worried about."

Becky glanced at the temperature probe lying across the patient's legs. Since the seizures had stopped, it was easy for her and one of the other nurses to place the rectal probe.

Tony watched as the temperature readout displayed at 99.8, and rapidly started to climb. He was distracted by the ECG tracing, which showed that rather than narrowing in response to the calcium, the QRS complexes had continued to widen. It looked more like a sine wave than an ECG tracing, and Tony knew the patient was minutes away from entering a non-salvageable rhythm.

"Shit! The potassium must be through the *roof*." He knew there were other treatments to lower serum potassium, and his mind scrambled as he tried to recall them.

"A hundred and six point four?" Becky hissed. "No way."

Tony's eyes jerked back to the temperature reading; his mind suddenly focusing on the first cocaine OD he'd ever treated. It was during his final year in medical school at U.C. San Diego that he'd seen a patient with such a high temperature. One of the bags had burst inside a body packer who'd been busted smuggling cocaine across the border. That patient had been in rhabdomyolysis, seizing and severely hyperthermic too—and his ECG had looked just like Metzger's did now. Despite aggressive treatment by the ER resuscitation team, the body packer had gone out twitching and sizzling, just like the egg in the old "here's your brain on drugs" commercial.

Although Castaic now remembered the tricks they had tried with the body packer, he knew it was too late. He was going to lose this patient too. Anything they did now would just be pissing in the wind.

"Push three amps of sodium bicarbonate," he said to Ann.

He turned to one of the nurses standing at the foot of the bed. "Grab some urine from the Foley and send it for a stat tox screen."

Tony checked the monitor again. The temperature was up to 107 degrees and the blood pressure had plummeted to 92/60.

The nurse who had drawn the ABG ran back into the room. "The pH is seven point oh four." She paused for a second and looked at the rest of the staff. "Potassium is ten point two." A buzz of astonishment passed through the team, but Castaic simply nodded, chewing on his mustache.

"See if you can't get some ice water and fans," he said to the tech.

Dr. Castaic lifted the patient's eyelid again. The pupil was still dilated, but now the light in the room reflected off the retina with the opalescent glimmer of brain death. Castaic shone his penlight into the eye, confirming what he already knew—there was no response. The elevated temperature had denatured the cellular proteins in Metzger's brain. His goose was, in a word, cooked.

But, since you can't simply walk away from a patient who still has a pulse, even if the outcome is hopeless, the team continued their efforts. They pushed drugs and tried to cool him off until he finally spiraled into a pulseless rhythm.

The ward techs had cleaned the room and were zipping the body into a morgue bag as Dr. Castaic, Becky and Ann sat at the nurse's station writing their notes. Any unexpected death would be a coroner's case, and careful documentation was needed. Tony was working on the assessment section of his note when he paused and leaned back. He tapped his pen on the page for a few seconds, and then turned to the nurses.

"Do you guys know if Metzger had a bowel movement while he was here?"

"What?"

"Bowel movement. Did Metzger take a crap the last few days?"

"Yeah," Becky said. "I had him up to the bedside commode last night at about eleven o'clock." She flipped back through the nursing notes. "He also had a BM yesterday morning. Why?"

"I'm pretty sure he died from a cocaine overdose, but I can't explain how. I was thinking he could have been body packing and it finally broke open, but that doesn't make any sense." He tossed his pen on the desk. "If he's had two bowel movements since he got here, there's no way it would've still been up his butt."

He mussed his hair and laced his fingers together on top of his head. "I just don't get it."

"Maybe it wasn't an overdose," Becky said. "What about sepsis? He did have a fever."

"Sure," Tony shrugged. "I definitely could be off base, but I'd be willing to bet two hours of uninterrupted sleep that it was an OD. I've seen it before, and it looked just like this."

"Why don't we call the lab and find out?" Ann said.

Dr. Castaic checked his watch. "It has been twenty minutes since we sent the urine over." He leaned across the desk to slide the telephone closer. "Let's see if it's done."

After talking to the lab tech, he hung up and turned back to Becky and Ann. "The preliminary screen was negative for cocaine, but the methamphetamine test lit up like a Christmas tree. They're checking specific levels, but that won't be done for a few hours."

"Amphetamine toxicity is basically the same as cocaine, isn't it?" Becky asked.

Tony nodded. "It's definitely what killed Metzger, but how did he get such a massive dose? The body packing theory makes even less sense for meth than it does for cocaine. Crank is dirt-cheap around here. They practically give it away down in south Sac. There's no reason to be packing it around like that. The autopsy will tell for sure, but he had to have been exposed to it some other way."

"How?" Ann asked. "He's a prisoner. The cops have been stationed outside his door since he got here—there's no way anybody could've slipped in and poisoned..."

"Oh no," Becky gasped, glancing at the two officers at the other end of the nurse's station. "About an hour and a half ago we were all in room B running a code on Mrs. Ettinger. When we were done, I saw Dr. Prescott coming out of Metzger's room."

"No way. Jake wouldn't do this," Tony said immediately, but as he considered what Metzger had done to Jake's family, the conviction in his voice faded. "He must've just been talking to the guards or something."

"He was *in* Metzger's room. I didn't think much of it at the time, but in light of what's happened..." Becky paused, looking back and forth between Ann and Dr. Castaic. "Well, I think we know how Metzger got the meth. And when the police get the autopsy report, they're going to remember him being in there too."

13

Chance shouldered the door closed behind him and put the cardboard box down on the carpet. The girl was still trussed up on the bed, watching him over her shoulder. Dried snot was smeared across her upper lip and her eyes were red-rimmed, but she wasn't crying. She glared at Chance through matted strands of hair, her jaw set. In that moment, Chance could envision what she would look like as an adult, and realized she would probably be a handful for her future husband. Then he remembered that she wouldn't be alive for any of that. He winked at her, laughing when she turned her head away.

"Don't be that way, sweetpea. Wait until you see what your dear old Uncle Billy Ray got you." He nudged the box with his toe. A rustling sound came from inside, followed by a thin mewing.

The girl looked back over her shoulder at the box, and then up at Chance.

"That's right," Chance leered, opening the box. "I got you a kitty."

He pulled a small calico from the box, holding it well away from his suit. The girl rolled onto her back, lifting her head to keep her eyes on the kitten.

"See how nice your Uncle Billy Ray is?" he asked, stroking the kitten. "Did your mommy and daddy ever get you a kitty?"

The girl held her lower lip between her teeth for a few seconds, and then shook her head. It was a small, almost imperceptible movement, but it brought a cold smile to Chance's face.

"I wonder why not. Kittens sure are friendly, and they're awfully easy to take care of. Your mommy and daddy must not like you as much as I do." Chance sat on the edge of the girl's bed. "Do you want to play with her?"

She nodded.

Chance held the cat out, and then pulled it back. "Do you promise to behave if I untie you?"

"Yes," she answered in a small voice.

"Good. Roll over so I can get you loose." Chance dropped the kitten onto the bed. It was only a few weeks old and high-stepped unsteadily on the mattress, its claws snagging in the stained bedspread.

When she was untied, the girl scooped the kitten into her arms. She hugged it tightly, and it began to purr.

"Well," Chance said after a few seconds. "What do you say, Kelly? Don't you want to thank your Uncle Billy Ray?"

"Thank you," she said softly.

"Thank you, Uncle Billy Ray," Chance said.

"Thank you, Uncle Billy Ray," Kelly repeated in a voice that had almost disappeared. She turned her back to Chance, shielding the kitten from him.

"Don't mention it." Chance stood up and moved over to the other bed, sliding the phone across the nightstand as he sat down. "I certainly can't understand why your parents never got you a kitten. This one sure seems to like you."

Chance picked up the receiver and dialed the direct line to Fowler's office. "Chance here. How's it going at the home front?"

Chance waited for a few seconds, but Fowler didn't respond. So much for pleasantries.

"I thought I'd give you an update on my progress out here." Chance had suffered through enough debriefings with Fowler to recognize his silence as a sign that he was in a particularly dangerous mood. Chance could almost feel Fowler's gaze boring into him, and decided to start with the good news.

"I took care of the Metzger problem this morning. So he won't be blabbing to anyone anymore. I made damn sure of…"

"Anymore?" Fowler cut in.

Chance held the phone away from his head and silently mouthed *shit,* before returning the receiver to his ear.

"…instructed you to eliminate him before he had a chance to say anything, did I not?"

"Yes sir, you did," Chance said, biting back the irritation he felt at having to grovel to Fowler. But his contracts with Harrison always paid top dollar.

"Well, what happened?" Fowler demanded. "Who did Metzger talk to?"

"Nobody. It was just a figure of speech. He still had a tube down his throat when I off'ed him, so he couldn't have said anything."

Chance glanced at the girl. She still had her back toward him and was hunched over, petting the kitten in her lap. Chance lowered his voice. "It's just that Prescott seemed to know our little meeting yesterday wasn't a simple ransom exchange. When I spoke to him the day before, it was obvious he had no idea what was going on. He bought the whole kidnapping story. But, by the time we met, he knew something was up. He came prepared. It seemed as if someone had..."

"You met Prescott yesterday?"

"Yes sir," Chance answered cautiously.

"Then I don't understand why this hasn't been settled."

"That's what I'm trying to tell you. He knew something was up and he pulled an end-run on me. He hired some private investigator who got the drop on me."

An oppressive silence weighed on the line. Chance could imagine Fowler's expression souring even more as he learned that another person was involved.

"And that's really what I'm calling about," Chance pressed on. "Your boys need to do a little digging for me. I need the names of all the PI's who've been licensed in the Sacramento area over the last ten years. Even if they're now out of business. Their physical descriptions too. Stuff I can't just get out of the local Yellow Pages."

"Why, I'd be happy to pitch in. It certainly sounds like you could use a rest. It must have been quite strenuous for you to foul things up so severely in such a short time."

"Listen, I know things haven't gone as smoothly as they could have, but give me some credit. You know I do good work. This assignment requires a little finesse. Simply killing Prescott would be a snap, but first we need to recover the documents. That's top priority, right?"

"Correct."

"Well," Chance continued, "since you had me ice Quince before we knew what he'd done with the original documents, I couldn't just kill Prescott the first chance I got. It would've been the wrong way to play it."

Silence.

"I mean, that's what you said, wasn't it? That retrieving the original documents was the primary objective? And that Prescott was our best shot at locating them."

"That would be the logical assumption. Quince would have known Prescott couldn't do any real damage without them." Fowler paused. "Why don't you sit back and put your feet up for a while. That way you won't screw things up any further. I'll get back to you with that list of private investigators."

Chance slammed the receiver back in its cradle, his gaze falling on the girl. She was still hunched over the kitten, her greasy hair hanging past her face.

"Get your ass in the shower," he said, lurching to his feet. He grabbed Kelly's arm and jerked her off the bed. The kitten scratched her as it scrambled away and shot under the bed. Chance pushed her into the bathroom and slammed the door behind her. "You look like crap."

14

Detective Nunes' desk on the second floor of the Joseph E. Rooney police station on Franklin Boulevard was next to a window with a western exposure. On summer afternoons, the heat blasted through with such intensity that Nunes had to keep the Venetian blinds closed. But since it was only mid-May and twenty minutes before noon, the blinds were up and the window was thrown wide. A delta breeze entered the room, ruffling papers on the desks of the six squad members. A long rectangular table was against the northern wall of the squad room. It was crowded with a computer, fax machine, coffee maker and the community property of the squad. The linoleum floor was scuffed and scraped from years of heavy use.

Nunes was leaning forward on the worn desktop. The sleeves of his white shirt were rolled up. The collar was undone, the burgundy tie loosened. His jacket was draped over the back of his chair. He was on the telephone with David Meredith—one of the top men in the Medical Examiner's office.

"Can you tell me how high the methamphetamine level was, Dave?"

Nunes whistled softly into the receiver. "Any chance that was accumulated residual from chronic use?"

He listened for a few more minutes before thanking Meredith and hanging up. He sat back and stared out the window. A Bonanza turned into its final approach to Sacramento Executive Airport. Nunes' black eyes followed it down until it disappeared behind the trees.

Over the past five years, Nunes had been trying to scrape enough money together to buy a small airplane. Nothing fancy, a used Cessna or Piper—just something to tool around in. Maybe in another year or so he'd have enough saved. He glanced at the set of clear Lucite picture frames on his desk. The twins would be off to college soon, and his dream of taking the family on a flying tour of the National Parks would probably go unrealized.

It would help if he got the promotion he was up for—and the raise that went with it. But you didn't get promotions in the Sac PD by gazing out your window daydreaming. You got promotions by closing cases.

Nunes straightened in his chair and looked at Detective Case. "The M.E. says Metzger died of an acute metham-phetamine overdose. He said it was the highest level he's ever seen."

Detective Case leaned back in his chair. He was dressed casually, his shirt and slacks a little loose. He'd been dieting since his divorce, but, in spite of having lost twenty-five pounds, he was still overweight.

"I thought that resident we talked to this morning … What was his name?" Detective Case picked up his pocket notepad and flipped back a few pages. "Castaic. I thought Doctor Castaic told us Metzger died from complications of his injuries."

"As I recall, he was careful to point out that he didn't know why, exactly, Metzger died. He did say that he wouldn't be surprised if the cause of death was related to his injuries— that it's not too unusual for apparently stable patients to die several days after a traumatic injury."

"That's right." Case scanned his pad. "Something about blood clots floating into the lungs. What'd he call that?"

"Pulmonary embolism. He also mentioned other potential complications like arrhythmias from bruising of the heart, or fluid accumulating in the lungs from a pulmonary contusion."

"Sure," Case said. He tilted his chair back, placing his foot against the edge of his desk. "He was rambling on about that stuff for quite a while. Like there wasn't any reason to question Metzger biting it. I'm no doctor, but I can't imagine any of the things Castaic mentioned looking too much like a meth OD." Case flipped his notepad onto the desk. "The ones I've seen really spaz out."

"They can be dramatic."

"Exactly." Case fingered the sparse mustache that clung to his upper lip. "There's no way that flipping a little blood clot into your lung is going to look anything like a crank OD."

"I suppose we should have another chat with Doctor Castaic."

"Absolutely. I mean we *are* talking about a homicide now, aren't we?" He let his chair drop forward. "There's no way Metzger could've gotten the crank himself—he's been chained to a bed for two days with tubes coming out every orifice."

Nunes nodded.

Case pointed at Nunes. "Castaic's hiding something, I can feel it. We definitely should drag his ass in for another little chat."

Detective Nunes picked up the phone. "We should also speak with the patrolmen who were guarding Metzger. Are they still downstairs?"

"I imagine so. They must have a stack of paperwork to do—wait until they find out it was a homicide." Case laughed. "Those poor bastards."

"Let's see if we can get them up here," Nunes said, dialing the extension for the desk sergeant downstairs. "Find out who was in Metzger's room this morning."

Detective Nunes spoke with the desk sergeant briefly, and then hung up. "It's Dougal and Long. They'll be up momentarily."

"Poor bastards," Case repeated happily, shaking his head.

While they waited, Detective Nunes gazed out of the window, but didn't see any more planes. The little kernel of tension he'd first felt when talking with the M.E. began to grow.

Metzger's murder added another layer of complexity to a case that already had him stymied. He and Case had interviewed Prescott's co-workers and neighbors, who all thought highly of the Prescotts and couldn't imagine why someone would want to hurt them. Nunes still needed to speak with the Prescott's extended family. These cases sometimes turned out to be an old family skeleton jumping out of the closet. Jake's parents were vacationing in Europe, but Sara's parents were due to fly in that evening. Jake had promised to call him once they were settled in. Since they lived across the country in Florida, however, Nunes didn't hold much hope that they would have anything meaningful to add to the case.

The crime scene crew hadn't had much luck either. Their report was sitting on Nunes' desk—no latent prints, or any other physical evidence in the Prescott home that would help identify Metzger's partner. The Folsom prisoner who had threatened Prescott in March had been a dead end also—he'd been extradited to Texas later that month.

Metzger had been their only lead as to where the Prescott girl was, or who had taken her. He hadn't given them anything during their written interviews, but interrogation is something of an art. Passing notes back and forth limits the process. Nunes had counted on getting more out of him once the tube was out.

There was usually some communication from the kidnapper. You could at least get an idea what kind of nut you were dealing with. But so far they hadn't heard a word. Nunes worried that this case was starting to look more like a child abduction, rather than a kidnapping for ransom.

He glanced back at the pictures on his desk. His eyes lingered on his children during their rafting trip down the American River six years ago. Nunes, like every other detective he knew, hated abduction cases. They struck too close to home and were depressingly difficult to solve. The first twenty-four to forty-eight hours were critical—if you were going to get the child back at all, it was usually within that time frame. They were well past that window.

And now this. The one person who knew what was behind the attack on the Prescotts was dead. It wasn't only the loss of their one solid lead that was gnawing at Nunes. It was also the growing realization that he'd probably made the wrong decision about Prescott in the ER the other day.

He had been certain that Prescott's aborted attempt to kill Metzger was a spur of the moment impulse. That once he had cooled down, he'd be fine—especially since he knew Metzger was their best shot at getting Kelly back. But Nunes knew that grief and revenge made people do things they wouldn't normally dream of. He should have known better. Now the odds of getting the girl back had widened dramatically, and Dr. Prescott might be facing a murder charge.

Officers Dougal and Long entered the squad room, interrupting Nunes' thoughts.

"Hey, boys," Detective Case said. They were still in uniform, looking rumpled and worn. Case gestured at a pair of metal folding chairs between his and Nunes' desks. It was where suspects usually sat. "Pull up a seat."

Detective Nunes stood up, shaking their hands before they sat down. Case remained in his seat, a wide grin on his face.

"You fellas finish your paperwork?"

The officer who had introduced himself as Dougal nodded. "Finally."

He was a handsome man, with dark hair and a strong jaw. He had the lithe build of a distance runner.

Detective Nunes could tell that Case took an instant disliking to him.

"We've had a little development," Case said. "You'll probably need to redo those reports."

Officer Dougal glanced at Long, who shrugged.

"I'm sure you'll want to pad them a little more," Case said. "Cover your asses a bit."

"What are you talking about?" Officer Long asked. At thirty-six, he was a little old for a first-grade patrolman. His hair was graying at the temples. "Exactly what 'development' are you talking about?"

"We just heard from the M.E. regarding Metzger's death," Nunes said. "It seems as if…"

"He was *murdered*," Detective Case cut in. He leaned toward Dougal and Long, letting the word hang in the air like a guillotine blade. "Last night, while you were supposed to be guarding him, someone slipped him a massive overdose of crank."

"What?" Officer Long said.

"No way," Dougal said at the same time. "They said he died from the fall. Something about a blood clot."

Case snorted.

"Apparently not," Nunes said. "The M.E. has determined that the cause of death was a methamphetamine overdose."

"He was murdered," Case repeated. "During your watch."

Officers Long and Dougal exchanged looks, then Long turned back to Detective Nunes. "How could that be? We were…"

"Look," Case interrupted. He tilted his chair back and laced his fingers behind his head, affecting an air of cama- raderie. "I know how it is. I've been stuck with hospital guard duty myself. You're sitting on your ass all night, making sure a prisoner who's practically in a damn coma doesn't escape. It's the worst detail you can pull. So to fight the boredom you go chat it up with a couple of the hot little nurses." Case winked at Dougal. "Who could blame you?"

"No sir. That didn't happen. We even staggered our breaks so that at least one of us was outside his door all night."

"Come on, Dougal. A good-looking guy like you? As soon as Long headed downstairs for a cup of coffee the nurses were probably falling all over themselves to get you into a back…"

"Knock it off, Stan," Detective Nunes interrupted. He usually let Case play his annoying little games—more often than not it worked on the suspects they were questioning— but these were fellow officers. "All we want to know is who was in Metzger's room this morning."

"Nobody," Dougal answered. "I mean besides hospital staff, he didn't have any visitors."

"Well then, why don't you tell us about the hospital staff," Case said, as if he were talking to a couple of third graders. "Somebody poisoned him. What we're trying to do here is find out who that might have been."

"His nurse was in there off and on throughout the shift. And a group of doctors went around to all of the rooms last night, right after we started our shift," Officer Long said. "I suppose any one of them could've slipped him something while they were in his room."

Nunes shook his head. "According to the M.E., the ratio of unmetabolized methamphetamine to its breakdown products indicates a fairly short time between exposure and death. The overdose couldn't have been given any more than a couple of hours before Metzger died."

Officer Long shrugged, then a thought occurred to him. "Hey, wait a sec. They have a flowchart at the bedside where they always record the patient's vital signs. I'm sure we could check it and find out what times the nurse was in there." He looked at Dougal. "But it seems to me that she hadn't been in Metzger's room for quite a while."

"That's right. I think it was about three a.m. She told me Metzger had finally gone to sleep—he'd apparently been a real pain in the ass."

"We're more interested in who it *could* have been, not who it wasn't," Case said.

"The only other person I remember is the janitor," Dougal said, shifting his weight uneasily on the metal chair. "He went through the unit that morning, emptying trash cans. He was only in each room for a few seconds, though." Dougal rubbed at his forehead as he thought about it. "Other than that I don't remember anyone else..."

"Hey!" Officer Long snapped his fingers and looked at Dougal. "What about that doctor?"

"What doctor?"

"Remember when the nurses and everybody ran into that old lady's room? Everyone except that doctor who went into Metzger's room, remember?"

"You're right. And he was in there quite a while, wasn't he?"

"At least five minutes. They'd finished working on the lady in the other room before he came out."

"What time was that?" Nunes asked.

Long and Dougal studied each other for a few seconds. "It must have been just a little before five," Long said. "I was waiting for the cafeteria to open so I could go down and grab a bite."

Detective Case narrowed his eyes at Long. "What makes you say he was a doctor?"

Long shrugged. "I assumed he was. There aren't many other people running around in a hospital in the middle of the night besides doctors and nurses."

"He was wearing scrubs and a white coat," Dougal added.

"Did he have a name badge?" Case pressed.

"Yeah," Dougal hesitated. "I suppose he did."

"Well, did he, or didn't he?"

Dougal looked down at his lap. "Yes. He did."

"What was the name on the badge, patrolman?"

"I'm sorry, sir, but I didn't notice."

Case snorted again. "A man walks right by you and kills the prisoner you're supposed to be guarding, and you don't even read his name tag?"

"Look, Case." Officer Long stood, carefully placing his palms onto Case's desk and leaning toward him. "We were there on guard duty, not witness protection. Our job was to make sure Metzger stayed in the room, not keep doctors out. Nobody told us he was at risk. Not even the detective investigating the case."

Nunes watched Long, impressed with his restrained strength. He'd probably make detective one day.

Long straightened away from the desk. The holster and equipment on his belt made that unique, creaking cop-sound that always took Nunes back to the days when he walked the beat on K Street. That was a long time ago. He suddenly felt tired and old.

"Look," Long said in a moderating tone, "we simply weren't anticipating somebody slipping in to kill the prisoner. We know we blew it. But we're trying to help out now as much as we can." Long sat back down.

Nunes cut Case off before he could respond. "You're correct, Officer Long. This finger-pointing is just wasting time."

Nunes studied his thumbnail. "Metzger was involved in a violent crime—we all should have been more aware that something like this might happen. Detective Case and I appreciate any help you are able to give us."

Nunes looked from Long to Dougal. "Do either of you remember what this doctor looked like?"

"He was kind of young, I guess."

"It's a teaching hospital. They're all young," Case said.

"How about you, Officer Long?" Nunes asked.

"White guy, about six feet."

Nunes resumed the study of his thumbnail. "Medium build?"

"Yeah."

"Brown hair?"

"Now that you mention it." Long looked at Dougal.

"That's right. Kind of reddish brown."

Detective Case looked at Nunes. He was trying to figure out where Nunes was going with this, and didn't like being left behind.

"What about his eyes?" Nunes reached down and opened the bottom drawer of his desk, pulling out a file. "Were they hazel?"

Case's face suddenly relaxed. Before Long and Dougal could respond, he pointed at the file. "Prescott."

"Do you recognize the man in this photograph?" Nunes asked, removing a copy of the family portrait from the file.

Long took the photo and held it so both he and Officer Dougal could see it. They both nodded. "That's him," Long said. "That's the guy."

Nunes looked at Dougal.

"Yes sir, that's the man. Who is he?"

"Doctor Jake Prescott. It was his home that Metzger broke into the other night. His daughter was kidnapped and his wife shot."

"Holy crap," Dougal exclaimed. "Do you think he's the one who gave Metzger the overdose?"

"What else do you think he was doing in there?" Case sneered.

"He certainly had a motive," Nunes said. He continued in a soft voice, as if he were thinking out loud rather than speaking to the other men. "I thought Prescott understood that Metzger was the only solid lead we had for finding Kelly—I guess I was wrong."

"Hey, for all we know, Prescott set this whole thing up," Case said, warming to the idea of Jake Prescott as a suspect. "And now he had to take Metzger out to protect himself. I thought there was something a little off about him. Probably got himself a hot little nurse and wanted his wife out of the way."

"I suppose we better get him in here for questioning," Nunes said.

"You bet your ass." Case jumped from his seat.

"Let me take care of that, Stan." Nunes reached for his telephone. "We're going to need to talk to Dr. Castaic and Metzger's nurse again. Why don't you set that up?"

Detective Case frowned at getting stuck with the scut work.

"How about the janitor?" Officer Long asked.

"That's right," Detective Nunes said as he finished dialing Prescott's home number. He held the receiver to his ear and looked at Case. "Track him down, too."

"Fine," Case muttered. He glared at Long. "Don't you guys need to redo your reports? We can take care of this mess from here."

Long and Dougal stood up.

Nunes nodded his thanks while he listened to Prescott's answering machine.

"Dr. Prescott, this is Detective Nunes. We would like to touch base with you. Could you call me at the station as soon as you get this message? It is now Monday, twelve-oh-five." He gave the phone number for the squad room and hung up, leaving his hand on the receiver. He thought for a few seconds, and then picked up the phone again.

"He's probably with his wife."

After speaking with the SICU ward clerk, Nunes looked at Detective Case.

"Nobody has seen him today," he said heavily. "But they expect him within a few hours. I guess we might as well both head over to the hospital."

15

As Luther hung up the phone, it occurred to him that he hadn't thought about Katherine for the last few days. It felt good to be free of the guilt for a while. He closed the Yellow Pages and stretched in his chair. He heard the guest room door open.

"Hey, Sleeping Beauty," he said, when Jake entered the study.

Jake grunted and dropped into a chair. His hair was mussed and, if anything, he looked even worse than he had a few hours ago.

"I just made a pot of coffee. You want a cup?"

Jake nodded.

When Luther returned from the kitchen, he handed Jake one of the mugs. "Well, I batted about 500. We've got a lead on Quince's package, but no luck tracking down Chance." He nodded at the phone book. "There's no Billy Ray Chance or David Brown registered at any of the area hotels. Must be using a different alias."

Jake sunk a little lower in his seat.

"When I tried Quince's home number it was disconnected. But I was able to locate his brother." Luther pushed on, wanting to get all of the bad news out of the way. "Quince is dead."

Jake froze, the cup of coffee half way to his lips.

"They're calling it a suicide. The brother thinks he was overwhelmed by his wife's death."

"How did he die?" Jake's eyes held Luther's. He already knew the answer.

"Gunshot wound to the head."

Luther sat on the edge of his desk. "After that I called several independent shipping services, claiming a package I was waiting for was overdue. We caught a break. There's a company called Mailboxes USA that's handling a parcel addressed to you, originating from Roanoke, Virginia."

"When's it arriving?"

"It's due this afternoon, or tomorrow morning at the latest. We need to go to the local office to find out when, exactly. I'll throw a couple of BLT's together and then we can head on over."

Jake glanced at his watch. "Chance is supposed to call me at the hospital today."

"That's right. You better get over there. I'll take care of Mailboxes USA." Luther stood up. "Come on. Let's get those sandwiches."

As Luther made the BLT's, Jake called the SICU. Except for Detective Nunes, they hadn't received any calls for him. Jake asked them to forward any calls to his pager.

"No word from Chance yet," Jake said, hanging up.

"How's Sara?" Luther handed him one of the sandwiches.

"She was asleep, but the nurse says she's doing well."

"Great."

They stood at the kitchen sink, eating.

"I was thinking I should swing by my place on the way to the hospital," Jake said around a bite of sandwich.

"Sara's parents are flying in tonight, and I'd like to get the blood stain out of the carpet."

Luther nodded and drank some milk. "It might be a good idea to put your pager number on the outgoing message of your home phone, too. We want to make it as easy as possible for Chance to reach you."

"Will do." Jake managed to finish half of his sandwich. "I better take off. I'll call when I hear from Chance."

Jake clutched the steering wheel, trying to keep the cold anxiety in check. The nap at Luther's had helped, but the familiar fear was closing in again.

Whenever a child abduction story was in the news, he had always watched in sympathetic dread. Now he knew that even his darkest fears had never come close to the actual horror. At least he knew what had happened to his daughter and, if Billy Ray Chance could be trusted, that she was still alive—for the time being. Many parents never heard another word, never had the thin sliver of hope to cling to that he had. How in heaven's name could they keep going?

As Jake turned the Citation off 43rd Avenue and into his housing tract, he suddenly realized his home was one of the few places that Chance knew where to find him. It seemed likely Chance would be there, waiting for him.

Jake's foot eased up on the accelerator. He slowed down, deciding to cruise the neighborhood first. If anything looked suspicious, he could always bail out. As he navigated the streets, Jake scanned the few cars parked at the curbs. Bikes and other toys lay scattered in the quiet yards. Everything looked normal. Jake was starting to relax as he turned onto the cross street toward Rivercrest.

Halfway down the block, his mouth went dry. A brown sedan was parked at the curb, just shy of the intersection. A man sat in the driver's seat, his head turned to the right. He would have a clear view of Jake's house, which was the third from the corner.

Jake slowed the Citation to a crawl and drifted to the left side of the road. He held his foot poised over the gas pedal as he coasted up to the other car. Although the man was still facing the other direction, Jake could now make out enough of his features to see that he was Asian. He was holding a CB microphone to his mouth, and Jake noticed the short, extra antenna on his car. Jake suddenly realized the man was a cop, and the breath he had been holding rushed from his mouth. It would make sense for the police to be watching his house in case Metzger's accomplice returned—and that meant it was safe for him to go home.

When the Citation drifted past the car, the man glanced at Jake and then did a classic double take. Giving him a wave, Jake smiled and swung into a right turn onto Rivercrest Drive and turned left into his driveway. As he got out of the Citation, Jake saw that the cop was leaning forward in his seat watching him, the microphone still at his mouth.

Jake changed from his scrubs into a pair of jeans and an In-N-Out Burger T-shirt. He clipped his pager to his belt and went to the telephone mounted on the kitchen wall. There were four messages. He pushed the play button.

"Jake, this is Mary Clemmons. I'm simply in a state of shock over what's happened. When the police came around the other day they said that Kelly is missing—is that true? I just can't believe something like this would happen on our street. I've called the hospital, and they tell me Sara's doing about as well as could be hoped for. So at least that's good news. You let us know if there's anything Frank or I can do to help, all right? Anything at all, just let us know. Well, our prayers are with you, Jake."

The machine beeped and played a message from Detective Nunes asking Jake to call him, then beeped again.

White noise hissed on the tape for a few seconds before the click of a hang up, followed by another beep.

"Jake. This is Tony. Listen up, cuz. The cops are looking for you. They got the preliminary tox report from Metzger's autopsy, and they know you were in his room just before he coded. Lord knows that *cabrón* deserved it, but…Shit, I don't know what to say. I just wanted to give you a heads-up and let you know they're all over the hospital looking for you. Give me a call, Jake. I can help you with this."

Jake's fingers fumbled on the repeat button. Autopsy? What in the hell was Castaic talking about?

It felt as if the kitchen floor were dropping from under his feet as the message played again.

Metzger had died?

Jake walked numbly back to the breakfast bar and sat on one of the stools.

He had killed Metzger.

His mind scrambled wildly. What went wrong? Maybe he miscalculated the dose of Versed. No, that was impossible. He had used one of the syringes from the ER airway box, and they were preloaded five-milligram doses. Even at double the dose, the only danger would be from suppression of the respiratory drive—and Metzger was on the ventilator.

Jake's eyes widened. Maybe he'd forgotten to…No, he clearly remembered going back and resetting the ventilator before he left Metzger's room. He thought about it for several seconds, and then shook his head. He was absolutely certain the ventilator had cycled a few times before he left the room. There was no way that Metzger should have died. Yet, apparently, he had. Jake couldn't figure out what went wrong, but whatever it was, the police thought he had intentionally killed Metzger.

Jake suddenly realized the cops weren't watching his house looking for Chance; they were looking for him. And if he was arrested, there was no way he could get Kelly back. Jake knocked the stool over as he ran to the window in the front room. He frantically scanned the street in front of his house. Nothing. He peered to the right to see if the brown sedan was still at the corner, but a hedge blocked the view.

Hurdling a laundry basket filled with toys, Jake ran from the family room, up the stairs and into the guest room that fronted onto the street. He spread the slats on the Venetian blinds and saw a squad car next to the brown sedan. Two uniformed officers were in the front seat, talking to the man in the sedan. The one on the passenger side had bright red hair and looked about eighteen years old. Jake saw the Asian man point down the street in front of him toward the levee that ran behind Jake's house. The cops in the squad car nodded, and the redhead got out. He squatted on his heels next to the sedan, resting a hand on the open window. The black and white pulled away and turned down Jake's street.

Jake stepped back from the window as the squad car drove past. After a few seconds, he peered through the window after the car. It pulled to the curb at the other end of the block and the driver got out. The driver and redhead both walked across to Jake's side of the street.

Jake ran downstairs and was at the back door when he remembered about leaving his pager number on the answering machine. He cursed and raced into the kitchen, his heart pounding. He punched the message record button, and the tape began to rewind.

"Come *on*," he shouted, slamming the wall next to the phone. The machine beeped. Jake spat out his name and pager number.

He ran out the back door, barely registering that one of its glass panels had been broken out. He sprinted across the yard and up the levee. His toe caught as he crested the top, and he sprawled onto the jogging trail. Rock fragments dug into his outstretched hands and he bit his lower lip with the impact. He got to his hands and knees and checked left and right. The cops hadn't made the top of the levee. He scrambled down the other side.

There was a sloping stretch of ground between the water and the base of the levee. A path wound through the tall weeds and brush down to the river. Bending over at the waist, Jake crabbed along the path as fast as he could, star thistle pricking through his T-shirt. It was less than a hundred yards from his house to the river, but Jake's breath was coming in tearing rasps as he ducked past one of the huge cottonwoods that lined the bank. He tilted his head back against the rough bark and looked at the river. The water was flat gray and calm.

Jake dabbed at his bloodied lip. His breath was coming easier. He peered around the tree. The policeman with the red hair was moving along the top of the levee, his hand on his gun. His attention was focused on Jake's house, but every few seconds he looked along the levee. The other officer was trotting up from the opposite direction. He pumped his palm at the redhead in a "slow down" gesture as he approached.

When they were positioned behind the houses next to Jake's, the older cop spoke into a hand-held radio. He drew his gun and nodded at the redhead. They moved down the slope, angling toward Jake's back yard.

The Asian cop would be making his move through the front door, and it would only take a few minutes before they realized Jake wasn't there. It wouldn't take them long to find him if he stayed where he was. He kicked off his tennis shoes, tied their laces together and hung them around his neck. Slipping into the water, he swam into the powerful current, allowing the river to carry him downstream. By the time he approached the other side, it felt as if his jeans were made of lead.

Jake's house was located on a bend in the river, and the current carved hard against the opposite levee. The steep slope had been reinforced with large chunks of fractured concrete, and Jake pulled himself onto one of the slabs that angled up from the water line. Squatting on the sun-warmed surface, he studied the opposite shore. He had drifted far enough around the bend so he couldn't see the roofs on his block. He pulled his shoes on, then scrambled and squished his way to the top of the levee.

South River Road runs along the western levee, and Jake walked down its crushed-cinder shoulder. To the west, the land spread out for miles in a checkerboard pattern of verdant fields. Before the levees were built, the entire area flooded each winter, forming a delta of dark, fertile soil. Jake looked out over endless fields of tomatoes, corn, sugar beets and beans, flourishing in the former flood plain. In the distance, a yellow crop duster trailed white mist back and forth beneath the blue sky. Pheasants cackled from across the valley. A chatter of birds came from the blackberry thicket next to the levee. The air was crisp, in spite of the warm sun. It was a beautiful spring afternoon in the Sacramento Valley, but it was lost on Jake.

The thought of Kelly's captivity being prolonged because Chance wouldn't be able to find him gnawed at his mind. With the police looking for him, he wouldn't be able to visit Sara in the hospital, nor would he be able to go home—and those were the only places Chance knew where to reach him. At least if Chance called his house or the hospital he would get his pager number and be able to…

159

Jake stopped abruptly and snatched the pager from his waistband. The display screen was filled with condensation. He fumbled at the power switch, but the unit was already on. He stared at the blank screen for several seconds, then threw it far out into the river. His panic faded as he remembered the hospital kept a supply of backup pagers in the house-staff office. The office was separate from the main hospital, and he was sure he could get in and out without the police spotting him. Jake continued down the road.

The river completed its bend and turned due south. Rounding the turn, Jake saw a network of floating platforms protruding into the backwater between two rock jetties. Less than half of the slips had boats in them. A gangplank connected the platforms with a dock built on pillars, well above the high water level. Picnic tables sat on the dock next to a building that fronted the empty parking lot. Jake passed beneath a sign spanning the entrance.

SCOTT'S MARINA—ESTABLISHED 1948.

A smaller sign above the door to the building read:

BAIT SHOP

BOAT AND JET SKI RENTALS

SNACKS

Jake walked in, a small bell announcing his arrival. Directly across the room, another door led out onto the dock. The floor space was crowded with display shelves. There was a dining bar, a grill, and a glass-fronted refrigerator stocked with beer, soda and bottled water.

The refrigerator buzzed loudly, vibrating a cardboard sign attached to its side advertising bloodworms for sale. An old man with thick, sun-bleached hair sat on a wooden stool reading a Louis L'Amour western. As Jake approached, the old man eyed his shoes.

"A mite early in the season for a dip, ain't it?" His voice was like dried bearings.

He pulled a paper cup from behind the counter, spat a stream of brown juice, and returned the cup to the shelf.

"I suppose." Jake looked down at his wet clothes, then turned his palms outward. "It wasn't exactly a planned activity."

"I reckon not." His lips split apart, revealing yellow teeth in what was probably supposed to be a smile. "What can I do ya' for?"

"I was hoping I could borrow your phone." Jake nodded at the telephone by the man's elbow. "It's a local call."

"Makes me no never mind." He slid the telephone over.

Jake lifted the receiver from the cradle and poised his finger over the keypad before he realized he didn't know Luther's phone number. He patted his hip pockets, but his wallet was still in the Citation.

"Do you have the White Pages?" he asked, replacing the receiver.

"I 'spect we got a copy round here somewheres." The old man pawed around behind the counter and pulled out a ragged phone book. The cover was crowded with hand written notes and telephone numbers. Dried bait was smeared across a corner.

Jake found Terry Luther's listing on Beechwood and dialed the number. He wasn't in. He left a message on the machine, asking Luther to call him at the marina when he got back. Hanging up, Jake thanked the man and told him he'd wait out on the dock for Luther's call.

Jake pulled a weathered chair over to several stacked crates at the dock's edge. He sat down in the sun, stretching his legs out in front of him. The crates shielded his body from the other side of the river. Peering between them, he watched the opposite shore. A couple of joggers went by on the levee, but Jake didn't see any police.

The sun slowly worked into his muscles, loosening the tension. The chunking sound of boats in their slips drifted up from the landing. Jake had just closed his eyes, resting his head against the back of the chair, when the old man's voice croaked out, "Now that looks like a mighty fine idea."

Jake lifted his head and saw the old man coming out of the bait shop with a bottle of Miller Genuine Draft in each hand.

"Perfect day for sitting in the sun and philosophizing," the man said. He transferred the beer so he was holding both bottles in his left hand and dragged a chair opposite Jake.

He spat his plug of tobacco over the crates and into the water, then sat down and held one of the bottles out. "Looks to me like you could use a brewski." When Jake hesitated, he added, "On me."

"Thanks." Jake accepted the beer. He took a long sip. "That does hit the spot. Thank you."

The man tilted his bottle at Jake in a beer drinker's salute and downed half of it.

He took another pull, and then used the bottle to point at Jake's feet. "Take it from a hard drinking fisherman. Your shoes'll dry out a sight quicker, you get 'em off your feet and set 'em in the sun. Spread your socks out on that crate and they'll be dry by the time your friend gets here."

Jake took his advice. He had another beer. The old man had another three. They sat and talked about nothing, waiting for Jake's socks to dry—and for Luther's call. Jake was grateful to the man for the conversation. It distracted him from his anguish over Sara and Kelly. After an hour and a half, a bell mounted on the outside wall of the bait shop began to ring.

"That'll be your boy." The man jerked his head at the store. "We don't get much action out here until summer."

Jake padded across the rough timbers in his bare feet, watching for stray hooks.

"Shag us another couple cold ones," the man called after him.

Luther knew where Scott's Marina was and said he would be there in half an hour. Jake went to the refrigerator and grabbed two more Millers before returning to the dock.

By the time Jake saw Luther's car approaching along South River Road, his socks were dry.

16

Billy Ray Chance parked the Lexus at the curb outside the next address on his list. Early that afternoon Fowler had called with the names of twenty-eight local PI's that were white males, between the ages of thirty and forty-five. He hadn't been able to narrow the search by height or weight—the database hadn't contained very specific information. Chance figured it would take him a couple of days to check them all out, but then he remembered Prescott's man had said he was retired. Chance called each agency on Fowler's list, pretending to be shopping around for a detective. If the investigator was available for consultation, Chance hung up and moved on to the next name. By the time he was done, he found four numbers had been disconnected, and two agencies had recorded messages saying they were not accepting any new clients.

That left Chance with only six names. The first one on his list had been a bust. The detective had been a thin man with sharp features. Nothing like Prescott's pal.

The next agency was Luther Investigations, and the address turned out to be in some hokey tourist trap called

164

Old Town. The front door was locked and had a FOR LEASE sign on it. He went to the photography studio next door. Some slob dressed like a cowboy was behind the counter.

"Afternoon," Chance said.

"Howdy, pardner. Ready to picture yourself in the Wild West?"

Chance glanced at the sample photos on the back wall. Pathetic tourists were dressed in ridiculous costumes. "I don't think so. I'm looking for the PI next door."

The man frowned. "Can't help you. He closed shop about half a year ago. Popular guy all of a sudden."

"How so?"

"Some kid was in here the other day looking for Luther, too. I'm glad he didn't have this much business when he was still open. He might've still been around to give me grief."

"I see." Chance paused. "This Luther, is he a big guy? Green eyes?"

"Yeah. Thinks he's some kind of Adonis."

"Sounds like the prick I'm looking for." Chance dropped his voice. "I caught him sneaking around me and one of my lady friends last year. Turns out he was working for my ex. The pictures he took cost me big in the divorce."

The man leaned on the counter, eyes wide.

"You wouldn't know how I could find him, would you?" Chance glanced at the door, then leaned in close to whisper, "I'd love to settle the score."

The man practically squealed with delight as he waddled out from behind the counter, his gut swinging over his belt like a wrecking ball. "I blew the kid off the other day, but I think I've got just what you're looking for." He draped an arm over Chance's shoulder and led him to an old roll-top desk. He pulled a business card for Luther Investigations from a drawer and flipped it face down on the desk. He poked a finger at the address written on the back.

"Mr. Luther asked me to forward anything important to his home." He winked at Chance. "I think this qualifies."

"Oh yeah," Chance said, copying the address. "This qualifies."

On his way to Luther's, he decided to get a different car. If Terry Luther was the guy, he would recognize the red Lexus, and Chance didn't want to tip him off. All he wanted to do for now was make sure Luther was the right cracker.

After a quick stop at the nearest Hertz, Chance drove a black Saturn to Luther's house and parked down the street. He pulled Zeiss binoculars from his duffel bag and settled in for a wait. A blue-haired woman in overalls carried a bucket and trowel out of the garage next door to Terry Luther's. Kneeling in the flowerbed between their front yards, she started weeding.

Thirty minutes later, a white car pulled into Luther's driveway. Chance trained the binoculars on the man when he got out and recognized him immediately.

Terry Luther was inside his house for only a couple of minutes before he hurried back to his car and drove off. Chance cruised by the house, avoiding eye contact with the old bat who was still rooting around in the dirt. The side-yard of Luther's house was screened by a large hedge and had a low fence. That was where he would go in, and then, so long Mr. Luther.

Chance stopped at McDonald's, formulating a three-step plan as he waited in the drive-through. First, it was time to shake Prescott up a bit. The more frantic he was at their next meeting, the better. Next, he would pay Terry Luther a visit and remove him from the equation. With Prescott alone and desperate, the final step of grabbing him up would be a breeze. Chance's spirits were high during the short drive back to the hotel. He unlocked the door and tossed a burger onto the kid's bed.

"How's it hanging, sweetpea?" He sat next to her and untied the knots. The kitten, which had been sleeping next to the girl's head, woke up, stuck its ass in the air and stretched its front legs. It yawned, clawed at the pillow, and then jumped up on the kid's side.

When she was untied, the girl sat up and grabbed the cat. She stiffened when Chance ran the back of an index finger along her cheek. Four long bruises were starting to show from when he'd had to backhand her that morning. His pinky ring had left a deeper, sharply rectangular bruise. He felt a sweet ache of anger as he saw silent tears stream from her eyes. All he did was untie her, and here she was crying again. He traced his fingernail from her chin down her neck, allowing his hand to linger on her chest. Her heart fluttered behind her ribs like a wild bird in a cage.

"Did you think of a name for your kitty yet?"

The girl remained completely still.

"Kelly," Chance said, allowing a dangerous edge to creep into his voice, "did you come up with a name yet?"

Kelly's nod was barely perceptible.

"Well?"

She pressed her lips together and turned her head.

Savoring the flash of rage as if it were forbidden fruit, Chance grabbed the hair at the back of her head, close to the scalp. "Don't get uppity with *me*, missy," he hissed, pressing his mouth against her ear. He twisted his fist, feeling hair pull out by the roots. "When I ask you a question, I expect an answer."

"Patches," she managed, her face contorted in pain.

"Well that's nice," Chance said, releasing his grip. "Patches is a nice name. Why don't you let me hold him while you go use the can and eat your lunch."

The girl reluctantly handed the kitten to Chance before going into the bathroom. Chance stood up, tossing the kitten onto the bed. It was time to turn up the heat.

He looked at the pad he'd left next to the telephone and called Sacramento General.

"SICU," a female voice answered.

"Hello, this is Officer Sloan," Chance said. "I'm wondering if Dr. Prescott is available. I'd like to speak with him."

"No, I haven't seen him all day," the woman said impatiently. "I've already told the detective I'd let you know as soon as he shows up. You don't need to be calling every five minutes."

"All right," Chance said after a moment's hesitation. "We appreciate your help."

He hung up and frowned at the telephone. He had told Prescott he'd be calling him at the hospital that afternoon to set up another ransom exchange—where the hell was he? He glanced back at his notes, and then called Prescott's home number. The machine picked up after several rings. In a rushed voice, Prescott identified himself and left his pager number.

Chance cursed out loud, slamming the phone down. What was Prescott thinking? How did he expect to get his daughter back if he was out screwing around? After a few seconds, Chance got one of the pencils out of the nightstand and redialed Prescott's home number. This time, he wrote the pager number on the scratch pad.

A recording informed him the pager he had called was out of service, but the party could be reached via a new number. The lead snapped as Chance was scratching out the old number and he had to dig around in the drawer for another pencil. The message repeated the new number and he got it down.

As he was dialing, Kelly came out of the bathroom. She got the kitten and burger from the bed and sat on the floor under the window. The kitten jumped around, playing with the wrapper as the girl ate. When the pager prompted him, Chance began entering the number printed on the front of the telephone into the keypad. After the fourth digit, he realized what he was doing and slammed the receiver into the cradle. He stormed around the room, cursing violently. Kelly grabbed the kitten and huddled against the wall.

He'd almost screwed the pooch that time. The desk clerk would answer any incoming call with the name of the hotel before putting it through to the room. Within a few minutes, Prescott would've had cops swarming all over the place.

As he thought about it, he realized the safest way to play it would be to use a pay phone far from the hotel, but then he wouldn't be able to use the first part of his plan. He really needed to be in the hotel room when he spoke with Prescott. He decided to have Prescott call him back on his cell phone. Since his cellular account was through an alias out of Salt Lake City, giving Prescott the number shouldn't be a problem.

Chance went out to his car, opening the door to get at his duffel bag on the back seat. He unzipped it and was rummaging around for the cell phone when he caught a blur of movement out of the corner of his eye. He looked over his shoulder in time to see the girl streak past the next room and around the corner of the building.

His shoes lost traction on the gravel and he went down on one knee before scrambling after her. By the time Chance rounded the corner, she was almost a third of the way to the street. She was running awkwardly, her arms clutched to her chest, and he was able to close the distance quickly. Glancing back at the sound of his approaching steps, her mouth ripped open in an unbelievably loud, high-pitched scream.

Within a few more steps, Chance grabbed her shoulder. She spun out of his grasp, but in doing so, lost her balance. She had to throw her arms wide to stay on her feet. The kitten flew from her arms and skittered across the gravel. Kelly quickly regained her balance, but hesitated as she looked back, screaming the kitten's name.

Chance delivered a full backhand swing at the girl's shrieking mouth and she sprawled on the ground in a motionless heap.

Chance's chest heaved with rage. The temptation to kick the shit out of the girl was like a physical force, and it took all of his will to resist it. Sure, he should have locked the door, but it was the kid's fault for betraying his trust. She deserved a pounding, but he needed her coherent.

Chance looked around to see if anybody was watching. Nobody had come out of the rooms, or even looked out a window to see why a kid was screaming bloody murder. A guy with a shopping cart full of junk was sitting at a bus stop across the street, his head turned in the other direction. Chance snorted appreciatively. He loved America.

The kitten spit loudly when Chance scruffed it. He held it away from his body as it writhed and clawed at the air. He toed the girl in the ribs. When she didn't respond, he used his foot to turn her over onto her back. Her eyes were rolled up under half-closed lids, the exposed whites as glassy as bottled milk. Blood oozing from her nostril looked almost black against her pale skin. Her slack lips were mashed.

Chance turned his head to the side, his flat eyes studying her as a fisherman might study a worm. He thought he could detect a slight rise and fall of her chest, but wasn't sure. It didn't seem as if he'd hit her all that hard, but with kids, who knows?

He laughed when it occurred to him that it was too bad her dad wasn't there to evaluate her injury. The sound of his laugh seemed to bring her around. Her eyelids fluttered, her face twisting in pain.

Chance hefted her onto his hip. He figured he must look pretty ridiculous walking back to the room—one arm extended in front of him holding a squirming cat, the other holding the limp girl close to his body like a sack of feed. He glanced across the street, but the bum was still staring off into space.

Back in the room, the girl started to moan. He dropped her onto the bed and tossed the kitten next to her. It shot across the bedspread and darted under the bed. Wetting a coarse washcloth in the bathroom sink, Chance sat on the bed and placed the rag on her forehead. She opened her eyes and looked at Chance with a bewildered expression. Comprehension forced itself back into her face like an unwelcome guest. She put a trembling hand to her swollen lips.

"I'm sorry you made me do that, sweetpea. Running off like that—you didn't leave me much choice, now did you?"

The girl glared at him so vehemently that Chance couldn't suppress a smile.

"Why don't you go clean yourself up?" He removed the washcloth from her forehead and held it out to her.

Kelly took the washcloth and then sat up, searching the room. "What did you do with Patches?" she demanded shrilly.

"Relax. He's under the bed."

She crouched next to the bed and, after a few minutes of coaxing, was able to retrieve the kitten.

"Listen, Kelly. I feel kind of bad for having to hit you." Chance smeared the thickening blood from under her nose with his thumb. "How about I make it up to you by letting you talk to your daddy?"

Kelly's head snapped up, her battered face brightening with excitement.

"You'd like that, wouldn't you?" he asked. "Why don't you go in the john and clean up? If you make yourself pretty, I'll let you talk to him."

She stood up quickly, steadying herself on the edge of
the bed for a few seconds before carrying the kitten into
the bathroom. Chance went back to his car and got his cell
phone, locking the door this time.

He called Prescott's pager and entered the number to
his cell phone. It took Prescott less than a minute to call
back. Chance let the phone ring several times before he
answered it.

"Is that you, Jake old buddy?"

"Where's Kelly, you bastard?"

"Why, Jake," Chance said lightly. "Here I've been
baby-sitting your little girl for you the past two days, and
that's how you thank me? I must say, I'm hurt."

"Is Kelly all right?"

"Oh she's *more* than all right. She's a fine little thing.
Ripe as a sweet Georgia peach."

"Damn it, Chance! What have you done to her?"

"Take it easy." Chance's laugh faded as a wisp of
apprehension moved in the back of his mind. "She's fine."

"Let me talk to her."

"Hold your horses. We've got some business to take
care of first."

The vague uneasiness Chance felt suddenly flared.
Prescott had called him by name! He thought back over the
past two days, but he was certain he hadn't let it slip. Prescott
must have found out some other way.

Metzger.

Chance's mouth hardened. He'd been too slow taking
care of Metzger. The huge advantage he had enjoyed with
Prescott was lost.

"Well?" Prescott's voice cut across the line.

"Well, what?"

"Let me talk to Kelly."

"First we need to work out the details of our next little
get-together. You still want to get your kid back, don't you?"

"Yes!"

"All right, then listen up. I found a nice little spot. You know the Yolo Causeway?"

"Yes."

"Good. We'll meet on the west side, just south of Highway 80, tomorrow morning at nine. And no unexpected guests this time, Jake. Don't try and screw me over again."

"Okay."

"I mean it," Chance said. "Your kid's life depends on it. I know your buddy's going to be there, so I want him out in the open where I can see him. If he isn't, I'm going to assume he's trying to take me out, and it's bye-bye Kelly. You follow?"

"Yes."

"Good."

Kelly stepped out of the bathroom and stood next to the door, eyes fixed on the cell phone in Chance's hand. She had combed her hair back and washed the blood from her face. The lopsided swelling of her lips, circles under her eyes and bruise on her cheek were stark against her pale skin. Chance gestured, and she stepped to her bed and sat opposite him, holding the kitten in her lap.

"All you have to do is bring the money," Chance said. "If you and your friend behave yourselves, everything will go smooth and you'll get your girl back. Good as new."

"I need some proof that Kelly's all right."

"Fair enough, Jake." Chance smiled. "How about if I let you talk to her right now? Would that satisfy you?"

"Yes!"

"Hang tight. I'll put her on."

Chance held the cell phone out to Kelly and patted the bed next to him. "Your daddy wants to talk to you, Kelly. Sit over here by me."

Kelly stood up and reached for the phone. Chance pulled it away, nodding at the kitten. "Let me hold Patches for you."

She gave him the kitten and took the telephone.

"Daddy?" she cried.

Chance held the cat in his left hand and, guiding the girl by her shoulder, made her sit down next to him.

"Daddy," she cried again. Tears began to flow from her eyes. "I want to come home!"

Chance held the kitten on his right thigh. He trapped the top of its shoulders in his left hand, his thumb and index finger encircling its neck. As Kelly was telling her father that she loved him too, Chance twisted the kitten's head off.

Kelly froze in horror. When the blood spurted, she shrieked hysterically and dropped the phone. Her screams filled the room.

Chance took a few steps toward the cardboard box and tossed the cat's body in. The head followed. Chance picked up the cell phone.

"See there, Jake old son? I told you she was all right. That's quite a set of lungs she's got on her. Be there tomorrow morning with the money." He shut off the phone and tossed it onto the bed.

"That ought to tighten the screws a bit," Chance said to himself.

17

Luther hung up the extension in the kitchen and went back to his office. Jake was still pleading and cursing into the phone. He pried the receiver from Jake's hand and replaced it in its cradle. Jake collapsed into the chair and hunched forward, holding his face in his hands. Luther stared at Jake. No words of comfort would erase Kelly's screams.

He picked up the pager and pushed the button to display the number Jake had just called. It began with an area code Luther didn't recognize. There had been a steady background hum during the call, and the staticky, tinny sound suggested a cell phone. Pushing the display button again, he studied the four-digit number that had come across a few minutes before the last page. The deep lines in his face relaxed. He copied the number onto a notepad and pulled the Yellow Pages from the bottom drawer of his desk.

"Take a look at this, Jake." Luther flipped the book open to the motel section and laid it on the desk. He dropped the notepad on top and jabbed at it with his finger.

"This is the partial number you were paged to just before Chance's page came through. It starts with three-seven-one, which is one of the prefixes in West Sacramento. And West Sac is crammed full of motels. I must've called over thirty of them this morning looking for Chance."

Jake lifted his face from his hands and stared at the number.

"I think Chance started entering the phone number for his motel, realized his mistake and paged you to his cell phone instead."

Jake leaned forward in his seat.

"But look here." Luther pointed at the number on the pad again. "The fourth digit's an eight. Assuming that this was Chance paging you with a partial entry, we can check the phone book for West Sac motel listings starting with three-seven-one-eight and…"

Jake lunged to his feet, leaning over the phone book to run his finger down the long list of motels. "Here's one on West Capitol," he exclaimed, his finger grinding into an entry near the top of the first column. "The Bonanza Inn."

Grabbing a pen from Luther's desk, he circled the number. He scanned the rest of the listings, circling two more entries.

"There's only three." Jake grabbed the phone book and headed for the door. "Let's go."

Luther unlocked the top drawer of the desk and removed his Beretta 92 FS. He clipped on its belt holster, grabbed a light jacket from the entryway closet, and followed Jake outside. They took Luther's Camry up Watt Avenue to Highway 80 and headed southwest. After connecting onto east bound Capitol City Freeway, they took the first exit at Harbor Boulevard.

Jake leaned forward against the seat belt as they crested the freeway overpass. His eyes searched ahead to the next cross street, which was West Capitol Avenue.

Luther nodded at the open phone book in Jake's lap as they approached the intersection. "What's the first address?"

"One-oh-four-three-eight."

Luther slowed and stayed in the center lane until he could read the block number on the street sign, then changed lanes to make a right turn.

East of Harbor, West Capitol had two lanes of traffic running in either direction, separated by a raised center divider. Turn lanes came at regular intervals, providing access to the businesses lining both sides of the street.

They passed the Bonanza Inn halfway down the third block. Luther pulled a U-turn at the next break in the island. The Bonanza was a rectangular, single level building with gleaming white stucco and green trim. Each room's front window had a green window box filled with violets. Station wagons and minivans crowded the parking lot.

Luther drove slowly to the end of the complex without spotting Chance's red Lexus. He turned around and drove back to the manager's office.

Before the Camry came to a stop, Jake opened the passenger door and started to get out.

"Hold on a second," Luther said, laying a hand on Jake's forearm. "Let's go over the game plan first."

He opened the console between the front seats and pulled out a small plastic file for business cards. "A little subterfuge will usually get you further than the direct approach." Fingering back to the tab marked Real Estate, he removed a card and dropped it into the breast pocket of his jacket. "If the managers smell trouble, they usually clam up. It can be a little tricky, so it might be best if you let me do the talking."

"No problem," Jake said, stepping out of the car. He waited impatiently.

Luther got out of the car and came around to Jake's side, squeezing his shoulder. "Try to relax, Jake."

They entered the manager's office. A counter dominated the small room. Two chairs were backed against the front wall, one on either side of the entrance. A couple of magazine racks stood on the burgundy carpet, displaying circulars advertising local restaurants and nightclubs. Muted clinks of silverware came from the door standing ajar behind the counter. The office was warm with the smell of curry. When Jake let the front door swing shut behind them, a chime sounded in the back room.

A few seconds later, an Indian woman came from the back room. Before she pulled the door closed behind her, Luther caught a glimpse of a turbaned man and two children eating supper.

"Good evening, gentlemen," she said in a precise, British accent. She reached behind the counter and then placed a blank registration card on top. "We have one very nice room available."

"Oh, no thank you, ma'am. We don't need a room." Luther stepped up to the desk. "We're hoping you can help us though. We're looking for one of your guests."

He pulled the business card from his pocket and laid it on the counter. "My name is Terry Luther. I met a man last night who was interested in buying a home in the area, and he asked me to show him my listings this afternoon. I was to pick him up at his hotel, and I believe he told me he was staying here."

The woman picked up Luther's card and studied it briefly before placing it back on the counter. "What is his name, please?"

"Well, that's just it. I can't recall, exactly," Luther laughed sheepishly, then jerked a thumb over his shoulder. "We met at a bar just down the street here. By the time we got out of there, I was pretty lit. I know he told me his name. I remember thinking it was a simple one—that I wouldn't have any trouble remembering it—but now I'll be dogged if I can think of it."

The woman looked past Luther at Jake, then back to Luther again. Her dark brown eyes remained impassive as she waited for him to continue.

"I was hoping if I describe him to you, you might recognize him. I'm a lot better with faces than I am with names."

"I will try."

"I appreciate it. He's an inch or two shorter than me." Luther held his hand out next to him, level with his eyes. "In his mid- to late-thirties. With light colored eyes and blond hair. He was wearing it in a short ponytail."

The woman turned and studied the key cabinet on the wall behind her, as if she could see the faces of her guests there. Then she faced Luther again and shook her head. "I do not believe your friend is staying with us."

Luther pursed his lips. "I'm almost certain he told me The Bonanza. He mentioned that he was traveling with his young daughter. Does that sound familiar?"

"No. It does not." She shook her head, then glanced at the door behind her.

"He was driving a red car—I think it was a Lexus."

Reaching back under the counter, she pulled out a small stack of registration cards and looked through them. "I am sorry. None of our guests have such a vehicle. Perhaps your friend is staying at one of the other motels. There is one called the Beaumont." She inclined her head slightly. "Perhaps you misunderstood."

"Well, that certainly is possible." Luther smiled. "I'll give the Beaumont a try. Thanks for your help."

Luther retrieved his card from the counter, then he and Jake returned to the car.

"What are the other two addresses?" Luther asked, starting the car.

Jake opened the phone book and read the other circled listings.

"It sounds like The Hacienda is closest, probably only one or two blocks back on the other side of Harbor," Luther said, pulling out onto West Capitol. He flipped his visor down against the afternoon sun. "Let's hit that one next."

Once west of Harbor, conditions deteriorated. The distance between West Capitol Boulevard and the Capitol City Freeway shrank to less than a block. The motels advertised that they rented rooms by the hour. The potholed street narrowed to a single lane in either direction. Gravel shoulders replaced the sidewalks. A guy in a greasy overcoat was pushing a shopping cart along the edge of the road.

When they drove past a mobile home park surrounded by a cyclone fence, Luther began to slow down. It was Jake who spotted the small marquee for the Hacienda. Wedged between a battery warehouse and a recycling center, the hotel was an L-shaped building, its short arm running across the back of the property.

Luther pulled into the gravel parking lot and drove around to the back, checking for Chance's car. Several rooms were obviously vacant. One had a door that hung open from its top hinge. The stucco was faded and webbed with cracks, several pieces flaking off in sheets. Graffiti covered the walls. A thin dog was sniffing garbage at the base of the wall bordering the freeway. The rear parking area was otherwise deserted.

Luther drove back to the manager's office. The front of the hotel was in slightly better shape. The larger cracks in the stucco were patched and the graffiti had been painted over. The office door was warped, and Luther had to give it a shove with his shoulder. The air inside was stale, as if it had been breathed too many times. The front window was covered with adhesive tinting. A flickering fluorescent bulb provided the only light. A doorbell buzzer was screwed to the front of the counter.

When Luther pushed the button, a grating buzz sounded in the back room, followed by a crash of breaking glass. Luther heard a muttered curse, but then there was no further sound from the back room. He pulled the real estate card from his breast pocket and tapped its edge on the counter as they waited. After twenty seconds, Luther shrugged at Jake and pushed the button again.

The door jerked open immediately, and a man in his early forties stepped out. He was short and very thin—his sallow skin stretched across the hungry bones of his face. Lank hair hung into his eyes. His pupils were dilated. He shuffled up behind the desk. A strong ether smell made Luther step back.

"What'cha want?" The man didn't seem to know what to do with his hands. They fluttered nervously across the desktop. His eyes crawled over Luther, lingering where his coat hung over his right hip. "You cops?"

Luther dropped the business card back into his breast pocket and unbuttoned his coat. The man flinched when Luther's right hand rested on top of the gun.

"Guy's pretty sharp, eh Jake?" Luther's face was blank. He allowed an uncomfortable silence to develop.

The man's hands began to flit about as he readjusted the way his loose shirt and pants hung on his bony frame. He suddenly looked down at his hands as if they belonged to someone else, then folded his arms across his chest, tucking his hands beneath the armpits. Almost immediately, his mouth began to work. Dark teeth chewed his lip.

"What's your name?" Luther asked.

"Paul. Paul Dupree," the man said rapidly. "I work here, man. I take care of the place, see? I'm the manager. Been in this shit-hole for two and a half months. You got no call comin' round here hassling me again. Ain't seen my old lady in weeks." He pushed the lower part of his face forward, trying to make something of his nothing chin. "If she says different, she's lying, man. I swear it. I haven't been anywhere near that..."

Luther held up his hand.

"Relax, Paul. We're here to ask about one of your guests."

"Yeah? Which one? Because I'll tell you right now, man. I don't know nothing about them. I take the cash, and clean up the trash." He shook his head. "That's it, man. I mind my own business. Keep my nose clean and mind my own business."

"Well, Paul, we don't want a complete bio on the guy. All we want is for you to tell us which room he's in."

Dupree sniffed loudly and pulled the front of his T-shirt up, wiping his nose. The movement exposed a swastika tattoo above his navel.

"He's white. Maybe an inch shorter than me. Blond hair pulled back in a little Steven Segal thing."

Dupree's eyes flashed when Luther described Chance's hair.

"Pale, yellowish eyes? What do you think, Paul? Sound familiar?"

"I don't know, man," Dupree answered, wetting his lips. "We get a lot of traffic through here. They all kind of blur together, you know? I guess someone like that may've been here, but I don't remember. Like I said, I don't get too cozy with the guests—they're all a blur."

Luther leaned across the desk. "This guy would stick out around here like a boil on a hog's ass. He wears fancy clothes. Drives a red Lexus. The Narc Squad tells us he's moving a lot of high-end coke. We also know he's doing business out of your place. So why don't you cut yourself a break and tell us what room he's in?"

"I told you man, I don't know him."

Luther turned to Jake.

"Looks like he wants to do it the hard way. I guess we'll have to go through all the rooms in this dump, see what we come up with. All of the rooms," he repeated, deliberately fixing his gaze on the door behind Dupree. "Find out what, exactly, Paul's got going on around here."

"Wait a second. Did you say a red Lexus? Yeah, sure. I remember that guy now. He got a room a couple days ago. Rented it for a week. But I don't know nothing about no drugs, man. I ain't even seen the dude since he checked in. He made it very clear he didn't want to be disturbed while he was here. He was real uptight about that. No maid service, no nothing." Dupree's eyes flashed from Luther to Jake, then down to his frantic hands. They were plucking at his clothes like a pair of grotesque moths. He trapped them beneath his arms again. "But that's nothing unusual around here. Most of our guests want a certain amount of, well, privacy, you know. So I didn't think nothing about it. Like I said, man. I mind my own business."

"What room is he in?"

"One of the back rooms. Room twelve." Dupree retrieved a key from behind the desk. He tossed it onto the counter. "Help yourself."

Luther picked up the key. He and Jake walked to the front door.

"And Paul," Luther paused with his hand on the door knob, "if we find out that you rang this guy's room—gave him a heads up—we'll have to pull you in on an accessory charge."

"Hey, don't sweat it, man." Dupree waved his hands. "It's bad enough I got to scrub the toilets and clean up the condoms they leave all over the place. I don't owe these low-lifes nothing."

Luther jerked the door loose and stepped outside. He paused on the stoop to clear the stale air from his lungs, but Jake pushed past him and began to trot toward the rear of the hotel. Running after him, Luther grabbed his arm.

"Let go," Jake barked, trying to break free. "What are you doing? Let's get Kelly out of there."

"Hold on, Jake," Luther said, maintaining his grip. "We can't just rush in there, hoping Kelly doesn't get hurt. Let's play it smart here. It'll just take a few minutes to check it out, and then we'll make our move."

"But she's right there!" Jake flailed his arm at the back of the hotel, his eyes burning.

"I know, Jake. And we'll get her back. But you have to trust me. It's better if we play it my way. I know what I'm doing. This is what I do."

Jake let his arms drop and bunched his fists. "You're right. We need to be careful."

"Let's just head back there and check it out."

They drove to the back of the lot, parking so they could see along the rear face of the building.

Room twelve was the middle of three rooms, and seemed deserted. The graffitied door was closed and drapes were pulled across the window. Nothing moved as they watched from the Camry. Jake leaned forward to see around Luther.

After a few minutes, Luther's fingers drummed a quick staccato on the steering wheel. "Well, his car's not here. I'll go take a closer look."

"Let's go," Jake said, opening the passenger door.

"Just a second, Jake. Why don't you sit tight while I check it out?" Luther opened the glove box and pulled out a cell phone.

"Here," he said, handing the phone to Jake. "I'll give you the high sign when everything's clear, but in case something goes wrong, call 911."

Jake took the phone and pulled his door closed, careful not to slam it.

Luther moved to the corner of the building. He pulled the Beretta from its holster. His heart was pounding and his mouth was dry. Old familiar responses, but it had been a while.

He stepped onto the narrow sidewalk that ran in front of the rooms. Two quick strides moved him through the gaping door of the end unit. Careful to avoid the bottles and trash, he crossed to the far side of the room. Luther pressed an ear to the wall and plugged his other ear against the freeway noise. He listened for a full minute.

Nothing.

He stepped back out onto the sidewalk. Holding his gun next to his thigh, he glanced back at the Camry. He flashed his palm at Jake, then dug Dupree's key from his pocket and held it between his teeth. He stepped over crumbled stucco as he moved along the sidewalk.

At the doorway of room twelve, he pressed back against the wall. Blinking sweat from his eyes, Luther reached for the doorknob. He turned it slowly. As soon as he felt the door give, he pushed through, diving for the floor.

He rolled quickly into a crouch, his gun up.

The room was empty.

He lunged to his feet and crossed the room to the bathroom, glancing behind the beds as he ran past. The bathroom door was open, the small room empty. Luther scanned the bedroom—there weren't any closets to hide in, just an empty tension bar in the short dead-end hallway past the bathroom.

He holstered his Beretta and walked to the front door. Jake was standing beside the Camry, watching. When Luther called, he ran over.

"What happened? Where is she?"

"It's empty," Luther said. "Looks like Chance pulled out."

"Kelly," Jake called, as he ran to the bathroom. "Come on out, honey." He came out of the bathroom after a few seconds and looked at Luther. "She's not here."

Luther shook his head. "No clothes or luggage either."

"Maybe they were never here. That crack-head was probably just telling us what we wanted to hear to get us off his back," Jake said, moving to the door. "We better get to the next place."

"Hold on, Jake. That drone in the background when you were on the line with Chance might have been this freeway noise. Let's at least take a quick look around, see if we can't find some evidence that they were here. Try not to touch anything if you can. We don't want to screw up any evidence for the crime scene boys."

Luther walked to the narrow space between the bed and the bathroom wall, got down on one knee and peered beneath the bed. He grabbed a crumpled piece of paper, but it was only a burger wrapper.

Jake gasped. Luther straightened and looked across the bed at Jake, who was on his knees between the two beds, his face pale. He was leaning back from his outstretched arm as he stared at his palm.

"What is it?" Luther asked, getting to his feet.

"Blood." He looked up as Luther came around the bed. "I was just going to check under the other bed and I put my hand in it. I didn't even see it on the carpet."

It took Luther a second to locate the dark stain on the dirty, multicolored shag in front of Jake's knee. The blood had clotted into a gel, but it was still wet—probably no more than an hour old.

"What did he do to her?" Jake closed his eyes. "Oh Jesus, my little girl."

Luther noticed smaller stains spaced across the carpet, and he followed them to a cardboard box in the corner of the room. A young kitten lay in the bottom of the box, its calico fur half buried in the trash. Using his pen, Luther pushed some of the paper aside and saw that it was decapitated. The head was under a Burger King bag in the corner of the box. A few small syringes with orange caps were scattered amongst the rest of the trash.

"Jake, step over here a second. I think I know why Kelly screamed. I don't think she was injured," he added quickly, noting Jake's expression.

Jake stopped a few feet short, leaning forward to peer over the edge of the box. "What is that?"

"A dead cat." He moved the trash with his pen again. "He popped the head right off."

"Why would he…?"

"I don't know."

Luther used a burger wrapper to pick up one of the syringes. "What do you make of this?"

Jake studied it briefly. The barrel was marked in gradations labeled with the letter U. He asked Luther to pull the orange cap off, and then nodded at the small needle.

"Insulin syringe. Addicts use them to shoot up."

Luther replaced the cap and dropped the syringe next to the box. He got down on one knee and began to remove pieces of garbage as Jake walked back to the beds.

Luther had three-quarters of the trash pulled out and spread on the floor when Jake called out, "Here we go, Luther."

He was next to the nightstand between the beds, holding a small pad of paper. "They were here," Jake said, flapping the pad at Luther. "This is my pager number."

Luther examined the pad. The number to Jake's replacement pager was written on the bottom of the paper, below a few numbers that had been scratched out.

"This is the place. Do you think they'll be back?"

"No. They're gone." Luther took the pad from Jake and put it back on the nightstand. "Let's leave this for the police. It establishes that Metzger's accomplice was contacting you—demanding a ransom for Kelly."

Jake looked around the room. "What now?"

"First, I want to have another little chat with Dupree. Find out what alias Chance used here and how he paid for the room. If we're lucky, he may have used a credit card and we might be able to track him from future charges on the account.

"After that, we better start getting set for tomorrow's meeting. We're not going to be able to do anything fancy this time—Chance knows about me now. He also knows that we know who *he* is, so he's going to be a lot more…"

Jake shot him a puzzled look.

"You used his name on the phone."

"I did?"

Luther nodded. "He's going to realize it was probably Metzger who gave him up, so he has to assume he spilled the whole story—that we know this is about Quince's papers and the whole Harrison thing. He won't be pussyfooting around tomorrow. He'll come at us pretty hard."

"Great. What can we do?"

"Plenty," Luther said. "Let's get going, I'll explain on the…"

Jake started suddenly, reaching for his right hip.

"What?"

"My pager," he said. "Maybe it's Chance again."

Jake pushed the display button and the unit stopped vibrating. He studied the screen for a second.

"Nope. It's Tony. A friend from work." He bit his lip. "I probably should get this—he put a nine-one-one behind his number."

"Hold on, Jake." Luther put a hand on Jake's arm as he reached for the telephone. "The cops might be able to lift a nice set of prints from that."

They went out to the Camry and Jake used Luther's cell phone to call Tony.

18

The moment Doctor Tony Castaic turned his 1970 Camaro Z28 onto Rivercrest Drive, he knew something was wrong. He couldn't quite put his finger on it at first. Jake's Citation was parked next to another car in his driveway, and his house looked quiet. The rest of the neighborhood seemed peaceful as well. But something nagged at Tony's mind like a half-remembered smell. It wasn't until he was slowing at the curb opposite Jake's house that he noticed the black and white parked at the other end of the block.

He cursed under his breath and shifted into second. As he pulled away from the curb, Tony took a closer look at the car parked next to Jake's Citation. He shook his head when he saw the extra antenna on the hood. He was slipping. He should've known as soon as he saw it. Only a cop would drive a plain brown piece of crap like that.

As he passed the squad car at the end of the block, he saw it was empty. He turned at the cross street and tooled along until he reached the next corner. Punching it as he hung a right, he raced down the block. The throaty roar from the glass-packs washed over him in a nostalgic wave. A hard smile compressed his lips as he felt the old tingle of excitement surge up from beneath his *cojones*. He pulled his Ray-Bans from the visor and put them low on his nose. Draping one wrist over the wheel, Tony leaned back in his seat, the self-caricature of his former posturing done only half in jest.

As he turned onto the connecting street back toward Rivercrest, he shifted into neutral and let the Camaro coast to a stop at the curb about ten or fifteen feet from the corner. He killed the engine and popped Stevie Ray Vaughan into the tape deck. He slid further down in his seat, watching Jake's house over the dashboard.

Within ten minutes, two black and whites and another unmarked police car drove past. One of the squad cars came back and parked at the base of the levee across the intersection from Tony. Two cops got out and double-timed it to the top of the steps. One guy was tall and powerfully built, with a shaved head. The other was lanky with brown hair. They paused on top of the levee for a few minutes while the bald guy spoke into a hand radio. Then he used it to point down the back of the dike. His partner gestured for a few seconds as if he didn't agree, but gave in and started down the other side. He had only taken a couple of cautious steps when he suddenly disappeared, a cloud of dust rising into the still afternoon air. The bald cop laughed, then began to walk along the levee toward Jake's house.

Tony smiled. With the cop car in the driveway, he'd worried that Jake had already been arrested. That didn't seem likely since they were still searching the area. He wondered where else he might look for Jake, but he'd already tried the hospital and gym. He decided to use his mobile phone to call Jake's pager again.

When he heard Jake's recorded voice instruct him to enter the numeric message, he punched in his number and pushed the pound sign. Fishing the adapter from the glove box, he plugged the phone into the cigarette lighter and waited for the return call.

Jake still hadn't called back after fifteen minutes. Tony repaged him, this time putting a 911 after his phone number. Tony dropped the phone on the passenger seat and reached for the ignition key. The 350 V8 rumbled to life. Tony slipped it into first, easing away from the curb. Driving past Jake's house again, he searched the windows, although he knew there was nothing there for him.

Tony's apartment was on the south side of The Pocket. It only took him a few minutes to get home. He pulled into his carport and got out, pausing to rest his hand on the dark green hood. He could feel the warmth of the engine as he let his eyes linger over the polished finish and broad, black-mat racing stripes coursing up the hood. He had acquired the car when he was fifteen. He'd probably spent more time under its hood than between the pages of medical books, yet he had never tired of its *machismo*.

He took the steps up to his apartment, threw together a couple of sandwiches and ate at the breakfast bar. As he was finishing, a thin teenager with dreadlocks walked in.

"Jamal," Tony said. "How was school?"

He shrugged, dropping his books on the couch. "Schaffer's an idiot."

Tony had already had a few conferences with Jamal's math teacher, and had to agree with the kid. Ideally, his mother would've gone, but those things didn't interest her. As his Big Brother, Tony had been the next best thing.

"There's a sandwich in the fridge. Why don't we burn through your homework after you eat, then we can change out the plugs on the Camaro?" Tony had been walking him through a basic tune-up over the past week.

As Jamal ate, Tony put out another call to Jake's pager, entering his home number.

When he was done, Jamal carried his plate into the kitchen, but left it next to the sink. Tony shot him a look, and he rinsed it off.

"Can I crash here again?" Jamal asked, opening the dishwasher.

"Sure."

Tony watched the back of Jamal's head, waiting for him to turn around, but he kept fiddling with the dishes.

"Your mom hasn't shown up?"

Jamal's mother enjoyed her heroin, and would disappear for days at a time.

Jamal shook his head.

"*Mi casa es su casa*," Tony said. "You know that."

Tony could barely hear Jamal's "Thanks."

They finished Jamal's schoolwork in a little over an hour. As Jamal got the tools from the hall closet, Tony decided to try Jake one more time.

When his call went through, an automated voice reported that Jake could be reached via a different pager. Tony called the new number and told Jamal to go ahead and get started on the car; he'd be down soon.

Within two minutes, the phone rang.

"Jake. Where you been? I've been trying to reach you all day."

"Long story. How's Sara?"

"We pulled the tube this morning. She's doing great. Listen, man. Did you get my message?" There was a steady droning sound on the other end of the line, and Tony spoke louder. "The cops know about Metzger. They're looking for you." He looked out the window and saw that Jamal had the hood up and was working with a socket wrench.

"Yeah, thanks. You saved my butt."

"No shit, cuz. I was just at your house. Cops are crawling all over the place." Tony sat on the couch. "A Detective Nunes cornered me a couple of times today. He's hot to lay his hands on you."

"I know."

"What are you going to do?"

"I don't know. I can't worry about that right now. I'm still working on getting Kelly back."

"Yeah, what's up with that? You never picked up the cash."

"Sara's parents wired me the money, but things went sour. Turns out the guy who's got Kelly is after something else. We're supposed to meet again tomorrow morning."

"What's he want?"

"Me."

"You?"

"It's complicated. I'm right in the middle of something here."

Tony waited for Jake to say more, but he didn't. He wondered why Jake was being so tight-lipped all of a sudden. "Where are you supposed to meet this *cabrón*? What time do you want me there?"

"No way, Tony. You can't get involved. This guy's dangerous."

"*I'm* dangerous," Tony said. "Where and when?"

"Tony. No."

"Where and when?" Tony said slowly. God love him, but Jake was a little dense sometimes. It was as if he didn't understand that they were *brothers*—that he would do anything for him. What could be simpler than that?

"Listen to me, Tony. This guy specifically said no surprises. If you, or the cops, or anyone else shows up, he's going to kill Kelly. I know you want to help, and I appreciate that, but you can't. There's nothing you can do."

"Bullshit." What the hell did Jake think the guy was going to say? Bring an army with you? "That's bullshit, man. You need someone watching your back. I'm going, cuz. That's all there is to it."

"No. We've got it covered, but I really do…"

"Who's *we*?"

"Hang on a second," Jake said, and then Tony heard another voice that was muffled and unintelligible.

Tony pulled the phone from his ear and stared at the earpiece. What the hell was this? Jake couldn't risk having him involved, but he had somebody else helping out? That was bullshit. Who was this guy? Had he slugged through the impossible hours of internship with Jake, or split Kelly's *Daddy and Me* swimming classes with him last summer at the rec center?

Tony put the phone back to his ear. If Jake thought he was going to sit back as some bastard used Kelly to put the squeeze on him, he was off his nut.

"You could do me a big favor, though, Tony," Jake said. "Sara's folks are flying in tonight. Could you meet them? I'm afraid the cops'll be at the airport, and I can't afford to run into them before tomorrow."

"Sure. No sweat. But who's…?"

"It's a United flight, out of Fort Lauderdale. Arrival's at seven-thirty. Thanks, Tony."

"*De nada.*" Tony paused for a second, stroking his mustache with his fingertips. "Listen cuz, Sara's parents are going to want to know what's going on. Where you are, what's happening with Kelly, why a bunch of cops are skulking around the airport looking for you—shit like that. What should I tell them?"

"I don't know. Just tell them I'm trying to get Kelly back and that I'll get in touch with them tomorrow. Drop them off at my place, and I'll catch up with them there."

"Where are you going to be?"

"I'll be around. I just can't go home until Kelly's safe."

"They're going to want to see you, man," Tony pressed. "Are you staying at a hotel or something? I could swing by on the way back from the airport."

"I'm staying with a friend, but the less you know about it the better. I'm sure Nunes is going to corner you at the airport."

"Hey, don't worry about me, man. I cut my teeth on LAPD Special Forces. These cow-town cops aren't going to give me any grief." Tony cleared his throat, deciding to try another tack. "This guy you're staying with, is he the one that's helping you with Kelly?"

Jake hesitated. "That's right."

"Is he any good at this sort of thing? I hate to think of you just hanging out there in the breeze tomorrow."

"Don't worry. He's a PI. He does this kind of stuff all the time."

"Yeah, well, I still think I should be there." A gleam brightened Tony's dark eyes when Jake mentioned the guy was a private investigator. It had to be the Life Flight patient Jake had been so hyped about last year. He hadn't been able to talk about anything else for weeks. "You sure you don't want me in on this?"

"Picking Sara's parents up will really help out. I need to get moving here, Tony. Thanks again."

"United. Seven-thirty, right?"

"That's it. Thanks again, man. I'll talk to you later."

Tony hung up, his hand resting on the receiver for several seconds as he tried to recall the name of Jake's Life Flight patient. He remembered that it was one of those two-first-name deals, but couldn't come up with it. He turned toward the front door. He'd have plenty of time to help Jamal with the sparkplugs and rent a video for him to watch until he got back. Then he'd get the low-down on Jake's PI from the hospital before heading to the airport.

Tony parked the Camaro in the short-term lot and was halfway to the terminal when he stopped and patted his breast pocket. The piece of paper he'd written Terry Luther's name and address on was still there. He'd only spent twenty minutes at Sac General getting the information he needed.

It had been easy money to review last year's Life Flight logbook and get the names of the gunshot wound patients transported during Jake's rotation. There were only seven of them, and Tony had immediately recognized Luther's name when he saw it. Once he had the name, he went down to the medical records department in the basement and pulled the file. The demographic sheet in the front of the chart had listed Mr. Luther's employer as Luther Investigations, and provided his telephone number and home address. Bingo.

Standing in the airport parking lot under the reddening clouds of early evening, Tony pulled the paper from his pocket and folded it in his hand. It was likely that he'd run into Nunes in the airport. He probably wouldn't strip search him, but it would be best if he didn't have Jake's hideout address on him. He started back to the Camaro. It wasn't even seven yet. He'd have plenty of time to make it to the gate to meet Sara's parents.

Ten minutes later, Tony sauntered into the United/ American Airlines terminal. Behind the Ray-Bans his eyes searched the crowd. Except for airport security, he didn't see any cops. He took the escalator at the back of the terminal up to the concourse and joined the line of people waiting to pass through the metal detectors.

As he neared the front of the line he saw the police. A couple of plainclothesmen were leaning against the walls of the concourse, just past the security station. They were pretending to read magazines. Tony suppressed a smile. As he walked through the metal detector, Tony studied the guy on the left. His eyes kept darting back and forth from his magazine to the crowd of people surging past. He probably had a picture of Jake taped to the open page.

Tony checked the flight monitor and headed toward gate twenty. As far as he could tell, there weren't any other cops around. He was approaching gate nineteen—confident he'd be able to get Sara's parents out of there without a hassle—when a man leaning against one of the concrete support pillars spoke his name.

"Detective Nunes," Tony said, trying to keep his voice light. "Fancy meeting you here."

How could he have missed him? Nunes had been standing right there out in the open. He was even wearing the same ugly houndstooth jacket he'd had on earlier that day.

Nunes scanned the concourse behind Tony. "Is Jake with you?"

"Jake? What would Jake be doing here?"

"It's imperative I speak with him." Nunes seemed to be staring right through the dark lenses of the Ray-Bans.

"Okay, okay," Tony said, dropping the act. He decided to play it as straight as he could, without actually giving Jake up. "He asked me to pick up Sara's folks, but he wouldn't tell me where he's staying."

"When did you speak with him, Doctor Castaic?"

"A few hours ago." Tony took his sunglasses off and put them in his pocket. The word doctor bothered him.

Like he was caught between two worlds, the street and the hospital—and not really belonging to either. "After you told me what happened at the hospital, I went to the gym and his house, but couldn't find him. I've been paging him all day. He finally called me back, but didn't say where he was."

"What gym?"

"Pardon me?" Tony said, kicking himself mentally. When dealing with cops, you always keep your answers to a minimum. You never give anything away for free.

"What gym does Jake belong to?"

"The 24 Hour Fitness on 43rd."

"Where are you supposed to take Mr. and Mrs. Haas?"

"Jake's place."

"Is Jake planning on meeting them there?"

"Not as far as I know."

"Are you supposed to meet him anywhere when you leave here?"

"No. Believe me," Tony said, allowing his irritation with Jake to show through. "I tried to find out who he was staying with, but he wouldn't say."

"What makes you think he's staying with someone?"

"What do you mean?" Damn it; he'd done it again. If only Nunes would blink his eyes once in a while.

"You said he wouldn't tell you who he was staying with. What makes you think he's not at a hotel?"

"I don't know," Tony said sharply. "It was just a manner of speaking. That's all." He immediately regretted his tone, knowing it would be a red flag for Nunes. He looked around the terminal, trying to distract Nunes from his blunder. "Where's your side-kick? What's his name? Case?"

"So you have no idea where Jake is? Is that correct?"

"He wouldn't tell me."

Nunes pulled the back of his hand along his jaw, waiting for Tony to say more. When the overhead intercom announced the arrival of United flight 618 out of Fort Lauderdale, he glanced at his watch. "Fine, Dr. Castaic." He put a hand on Tony's back, directing him toward gate twenty. "Why don't you introduce me to Sara's parents?"

They stopped at the back of the crowd and watched through the glass wall of the concourse as the plane taxied up to the gangway.

"The reason I want to find Jake is because I have some good news for him," Nunes said casually.

Tony shot him a look. "What good news?"

"Do you know what Sara's parents look like?" Nunes asked.

"I met them last year. What good news?"

"That he's off the hook for Metzger's murder."

"What do you mean?" Tony turned to face him.

"They found the body of one of the janitors in a storage closet at your hospital a few hours ago. He'd been given a nasty blow on the head and stripped to his shorts."

"You think that had something to do with Metzger's death?" Tony remembered the guy in the ill-fitting coveralls bursting out of the SICU that morning.

"We don't know," Nunes shrugged. "My guess would be that Metzger's partner wanted a way to get in the SICU to silence him."

"So Jake didn't do it?"

"No. The guards outside Metzger's room say a man dressed as a janitor was in there after Jake. So you see," Nunes held his hands out in front of him, palms up, "Jake is in the clear. That's why I need to find him, so I can let him know he's no longer a suspect. We can concentrate on getting his girl back."

"Well, I'll be sure to give you a call if I hear from him again," Tony said, turning back to watch the people exiting the plane. "I've still got your card from earlier today." He'd learned long ago never to take anything a cop said at face value, and Nunes' story didn't ring true. If he wasn't here to grab Jake up, why the clowns back at the metal detectors?

Besides, Tony suddenly realized, Jake's reaction to the news that the cops were after him would've been very different if he hadn't actually killed Metzger. He hadn't made any denials, or even seemed surprised. All Jake did was thank him for the heads-up. Nunes was obviously just feeding him a load of crap.

Cops.

Tony was shaking his head when he spotted Sara's parents coming out of the gangway. Mr. Haas towered above his wife and moved with the ramrod straight gait of a drill sergeant. Barbara Haas was a slight woman with short gray hair and a deep tan.

As they approached, Tony stepped away from Nunes. "Mr. and Mrs. Haas. It's me. Tony Castaic. Jake and Sara's friend."

"Of course," Mrs. Haas said, her face brightening. "Anthony. How are you?" She gave him a quick hug.

Mr. Haas shook his hand and gave him a brusque nod. "Castaic. Good to see you, son." William Haas always addressed people as if he were in the midst of a high-power board meeting. His bushy white eyebrows bristled as he looked past Tony's shoulder. "Where's Jake?"

"He couldn't make it, sir. He asked me to pick you up."

Mr. Haas' expression soured.

"He's tied up with trying to get Kelly back," Tony explained softly as Nunes approached them. Wanting to make it clear that they were not together, he let Nunes wait at his elbow for several seconds before introducing him.

"This is Detective Nunes," Tony said. "He's the lead investigator on the case."

"Mr. Haas. Mrs. Haas," Nunes said, shaking their hands. "It's unfortunate to have to meet under such difficult circumstances."

"Who shot my girl, Nunes?" Mr. Haas took a step closer. "Who's got my granddaughter?"

Tony moved away from Nunes, almost feeling sorry for him. Haas had started his family late in life and, although Sara was only twenty-seven, he was nearing seventy. Tony had recognized the early signs of Alzheimer's when they'd met last year. As with most patients suffering from the disease, Mr. Haas' psyche had tried to adjust to the loss of control by intensifying its inherent defense mechanisms. In his case, the aggressive energy that had served to sharpen his competitive edge during his corporate years was distorting into the first ravings of early dementia. The look in his eyes as he faced off on Nunes gave testament to the rapid progression of the disease.

"We're working on that, Mr. Haas. Unfortunately, the kidnapper hasn't made contact with us yet."

"That's not good enough." Haas waved a long index finger in Nunes' face as he leaned over him. "You're just sitting on your ass waiting for this maniac to give you a ring? That's not good enough by a damn sight."

"Our investigation is moving forward," Nunes replied calmly. He seemed unaware of Haas' aggressive posturing. "We experienced a setback this morning when the suspect we had in custody was killed. We'd hoped he would be able to tell us more about the man who is holding Kelly, but we're still moving forward."

"Setback?" Haas yelled. "Is that what you call it? A setback? I'd call it a travesty. How the hell does a suspect in a murder investigation get killed while in custody?"

Mrs. Haas was standing behind her husband, her eyes darting from him to Detective Nunes. She touched her husband's shoulder, "It's not a murder investigation, dear. Sara wasn't killed. She's doing well, isn't that right, Anthony?"

She looked at Tony, and he could read the realization in her face that the man she had known for over thirty years was slipping away. Tony was glad to see she hadn't rushed him into a nursing home at the first sign of the disease. It was something he still hadn't been able to get used to since leaving the *Barrio*—how quickly rich people unloaded their elderly.

Before Tony could answer, Mr. Haas waved a dismissive hand in her face, his eyes never leaving Nunes. "Yes, yes Barbara. Of course it's not a murder. I understand that, for crying out loud. What I don't understand is why this so-called detective is doing nothing to catch the man who is responsible."

Nunes started to respond, but stopped when Mrs. Haas gave him a small head shake.

"Bill, try to calm down. I'm certain that Detective Nunes is doing…"

"Calm down?" Haas exclaimed, turning abruptly on his wife. She steeled herself without actually flinching. Tony saw that Mr. Haas was one of those Alzheimer's sufferers who would eventually become physically violent. He could see that Mrs. Haas knew that day was coming, too. "Don't tell me to calm down, Barbara. Suzy's been shot, for crying out loud."

"That's right, William. Sara has been hurt." She laid her palm against his chest, putting a subtle emphasis on Sara's name. "That's what's important right…"

"I know which one of my own daughters was shot, for crying out loud. What is wrong with you lately? Why must you insist on correcting me all the time?"

"What's important is that she's hurt," Mrs. Haas continued soothingly. "That's what we need to focus on right now. Why don't we let Detective Nunes do his job, and we'll go visit Sara." She glanced at Tony. "We can do that, can't we, Anthony?"

"Of course we can, Barbara. Don't be asinine." Haas threw his shoulders back, trying to maintain his bluster, but his anger was starting to fade. "She's our daughter. Of course we can go see her."

"Visiting hours are until nine," Tony said. He turned toward Nunes. "Unless Detective Nunes wants to detain us for some reason, I can drive you right over."

Without saying a word, Mr. Haas spun around to face Nunes, challenging him to try and interfere.

"I have no problem with that, Mr. Haas," Nunes said. "Why don't you and Dr. Castaic pick up your luggage? Mrs. Haas and I can follow along, and I can fill her in on what we've learned so far."

Haas glared at Nunes for several seconds, then cleared his throat. "All right, then." He nodded to himself as if he'd just executed a hostile takeover. "Come on, Castaic," he commanded as he shouldered past Nunes.

19

Jake had only been asleep for a few hours when he suddenly jarred awake. Throwing the covers off, he jumped to his feet and stood next to the unfamiliar bed, wild eyes searching the dark corners of the room. His mind was still caught in the dream that had awoken him. In spite of running as hard as he could, he hadn't been able to close the gap between himself and Kelly. She was standing frozen on a road as a speeding eighteen-wheeler barreled toward her. The truck's horn was still blasting in his ears.

After a few seconds he cleared his head and sat on the edge of the bed, his damp T-shirt stuck to his body. He was in Luther's downstairs bedroom; the digital clock on the dresser read 3:17—a little over five and a half hours before their meeting with Chance. Lying back down, Jake stared at the ceiling, listening to his heart thump.

Luther had kept him so busy after leaving the motel that he hadn't really had time to worry about Kelly. Their first stop was Luther's place. They picked up one of his spare handguns—a 9mm Glock—and headed to an indoor firing range on Watt and Fruitridge. Luther coached Jake and by the time the range closed, he was able to group his shots within the size of a dinner plate at fifty feet. Luther was impressed, assuring Jake that handguns were close-range weapons—anything greater than fifty feet was strictly for the movies.

After that, they discussed strategy over a couple of Reuben sandwiches and pints of Amber Ale at the River City Brewing Company in the Downtown Plaza. Luther recommended they keep the plan as simple as possible. Quince's package was due at the Florin Road branch of Mailboxes USA the following morning. They would make copies of a few documents to bring to the meeting, and then drop the originals off at Luther's house before heading out to the Yolo Causeway. Once they knew Kelly was all right, they'd show Chance the copies of Quince's papers and leave it up to him. He could exchange Kelly for the twenty thousand and be done with it, or, if he wanted Quince's papers, he'd have to play by their rules. He would have to trade Kelly for Luther, who would wait with him as Jake took Kelly to a safe place and brought the papers back.

Luther cautioned Jake that they should be prepared for the worst. Chance had been quick to get his gun into play at their first meeting. It would be best if they spread out quickly and kept Chance between them.

As he lay in bed, Jake ran over the scene in his mind. He worried that if things suddenly went bad, he wouldn't be able to pull his gun in time. Maybe he should have his gun drawn right from the start, but that might only precipitate trouble. He turned his head, watching moon-shadows sway across the wall as he tried to decide what to do. An abrupt noise interrupted his thoughts.

It wasn't until the noise was repeated in rapid succession that Jake recognized it as the goose honking in the back yard. He propped himself up on his elbows, staring through the dark bedroom doorway. The goose's tone became increasingly strident, then was suddenly cut off. Jake got up and moved to the door. He hesitated, not sure what to do. Gus had certainly sounded pissed off, but with a goose, who knows? Jake wondered if Luther had heard it from his upstairs bedroom. He considered going up to ask him about it, but after listening for several minutes without hearing anything else, he decided he was overreacting and went back to bed.

He was trying to clear his mind so he could get back to sleep when a muffled sound came from the back of the house. Jake slid out of bed again and moved quietly across the room.

Pausing in the bedroom doorway, he peered into the darkness of the living room. Enough moonlight filtered in from the skylights to make out the furniture. He had taken one tentative step forward when a dark shape darted across the far side of the room.

An icy fear washed over him. He fumbled with the top drawer of the dresser, cringing at the sound of the Glock rapping against the wood as he pulled it out. The gun was cold in his hand. Something heavy slammed into a wall and the light in the front room blazed on.

Looking around the doorframe, he saw Luther, shirtless and barefooted, sandwiching a man between himself and the wall. The man's head was turned away from Jake, his left cheek mashed against the wall.

Luther levered the man's arm up high behind his back and clamped his free hand over his gun.

"Let go of the piece," Luther said. Deep scars distorted the muscles in his back.

"Why don't you eat…?" The words cut off abruptly as Luther cranked his arm. Jake recognized the voice immediately. Billy Ray Chance.

"Aaatta boy," Luther said, dragging out the vowels as if he were spreading gravel. He took the gun from Chance and released his arm. Luther quickly stepped back, transferring the gun to his right hand.

Chance slowly turned, rubbing at his shoulder. His eyes fell to his gun for a few seconds, then fixed on the colostomy bag just above the waistband of Luther's boxers. "That's rich," he snorted. "The hero PI has to crap in a bag."

Luther smiled without humor. "You may be needing one before the night's over."

"We'll see," Chance said. He shook his head. "A damn *goose*. I thought there were city ordinances against that sort of thing."

"There are." Luther angled the gun at Chance's head. "But we all take risks of one form or another."

"Well then, I guess I did you a favor. You won't have to live in fear of a raid by animal control anymore."

Luther slowly nodded at Chance, as if he were committing something very important to memory.

Chance glanced around the room. He saw Jake standing in the back hallway. "Some bitch. Dr. Prescott. Isn't this cozy? I'm a little hurt I wasn't invited to your little sleepover."

"We must have misunderstood you," Luther said. "We thought we were going to meet out at the causeway later this morning at nine, not in my living room at three-thirty."

"No, no. You got it right. I only stopped by to make sure you were going to be able to join Jake and me later today." Chance smiled. "I had a premonition that your health might take a sudden turn for the worse. I was worried about you, Mr. Luther."

"Thanks for your concern." Luther waggled the gun a bit. "But *I'm* not the one in any immediate danger."

"Yeah, I guess not." Chance rubbed at his deltoid again, and then rotated the arm at the shoulder a few times.

"Now that I know you're all right, I might as well be on my way." Clicking his tongue, he shot Luther a gunman's salute. "I'll catch'ya later."

"No way!" Jake blurted out. He brought the Glock up in the two-handed Weaver stance Luther had taught him. "There's not a chance in hell you're walking out of here. So help me, I'll put a bullet through your brain if you don't take us to Kelly right now."

Chance turned to Luther and shook his head slowly. "I thought we already went over this the other day. Maybe you can explain it to him." He spoke in the tone of one parent appealing to the other for help with a slow child.

"He's right, Jake," Luther said after a few seconds of heavy silence. "We've got to let him go."

"No way, Luther." Jake advanced rapidly across the room, arms stretched out in front of him as if the gun were pulling him. He didn't stop until the muzzle was digging into Chance's temple. "He was going to kill you."

"I know," Luther said softly. "I know. But if you kill him, we'll never find Kelly."

"Listen to him, son." Chance cut his eyes along the Glock at Jake. "You may have all the guns, but I've still got my hole card. And she's in a hole so deep nobody will ever find her until it's way too late."

"Put the gun down, Jake," Luther said. "We've got to let him go."

"Not again. Not this time."

"Think, Jake." Luther moved next to him. "Before you do anything, just take a few seconds and think. I know it would feel good to take him out right now. I understand that. But you've got to focus on Kelly. To get her back, you've got to let the anger go."

At the core of Jake's being, a hard realization crystallized around the rage and anxiety that hounded him: he could actually kill a man. The urge was almost irresistible.

Luther draped his left hand over Jake's gun. "Put it down, Jake."

Jake slowly allowed his arms to drop, the gun dangling from his hand.

"Smart move, Doc," Chance said. "You just do as you're told, and things'll work out fine. Now if you'll excuse me, I've got to be getting back to my girl. I'll be sure to give her your love." He stepped past Luther, walked to the front door and out into the night.

Jake and Luther remained motionless for several seconds, and then Luther led Jake to the couch. He dropped into a chair. "We didn't have a choice."

"I know," Jake said quietly. He stared at the gun in his hand. "He's not going to let her go. He came here tonight to kill you. He wanted you out of the picture so he could get Quince's papers from me and then finish it. Kill Kelly, me, and Sara too—anybody who could identify him, or knows about the papers."

Luther ejected the clip from Chance's gun. He jacked the slide to eject the chambered round and laid the gun on the broad armrest of his chair. "You're right, Jake. He's deadly serious about silencing this leak. He has no intention of letting us walk away from this thing. We're going to have to modify our plan."

"What can we do? As long as he's got Kelly, we're powerless."

"Well, not entirely. Let's not forget *our* hole card—Quince's documents. Until he gets his hands on them, we've got some juice, too." Luther thumbed the cartridges from the magazine clip and jiggled them in his hand. "If we play it right, we should be able to use them to pressure him into giving Kelly up. I'm not saying he's just going to hand her over as soon as we wave the documents in his face, but maybe we can maneuver him into a vulnerable position."

"What do you mean?"

"Let's look at it realistically. Cut the equation down to its basic elements, then take a hard look at it. On one side," Luther held his left hand out, bobbing it up and down as if he were estimating the weight of the cartridges, "we've got the documents and want to get Kelly back. On the other side," he took half of the cartridges from his left hand and held them out in his right, "Chance has Kelly and wants to get the documents back." He raised his eyebrows at Jake and seesawed his hands up and down slightly to indicate equal weights.

"Sure."

"If that were all there was to it, a simple exchange would solve the problem. But its pretty clear that Harrison Tobacco also wants us dead." Luther let his right hand drop, the left moving up an equal distance.

Jake nodded.

"So, if we factor Kelly and the documents out of the equation," leaving his arms in the unbalanced position, he tilted his hands, letting the cartridges spill to the floor, "what we're left with is that, once Chance has the documents, he's going to try to kill us. I can only think of one way to balance out the equation," Luther continued, slowly leveling his hands out again.

They stared at each other.

"So you're saying that once we get Kelly back, we have to kill him before he kills us."

"Well, not exactly." Luther shook his head. "That was my first thought, too, but think about it. Let's say we get lucky today and manage to get Kelly back and kill Chance without getting hurt. All that really would buy us is a little time before Harrison sends out another goon. The only way I can see to truly balance the equation is to eliminate their need to silence us."

"How are we going to do that? We'd never be able to convince them that we wouldn't talk. They'd never take that chance."

"You're right. But if the story were released—Quince's documents made public—there would no longer be any need for them to kill us. The horse would be out of the barn. In fact, things would only get worse for them if the guys who broke the story suddenly turned up dead."

"Sure. I've thought about that." Jake shrugged. "But we'd still have to get Kelly back first. There's no way Chance is going to let her go if we give the story to the press."

"I know. But I think there's a way we can orchestrate it so that we can get Chance to release Kelly first."

"How?"

"Well, we stick with our original plan of making a few copies of Quince's documents to take with us to the meeting. But, instead of leaving the originals here at my house, we stash them in a locker at the bus terminal. Then we put the key in an envelope addressed to John Faraday and drop it into…"

"John Faraday?"

"He's an investigative reporter at *The Bee* I've worked with on other cases. We drop the envelope addressed to Faraday in the mailbox of one of the houses in my neighborhood. Our mailman comes by in the early afternoon and, unless Chance is willing to play ball, it'll get picked up for delivery. We tell Chance that if he wants to keep the story from breaking, he'll have to go along with our plan to exchange Kelly for myself."

"Why would we still exchange you for Kelly? We just tell him he doesn't get the address unless he hands Kelly over, free and clear."

"He'd never go for that. He's going to need *some* assurance that he's actually getting the documents, and not just a key to an empty locker somewhere."

"I suppose." Jake rubbed his eyes. "But then what? We're still basically back where we started. Once I stash Kelly somewhere safe, get the key out of the mailbox and bring the documents back to trade for you, what's to keep him from killing us then?"

"Nothing," Luther said soberly. "He *is* still going to try. Especially since we've decided we can't actually let him have the original documents, no matter what."

"Then what's the point of the whole key-in-the-envelope gimmick? If it's going to come down to a shoot out anyway, why go...?"

"Because that's the only way we can get Kelly out of harm's way, which is the critical factor. And as far as I can figure it, that's about the best we can hope for."

"That's crazy," Jake said, his mouth suddenly dry. "There's got to be another way to play it. Some way where you don't have to be traded for Kelly."

"I don't see how. I'm open to suggestions of course, but I don't see how else we can get Kelly back without turning over the documents." Luther smiled reassuringly in response to Jake's obvious apprehension. "I imagine my job is a little like an oncologist's. A complete cure is often unobtainable. And sometimes the cure itself is lethal."

Jake shook his head.

"Don't worry," Luther said lightly. "I've been doing this kind of thing for years. I've still got a few moves left in me. I think I can handle Mr. Billy Ray Chance. In fact, I'm kind of looking forward to it." He stood up and slapped Jake on the back. "I've got to attend to Gus. Why don't you try to get some rest?"

20

Tony Castaic was already up and pulling on his jeans when his alarm clock went off. He buttoned his shirt and then opened the small fire safe he kept in his closet. Moving his medical license and diploma to one side, he removed a box from the back. The box contained his old bandana and gun. Tony folded the red bandana into a do-rag, tying the knot at the back of his head. He hadn't held the Colt more than five times in the last eight years, but when he picked it up, it felt more natural in his hand than a stethoscope. After loading it, he pocketed a spare clip and stuck the Colt in his waistband.

Jamal was on the couch in the front room. He watched the young man sleep, thinking about how they had formed an abiding friendship. A familiar nervous jab took him, like before a gang fight. There was danger in what he was doing. After a few moments, he wrote a note for Jamal.

He grabbed the slip of paper with Terry Luther's address on it and stepped out into the pre-dawn morning.

Since they live in the flood plains of both the Sacramento
and American Rivers, Sacramentans have, over the years,
constructed an intricate network of levees and spillways to
protect home and property. Although it stands dry most
years, during flood conditions the Yolo Spillway diverts a
vast amount of water around the city to the west.

The three and a half mile raised section of Interstate
80 that spans the spillway between Sacramento and Davis
is known as the Yolo Causeway. During his four years at
the U.C. Davis School of Medicine, Jake had commuted
across it regularly. The Davis campus also has a strong
Wildlife and Fisheries program, and the many bird-watching
enthusiasts in the area enjoy the 3,700-acre waterfowl refuge
that has been established in the sloughs and marshes of the
spillway.

Flocks of mallards and pintails arrowheaded north
across the crisp morning sky as Jake and Luther drove the
long stretch of raised highway in silence. They were unaware
of the forest green Camaro several cars behind them. Immediately after crossing the spillway, Luther took the Road 32A
exit, looping back under the freeway. He turned onto the
gravel road that cut up the side of the spillway's western
levee. They passed a large sign proclaiming VIC FAZIO YOLO
WILDLIFE AREA as they crested onto the levee-top road and
headed south.

After driving a few hundred feet, they approached a
road angling down to the flat spillway bed. The short spur
ended in a small parking area next to the base of the levee.
A black Saturn was parked at the far end of the otherwise
deserted lot. Jake's heart skipped a beat when he saw Kelly

lying on the gravel next to the Saturn. She was on her side, her arms and legs pulled behind her. Billy Ray Chance was squatting on the ground behind her.

For a panicked second Jake was certain she was dead, but as Luther eased the Camry down the spur, Kelly lifted her head to watch their approach. Despite the contusions distorting her features, Jake had never seen anything more beautiful than her face at that moment.

He saw Chance hold a gun up for a few seconds before pushing Kelly's head to the ground with the muzzle. He kept the barrel against her temple as Luther pulled into the parking area. Chance was wearing a gray suit, his hair hanging loosely onto his shoulders.

Jake reached for the door handle, but glanced at Luther before opening the door. Luther was studying the layout. The small parking area was the head of a nature trail, and a thick growth of blackberries bordered its three non-levee sides. A few poplars rose out of the thicket, providing patches of shade that, in the morning light, were falling across the lot and onto the steep slope of the levee.

"He's positioned himself so we won't be able to flank him very well," Luther said. "We'll just have to spread out as much as we can and go from there." He grabbed the folded copies of a few of Quince's memos from the dash-board and tapped them a couple of times on Jake's thigh. "All right, let's do it." He opened his door and stepped out.

Jake got out of the Camry and moved cautiously toward the base of the levee, a rubbery, dreamlike feeling in his legs. The traffic on the causeway thrummed like blood through an artery, rushed and urgent beneath the raw skin of his awareness. When he stopped in the shade of a tree, Kelly and Chance were contrasted sharply in the sunlight. The holster dragged at his hip.

Luther angled away from him, walking slowly toward the Saturn. Chance waited behind Kelly, tripodding with his left hand on the ground, the gun resting almost casually against her head.

"That's far enough," he called out when Luther was about halfway between him and the Camry. "Why don't y'all just hang right there while we lay down a few ground rules."

Luther stopped.

"First of all, it's Jake I'm dealing with, not you. You're just a spectator. And, Jake, you're going to do what I say, when I say, or it's lights out for your little girl. You understand?"

Jake nodded.

"I *said*, do you understand?"

"Yes. I understand."

"Good, then let's get down to it. As you can see, I held up my end of the bargain. Here's your little sweetpea, none the worse for wear." Kelly remained perfectly still, her pleading eyes fixed on her father. "But I don't see the money anywhere. What's the deal?"

Jake jerked his head in the direction of the Camry. "It's in the car. But let's cut the crap," he said, failing to control the quaver in his voice. "We all know this isn't about the money."

"Oh no?" Chance's pale eyebrows arced upward in mock surprise. "What's it about, then?"

Jake glanced at Luther, who gave him a small nod.

"It's about Winston Quince. And Harrison Tobacco."

Chance smiled. "Assuming I know what the hell you're talking about, what do you propose to do about it?"

"Well, to start with, we brought copies of a few of the documents that Quince sent me." Jake pointed at the papers in Luther's hand. "Just to let you know that we have them and are willing to trade."

"Go on."

"We stashed the originals in a public locker and sealed the key in an envelope that's addressed to a reporter at the

Sacramento Bee. That envelope's in a mailbox in a neighborhood where the mailman makes his rounds in the early afternoon." Jake paused as a large smile creased Chance's face. It wasn't the reaction he was expecting. "The plan is that you hand Kelly over, I take her someplace safe, and then get the key and bring it back to you. Mr. Luther is willing to stay here with you, as insurance that I'll bring the key back. That way, you get Quince's papers back, and I get Kelly.

"If you don't do as we say..." Jake hesitated, unnerved by Chance's chuckle. "If you don't do as we say, the key gets mailed to the reporter and the whole story..." Jake trailed off again, his voice drowned out by Chance's laughter. The cold, hard sound was somehow more threatening than the gun pressed against Kelly's head.

Jake felt a sinking in his gut as he waited for the laughter to stop. He looked at Luther and saw that Chance's reaction had him worried as well. He was leaning forward in a slight crouch, his right hand hovering near the gun on his hip.

Laughter animated his face, but Chance's pale eyes remained stonily on Jake. "Whoo-wee," he exclaimed when he finally stopped laughing. "That was rich. Secret lockers? Mailing keys to reporters? Y'all get an A-plus for creativity. But I gotta tell ya," Chance lifted his left fist from behind Kelly's body and rested it on her shoulder, "I figured Metzger spilled his guts and you'd try to pull something like this."

Chance pushed down on Kelly's arm as he dropped his thumb in a plunger-type movement. Kelly flinched. Jake immediately understood what had happened, even before Chance opened his hand to show him the small syringe.

"Now don't get excited," Chance said, crouching a little lower as Jake took a few steps forward. Jake froze at the sound of Chance cocking his gun. "That was insulin, not meth. She's got a little more time than Metzger did."

Chance dropped the syringe and picked up a plastic vial. He tossed it at Jake and it bounced to a stop at his feet. "But make no mistake, twenty units of insulin will kill her just as dead—it'll just take a tad longer."

Jake saw that Luther had dropped to a one-kneed crouch, his gun out and leveled at Chance. Although he was definitely within Chance's peripheral vision, Chance didn't even give him a second look. Instead, he ran his eyes up and down Kelly's body a few times before looking back at Jake.

"I don't know, I'd guess she weighs, what, about forty-five pounds? That would be around twenty kilograms. And at one unit per kilogram body weight, I'd figure she's got about…" Chance pursed his lips as if he were trying to calculate the price of a melon in a produce scale. "Oh, I don't know, twenty to thirty minutes, give or take, before her glucose bottoms out and she goes into shock. And then, what, about another five or ten minutes before we start getting into the whole irreversible brain damage and death thing?"

Chance snorted a laugh. "Would you listen to me? Lecturing a doctor about the finer points of insulin and glucose metabolism?" He dropped his smile. "Let's just say that I don't think she's got the time for us to haggle about what we're going to do here. If you drive like hell, you just might be able to make it back here with Quince's papers before your little darlin' checks out. So what I suggest is that you get back into your car and…"

"Listen, Chance," Luther interrupted. "We're willing to hand over Quince's papers. There's no need for this…"

Jake was watching Chance the whole time, but his mind didn't connect the casual flick of his gun with the explosion that ruptured the morning calm. In the same instant, Luther lurched grotesquely in Jake's peripheral vision. He turned and saw that Luther must have somehow lost his balance and fallen, because he was scrambling wildly to get to his feet. At first, Jake thought it was just the loose gravel giving him trouble, but then he saw that his right leg was flopping freakishly, a dark stain forming on the front of his lower thigh. Luther made it about halfway up, but when he put weight on his leg, it folded backwards under him like a bird's leg. As Luther collapsed, a sodden, splintering sound carried across the unnatural silence following the gunshot.

Jake ran to Luther's side and called his name, but he was unresponsive. His respirations were shallow, and a clammy sheen accentuated the sudden pallor of his skin. Jake straightened the leg, cringing as he felt the bone fragments grind together. He quickly removed Luther's shoe, but was unable to locate the pulse in the top of his foot. Feeling Luther's thigh, his fingers quickly found the hole in his jeans just above the knee. Chance's bullet had shattered Luther's femur at the level where the femoral artery ran right next to the bone. The large vessel had obviously ruptured, the muscle compartments already turgid with blood.

Jake knew that people could bleed to death from a lacerated femoral artery, but it would take longer than one or two seconds to lose enough blood to develop hemorrhagic shock. His experience with trauma resuscitation should have reassured him that Luther had simply fainted from the pain of a major bone shattering, but he still had to fight back the irrational thought that Luther had already bled out. His panic intensified when he moved up to Luther's neck and was barely able to feel a pulse in his carotid artery.

Slowly, the pulse started to strengthen. Luther's blood pressure was starting to come back up. He moaned just before Chance called out.

"Best forget about him, son. I gave him fair warning to stay out of it, but he wouldn't listen. You ought to focus on your girl here—you may still be able to save her, but time is running out."

Jake removed Luther's belt. He looped it around Luther's upper thigh several times and leaned back to cinch it as tight as he could. Securing the tongue of the belt in the buckle, Jake removed the Glock from his own holster before turning to face Chance.

"Drop it, old son," Chance said when Jake took a step toward him. He thought he had screened his movements, but Chance had obviously seen him pull his gun. "Just go ahead and drop it right there."

Jake tried to decide what to do. Scenes from innumerable cop movies played through his mind. The silver-screen credo was that you never gave up your weapon, no matter what.

Chance must have seen something in his expression, because he quickly lowered himself as flat as possible behind Kelly. His thin smile invited Jake to make the call.

The seconds dragged out, distorted time punctuated by the call of meadowlarks. Jake couldn't risk taking a shot. The odds that he'd be able to get his gun up and shoot Chance without hitting Kelly—all before Chance simply pulled the trigger and killed him—were ridiculously small. He opened his hand and let the Glock drop to the ground.

So much for the movies.

As Chance got to his feet, Jake thought he saw a flash of movement on top of the levee—a sudden absence of a half-seen form. Chance caught his look and spun around, but nothing was there. Before Jake could even think to go for his gun, Chance turned back.

"Nice try, kid." He shook his head. "The old 'someone's behind you' bit is not particularly original, but very convincingly played." He gestured at Jake with his gun. "Now step away from your gun. I wouldn't want you to get yourself hurt."

Jake took a few slow steps to his right, his mind struggling to come up with a plan. Kelly didn't have much time.

"Keep going," Chance said, when Jake stopped only a few yards away from his gun.

"Look, Chance," Jake pleaded. "You can have Quince's papers. Just let Kelly go. I swear I won't…"

Another shot exploded from Chance's gun, the bullet kicking gravel at Jake's feet before ricocheting past with a hungry whine.

"I said move, damn it!"

As Jake took several quick steps away from his gun, a crouched figure scurried across the top of the levee, about fifty yards behind Chance. It took everything Jake had not to look directly at the figure as it started to move down the slope. Jake forced his eyes to remain fixed on Chance's face as he tried to will himself to increase his peripheral vision. It felt as if his eyes were bulging like a thyroid patient's, but the only thing Jake could make out was that it was a man, wearing a red bandana.

Jake moved away from his gun. Chance stepped to the front of the Saturn. He glanced down to wipe the dust from the fender, and Jake took the opportunity to shoot a quick glance at the person creeping along the slope of the levee.

His heart skipped.

Tony Castaic.

He was wearing black jeans and a gray flannel shirt buttoned up to the neck. The red bandana was tied low on his forehead and pulled back, concealing his hair. His Ray-Bans reflected the morning sun. Even though Jake had never seen Tony wearing his old colors before, it looked as natural on him as spots on a jaguar. Jake caught a glimpse of a large gun in Tony's hand before he shifted his gaze back to Chance.

"So, Doc," Chance said, leaning on the fender. "Here we are, at long last. No pesky PI's or other distractions to get in the way."

Jake didn't say anything, but continued to move slowly away from his gun. He altered his course slightly, trying to bring himself closer to Chance and Kelly, without putting himself in Tony's line of fire.

"Lord knows I'd love to savor the moment," Chance continued, tilting his head in Kelly's direction, "but since you're probably feeling a little pressed for time, I'll cut to the chase. Here's how it's going to go. We're going to toss the kid in the back of my car, then you're going to drive me to wherever the hell it is you stashed Quince's papers. Once I make sure everything's there, you and your little darlin' will be free to go." He smiled, not even bothering to feign sincerity. "You've got my word on it."

"Sure," Jake nodded, trying to come up with something that would distract Chance. Tony had covered about half the distance creeping along the base of the levee, and Jake hoped he could buy him enough time to get a little closer. Although it didn't seem particularly important, the only thing that came to mind was to ask, "What was it you said about Metzger? That you're the one who killed him?"

"That's right."

"Because the police think I did it. I've been dodging them ever since yesterday morning."

"Oh man, that's rich," Chance laughed. "The cops have been spinning their wheels trying to find…"

His voice cut off in a sudden grunt as his left shoulder jerked back.

In the same instant, an explosion burst from behind Jake. He turned to see Luther propped up on his left elbow. His red hair was glistening with sweat, his jaw hanging slack. He was paler than any conscious person Jake had ever seen, and his extended gun arm was weaving around as if he were trying to aim at an airborne fly. Luther squeezed his eyes shut in an exaggerated blink, the way drunks will do to clear their swimming vision. Out of the corner of his eye, Jake saw that Chance had regained his balance and was raising his gun. Before Luther could steady his aim, he was thrown back by Chance's next shot.

Jake rushed at Chance, screaming for him to stop shooting, but he immediately skidded to a halt as Chance swung the gun on him, his left arm flopping at his side. Chance's face contorted in anger and pain as he opened his mouth to say something, but a new gunshot obscured his words. The blast came from behind Chance, and his left ear disappeared in a burst of blood.

Chance spun into a crouch, leveling his gun at Tony over the hood of his car. Tony was in an awkward stance, one leg hiked up on the bare slope. The closest cover was the blackberry thicket between him and Chance.

Jake ran at Chance, but he had only taken a few steps when both guns fired. Part of Tony's skull blew away, his Ray-Bans flipping high into the air. The tattered bandana fluttered to the ground as Tony's body straightened—horribly erect as it arched back on its heels for an eternal instant—before collapsing down the slope.

The last thing Jake saw before he slammed into Chance was that Tony's bullet had gouged a harmless groove out of the Saturn's hood. Jake's impact knocked them both to the ground, Jake landing on top, straddling Chance's chest. He grabbed fistfuls of Chance's hair and began pounding the back of his head into the gravel.

Jake's mind was blank, drowned under waves of primal rage. He didn't realize he was too high up on Chance's torso.

By arching his back and yanking on Jake's shirtfront, Chance was able to throw him off, over his head. Jake's face bit into the gravel, his mouth filling with grit. After a stunned second, he scrambled to his hands and knees, spinning around to face Chance, a raw scream ripping from his throat.

Chance had recovered his gun and was pointing it at Jake. His head looked lopsided, a bloody stump where his left ear used to be. Demonic fury burned white hot in his shallow irises.

It was the first time Jake had seen any emotion in those lifeless eyes, and in that instant, he knew it was over. He stared into the muzzle of Chance's gun. A small, detached portion of himself was surprised to realize that he wasn't afraid. The only thing he felt as he waited for Chance to pull the trigger was regret.

He had failed to save Kelly. It had cost Luther and Tony their lives, and he still hadn't been able to save his daughter.

Inexplicably, the seconds ticked by; a heavy silence marked only by Chance's rasping breaths. His nostrils flared and the corners of his mouth turned downward, a vicious internal struggle contorting his features. He opened his mouth to speak several times, but no sound issued from his throat. The gun in his hand began to tremble.

"I need those papers," he managed to hiss.

Chance jerked the muzzle of the gun upward. "Let's go." He stood up, his left arm dangling uselessly.

As Jake got his feet under him, he realized he had nothing to lose. He drove forward from a lineman's crouch, launching himself at Chance. The gun bellowed flame, burning his face as his shoulder slammed into Chance's gut.

A sudden numbness deadened Jake's left leg from the hip down, but there was enough force in the blow to throw Chance into the side of the Saturn. The impact must have weakened his grip, because when Jake grabbed his wrist and gave it a violent jerk, the gun flew loose. It skittered across the gravel under the car.

Chance pushed Jake away. His right fist exploded against the side of Jake's head.

Jake fell, landing on his back. He sat up, but before he could rally, Chance had landed two more punches to his face. Blood ran into his eye, and he could feel the upper lid swell. Jake swung blindly, but didn't connect.

Through the swirling daze, Jake understood he was horribly outclassed. He tried to get his feet under him again, but his left leg was slow to respond. He managed to get to his knees before Chance kicked him in the stomach. The sudden nausea doubled Jake over, and he clawed wildly, managing to grab Chance's arm. Digging in with every shred of strength, Jake pulled himself forward, clinching with Chance. His only thought was to keep Chance from delivering any more blows, and he wrapped his arms around his torso, pinning Chance's arms.

Chance threw himself backward, but Jake managed to hang on. They rolled in the dust, Chance yelling a steady torrent of expletives in Jake's ear. Jake simply held on, wishing he'd taken Sara up on her invitations to join her tae kwon do class. His self-disgust at being nothing more than a candy-assed intellectual—unable to hold his own in a fight with a one-armed opponent—suddenly gave rise to the idea that he might be able to use his medical knowledge to some advantage.

He would attack the most vulnerable part of the human body. But before he could act, Chance drove a head-butt to his chin, and Jake went spinning down in a whirling checkerboard of red and black.

As the whirlpool slowed and flattened, Jake became aware that he was on his back, his arms thrown wide. A heavy weight was crushing his chest, and someone was rhythmically pounding on either side of his face with a sledgehammer. With the next blow, the checkerboard dissolved completely and Jake saw that Chance was now straddling his chest, using his right arm to deliver jarring slaps to his face.

They had rolled several yards and were now in front of Kelly. Even though he was only a few feet from her battered face, the roaring in his ears kept him from hearing the scream that was tearing her mouth apart. His vision, however, was surprisingly clear—he could see that her skin was pale and clammy. Her blood sugar had started to drop.

Time was running out.

Chance was putting everything he had into the blows, and the follow-through of his next backhand swing carried his arm high and away, exposing his torso.

Jake knew this was his last chance. His right hand shot up to Chance's neck, clawing for his voice box. He didn't try to enclose Chance's entire neck in his hand; he let his fingers dig into the front, searching for the windpipe itself.

The human larynx is a delicate structure, composed primarily of cartilage and a few thin muscles. It sits out there in the front of the neck with nothing to protect it. Over the years, Jake had seen several fatalities from relatively mild trauma to the larynx.

Chance's neck was slippery with blood running from his injured ear, but Jake was able to dig his fingertips and thumb between the voice box and the strap muscles on either side. When he crushed his hand closed, he felt Chance's larynx lift and twist from between the muscles.

Chance's eyes opened wide in panic, and he grabbed Jake's wrist. Jake's hand clawed closed in desperation, almost completely encircling Chance's airway. All Chance's one-handed grip served to do was add strength to the wrenching action Jake was applying to his windpipe. Chance let go of

Jake's wrist and frantically tried to scramble away, his breath coming in raw, whistling gasps.

Jake hung on, and Chance's backward struggle pulled him up to a seated position. He glanced over at the Saturn and saw the gun lying underneath, but realized he couldn't trust his leg to get him there before Chance. His only option was to finish it.

Jake knew that flexing the elbow increases the grip strength of the forearm muscles. He grabbed the lapel of Chance's suit with his left hand and pulled him close, allowing his right elbow to bend. From only a few inches away, Jake stared into Chance's frenzied eyes as he squeezed with all of his strength. The thyroid cartilage popped in his hand like a rotten gourd.

There is nothing more terrifying than being unable to breathe, and Chance thrashed wildly. Jake maintained his grip, long after he knew it was all over. Chance's wide-mouthed efforts to move air through a crushed airway only resulted in harsh, gurgling gasps.

The sound summoned Jake back across the years to his grandfather's deathbed, his last agonized breaths cutting deep memories into Jake's childhood mind. He jerked his hand from Chance's neck and dragged himself away.

Kelly had been watching through drooping eyelids. He pulled himself to her side.

"I'm here, honey." Jake kissed her. Her dark hair was limp and wet beneath his lips. "Daddy's here."

"I'm sorry, Daddy." She turned her head to look at him, tears forming in her unfocused eyes.

"Don't be sorry, sweetheart." Jake cupped her cheek in his hand, the skin alarmingly cool. "There's nothing for you to be sorry about."

"Mommy. He hurt Mommy," she murmured, as Jake began to work on the clothesline binding her wrists. "I hid. I was scared..."

Her voiced faded.

"It wasn't your fault. You didn't do anything wrong."

As her head slowly sagged to the ground, she began to shiver. Jake realized that getting her untied right away wasn't critical. What she needed was sugar. He glanced around the barren gravel lot. She didn't have much time.

He'd have to get to the car and use the cell phone to call for help. He pulled himself to his feet and found that although it shot searing pain down his thigh, his left leg was able to support his weight. He hobbled past Chance's lifeless form without giving him a second thought, but when he saw that Luther's face lay in a pool of blood, a jolt of new panic hit him. He altered his course toward Luther for a few steps, but then realized that without any equipment, he wouldn't be able to do much for him. The first thing to do was call 911.

By the time he collapsed against the side of the Camry, Jake's leg was buckling under him, his pants soaked with blood. He fell into the passenger seat, grabbed the phone and dialed 911. He gave the operator their location and described the injuries: one patient in hypoglycemic shock, two with critical gunshot wounds. He forgot about his own injury and didn't consider Chance a patient. He requested the Life-Flight helicopter and, even though he knew every EMS rig was equipped with them, he stressed that the first responders needed to bring oral and IV dextrose.

He dropped the phone and started digging through Luther's glove compartment for a candy bar or other carbohydrate source when he heard sirens. Lurching out of the Camry, Jake saw several cars racing down the levee. Nausea hit him and he had to lean on the door. He watched the cars. There was no way they could have responded that quickly to his call. Jake recognized the lead car as Nunes' brown Taurus. Jake managed to wave his arms, but they had already slowed to make the turn down to the gravel lot.

Before the Taurus had come to a sliding stop, Detective Nunes was out. His eyes swept the scene as he ran to Jake.

"How did you get here so fast?" Jake asked, his mouth dry.

Nunes glanced at Jake's leg, then placed a hand on his shoulder. "Sit down, Jake." He guided him back to the Camry's open door. "We heard the EMS call go out as we were pulling off the freeway. They'll be here any minute."

"Kelly needs sugar." Jake tried to shake off Nunes' hand, but his grip was strong as he forced him down onto the passenger seat. A deep fatigue had flooded Jake's muscles, and he had to admit that it was a relief to sit down. "Chance gave her an overdose of insulin."

Nunes looked at his partner. Jake tried to recall his name, but his mind wouldn't focus. All he could remember was that he didn't like him very much.

"We need your stash of Power Bars, Stan," Nunes said. "See if you can get the girl to eat one."

Turning to the officers who had come up behind him, Nunes pointed to Luther and Chance lying on the gravel. "See what you can do for them." He looked around the small lot. "Where's Castaic? He called us and told us what was happening. I thought he would be here."

Jake tried to point to the south, but his arm was ridiculously heavy and he could only lift it halfway. The Camry started spinning, and the red and black checkerboard returned. Jake shook his head slowly. He tried to tell Nunes that it was too late, that Tony was dead, but the only thing that came from his mouth was a ludicrous, garbled sound that echoed in his ears.

The sound continued to reverberate, waxing and waning in intensity, and he felt strong hands lower him into the swirling whirlpool. The spinning black squares consumed the red ones, and time was suspended in a dark vortex of remorse. The noise inside his head eventually changed into a steadily increasing thwapping. It quickly overwhelmed him, blowing away the few remaining red squares, until all that was left was blackness.

A murmur of fiendish voices began to jabber at him, and a tightness grew around his bicep. The last thing that Jake was aware of was a stabbing pain in the crook of his arm.

Epilogue

Jake grimaced as he leaned forward to raise the leg support on his wheelchair. The swelling had decreased enough so he could wear his suit that morning, but the pants were tight around his upper thigh. Jake looked up and saw that Sara was awake.

"Hi, hon," he whispered.

They had extubated her a few days ago, but she still had to swallow a few times before speaking. "How is she?" she asked, looking at Kelly. Her voice felt raw.

"Fine. Tired, but fine."

Sara's eyes lingered on Kelly, and a smile touched her face. "She looks like a doll. That's quite a job you did on her makeup, Mister Mom. You can hardly see the bruises. Maybe you could give me a touch up later. I'm sure I need it."

"That was your mom's handiwork. You look fine. Beautiful."

Sara rolled her eyes.

Jake nodded at the foot of her bed. "How was PT?"

Sara had started getting some movement back in her legs the previous morning, and Dr. Watney had ordered aggressive physical therapy.

"They've got this Brunhilda coming in here twice a day. She's brutal." In spite of her complaint, Sara lifted her legs off the bed, pleased with her rapid improvement.

Jake smiled. "No pain, no gain."

"Don't I know it."

Sara fingered the top of her blanket for a few seconds. "How was the funeral?"

"Nice. Jamal took it pretty hard, though. Tony left him a note saying if anything happened to him the Camaro was his. Maybe he had a premonition, I don't know. I just know I'll never forget him." Jake kissed the top of Kelly's head. "If it hadn't been for him we wouldn't be together now."

"Have you spoken to USC yet? Are they going to let you take Tony's spot?"

"They want me to send down my CV, but said it was only a formality. I'll be able to start as soon as residency is over."

"Tony would've liked that," Sara said. "I wish I could've made the service."

"I know. Several of Tony's old friends from L.A. were there. They helped keep the reporters out." Jake shook his head, "I swear, those vultures are unbelievable. They wanted to televise the service. Live and Nationwide. You'd think yesterday's press conference would've been enough. They've all got copies of Quince's papers by now, and I already told them everything there is to say."

"It's a big story," Sara shrugged. "They're going to run with it." She nodded at the dark television mounted on the wall opposite her bed. "I caught your interview this morning. You look pretty hot on TV."

"It's out of control. Your nurse told me that one of the reporters pretended to be Luther's brother so he could sneak in to interview him last night."

"Tell me about it. You should've heard the noise as the cops were dragging him out. Woke me up."

"I hope they arrested him. Luther was in the OR for eight and a half hours yesterday getting his leg and face put back together. He's got about a mile of wire holding his jaw shut."

"My nurse says he's going to be fine, though." The inflection in her voice made it a question.

"Oh, yeah. He's doing great. They're going to move him to the ward tomorrow. We'll all be going out for pizza in a couple of days. Luther'll just have to eat it through a straw, is all."

Sara's smile faded as she moved her hand to her chest. Her fingers lingered on her gown where the long thoracotomy incision was. "So...it's all over?"

"Absolutely." Jake wheeled his chair closer to Sara's bed. He gave her hand a squeeze. "It's over. We don't have to worry about Harrison Tobacco anymore. They wouldn't dare touch us now. That's where all this publicity is doing some good.

"I've just got to give the police my formal statement about Billy Ray Chance's death, and that'll be it. Nunes says the DA has no interest in pursuing self-defense cases, so once that's done, we can sit back and watch the lawyers tear Big Tobacco apart."

"It's already started." Sara said. "One of the executives at Harrison was arrested yesterday. Some guy named Fowler.

He's apparently going to turn state's evidence. And a bunch of politicians are demanding a federal investigation. I wouldn't be surprised if the President jumped on the bandwagon. From what was in those documents, I can't imagine that Harrison is going to be around much longer." Sara returned Jake's hand-squeeze. "And didn't Harrison make Ease, the brand your grandfather smoked?"

Jake's eyes jumped to Sara's. "You're right. I'd forgotten." A slow smile spread over his face. "That's perfect. That is absolutely perfect."

DURBAN HOUSE

EXCEPTIONAL BOOKS
BY
EXCEPTIONAL WRITERS

Check out these other fine titles by
Durban House at your local book store.

AFTER LIFE LIFE   Don Goldman

BASHA   John Hamilton Lewis

DANGER WITHIN   Mark Danielson

DEADLY ILLUMINATION   Serena Stier

DEATH OF A HEALER   Paul Henry Young

HOUR OF THE WOLVES   Stephane Daimlen-Völs

A HOUSTON WEEKEND   Orville Palmer

JOHNNIE RAY & MISS KILGALLEN   Bonnie Hearn Hill & Larry Hill

THE LATERAL LINE   Robert Middlemiss

LETHAL CURE   Kurt Popke

THE MEDUSA STRAIN   Chris Holmes

MR. IRRELEVANT   Jerry Marshall

OPAL EYE DEVIL   John Hamilton Lewis

PRIVATE JUSTICE   Richard Sand

ROADHOUSE BLUES   Baron Birtcher

RUBY TUESDAY   Baron Birtcher

SAMSARA   John Hamilton Lewis

SECRET OF THE SCROLL   Chester D. Campbell

SECRETS ARE ANONYMOUS   Frederick L. Cullen

THE SERIAL KILLER'S DIET BOOK   Kevin Mark Postupack

THE STREET OF FOUR WINDS   Andrew Lazarus

TUNNEL RUNNER   Richard Sand

WHAT GOES AROUND   Don Goldman

Nonfiction

FISH HEADS, RICE, RICE WINE & WAR: A VIETNAM PARADOX

Lt. Col. Thomas G. Smith, Ret.

MIDDLE ESSENCE—WOMEN OF WONDER YEARS   Landy Reed

WHITE WITCHDOCTOR   Dr. John A. Hunt

PROTOCOL   Mary Jane McCaffree, Pauline Innis & Katherine Daley Sand

For 25 years, the bible for public relations firms, corporations, embassies, governments and individuals seeking to do business with the Federal government.

AFTER LIFE LIFE   DON GOLDMAN

This murder mystery takes place in the afterlife. Andrew Law, Chief Justice of the Texas Supreme Court, is the picture of robust health when he suddenly dies. Upon arriving in the afterlife, Andy discovers he was murdered and his untimely death has some unexpected and far-reaching consequences–a world wide depression among others. There are all sorts of diabolical plots running through his hilariously funny, fast-paced whodunit with an ending that's a surprising double cross.

BASHA   JOHN HAMILTON LEWIS

Set in the world of elite professional tennis and rooted in ancient Middle East hatreds of identity and blood loyalties, Basha is charged with the fiercely competitive nature of professional sports and the dangers of terrorism. An already simmering Middle East begins to boil and CIA Station Chief Grant Corbet must track down the highly successful terrorist, Basha. In a deadly race against time, Grant hunts the illusive killer only to see his worst nightmare realized.

DANGER WITHIN   MARK DANIELSON

Over 100 feet down in cold ocean waters lies the wreck of pilot Kevin Hamilton's DC-10. In it are secrets which someone is desperate to keep. When the Navy sends a team of divers from the Explosives Ordinance Division, a mysterious explosion from the wreck almost destroys the salvage ship. The FBI steps in with Special Agent Mike Pentaglia. Track the life and death of Global Express Flight 3217 inside the gritty world of aviation and discover the shocking cargo that was hidden on its last flight.

DEADLY ILLUMINATION   SERENA STIER

It's summer 1890 in New York City. Florence Tod, an ebullient young woman, must challenge financier, John Pierpont Morgan, to solve a possible murder. J.P.'s librarian has ingested poison embedded in an illumination of a unique Hildegard van Bingen manuscript. Florence and her cousin, Isabella Stewart Gardner, discover the corpse. When Isabella secretly removes a gold tablet from the scene of the crime, she sets off a chain of events that will involve Florence and her in a dangerous conspiracy.

Hour of the Wolves Stephane Daimlen-Völs

After more than three centuries, the *Poisons Affair* remains one of history's great, unsolved mysteries. The worst impulses of human nature—sordid sexual perversion, murderous intrigues, witchcraft, Satanic cults—thrive within the shadows of the Sun King's absolutism and will culminate in the darkest secret of his reign: the infamous *Poisons Affair*, a remarkably complex web of horror, masked by Baroque splendor, luxury and refinement.

A Houston Weekend Orville Palmer

Professor Edward Randa11, not-yet-forty, divorced and separated from his daughters, is leading a solitary, cheerless existence in a university town. At a conference in Houston he runs into his childhood sweetheart. Then she was poverty-stricken, neglected and American Indian. Now she's elegantly attired, driving an expensive Italian car and lives in a millionaires enclave. Will their fortuitous encounter grow into anything meaningful?

Johnnie Ray & Miss Kilgallen Bonnie Hearn Hill & Larry Hill

Johnnie Ray was a sexually conflicted wild man out of control; Dorothy Kilgallen, fifteen years his senior, was the picture of decorum as a Broadway columnist and TV personality. The last thing they needed was to fall in love—with each other. Sex, betrayal, money, drugs, drink and more drink. Together they descended into a nightmare of assassination conspiracies, bizarre suicides and government enemy lists until Dorothy dies…mysteriously. Was it suicide…or murder?

The Lateral Line Robert Middlemiss

Kelly Travett is ready with an Israeli assassination pistol and garlic-coated bullets to kill the woman who tortured and murdered her father. Then the CIA calls with a double warning: she ought to know about Operation Lateral Line and her enemies are expecting her. Revenge is not so simple in the ancient killing alleys of Budapest. There's a Hungarian Chief of Police and his knife and a smiling Russian Mafia boss who has a keen interest in her Israeli pistol…

Lethal Cure Kurt Popke

Dr. Jake Prescott unearths a deadly secret that has one of the most powerful companies in the United States desperate to silence him. A botched attempt to assassinate him gets Jake's wife critically injured and his daughter is kidnaped. In a more successful attempt to get rid of Jake his enemies frame him for the murder of their own hit man. Hopelessly outgunned, Jake turns to a former patient, a retired PI, for help. Together they match wits with the cold-blooded assassin hired to eliminate Jake and his family.

The Medusa Strain Chris Holmes

A gripping tale of bio-terrorism that stunningly portrays the dangers of chemical warfare in ways nonfiction never could. When an Iraqi scientist full of hatred for America breeds a deadly form of anthrax and a diabolical means to initiate an epidemic, not even the First Family is immune. Will America's premier anthrax researcher devise a bio-weapon in time to save the U.S. from extinction?

Private Justice Richard Sand
winner of the Ben Franklin Award for Best Mystery 2002

After taking brutal revenge for the murder of his twin brother, Lucas Rook leaves the NYPD to work for others who crave justice outside the law when the system fails them. Rook's dark journey takes him on a race to find a killer whose appetite is growing. A little girl turns up dead. And then another and another. The nightmare is on him fast. The piano player has monstrous hands; the Medical Examiner is a goulish dwarf; an investigator kills himself. Betrayal and intrigue is added to the deadly mix as the story careens toward its startling end.

RUBY TUESDAY   BARON BIRTCHER
Mike Travis sails his yacht to Kona, Hawaii expecting to put LA Homicide behind him: to let the warm emerald sea wash years of blood from his hands. Instead, he finds his family's home ravaged by shotgun blasts, littered with bodies and trashed with drugs. Then things get worse. A rock star involved in a Wall Street deal masterminded by Travis's brother is one of the victims. Another victim is Ruby, Travis's childhood sweetheart. How was she involved?

SAMSARA   JOHN HAMILTON LEWIS
A thrilling tale of love and violence in Post World War II Hong Kong. Nick Ridley is the survivor of a POW camp in Changi. After the war, he moves to Hong Kong and purchases several U.S. Army surplus C-147's. Years later his Cathay Airlines is a world-class company and he's about to realize his crowning ambition when suddenly his world begins to unravel. When the love of Nick's life is kidnaped, he must once again face the man responsible for the horrors of Changi. An unforgettable climax.

SECRET OF THE SCOLL   CHESTER D. CAMPBELL
Colonel Greg McKenzie has unknowingly smuggled a first century Hebrew scroll out of Israel into the U.S. Someone wants it back. McKenzie's wife Jill is taken hostage: her life for the scroll. A Nashville wants to know why McKenzie hasn't filed a missing persons report on his "missing" wife. And the secret of the scroll has the potntial to turn the Arab-Israeli disput into a raging holocaust.

SECRETS ARE ANONYMOUS   FREDERICK L. CULLEN
Bexley, Ohio is a quiet, unremarkable town in the heartland of American. But its citizens have secrets and amitions which they reveal in interesting ways: chat rooms, instant messaging, e-mails, hypnosis, newspaper articles, letters to the editor, answering machines, video tapes, eavesdropping, vanity plates and coctail napkins. All-American "unremarkable" Bexley is suddenly beseiged by The National Security Agency, the FBI, the Securities and Exchange Commission and a drug cartel—and the guy who runs the ice cream parlor lets them all use the restroom—at a price. What's going on?

THE SERIAL KILLER'S DIET BOOK   KEVIN MARK POSTUPACK
finalist in *ForeWord Magazine's* Fiction Book of the Year
Fred Orbis is fat—very fat—but will soon discover the ultimate diet. Devon DeGroot is on the trail of a homicidal maniac who prowls Manhattan with meatballs, bologna and egg salad—taunting him about the body count in *Finnegans Wakean.* Darby Montana, one of the world's richest women, wants a new set of genes to alter a face and body so homely not even plastic surgery could help. Mr. Monde is the Devil in the market for a soul or two. It's a Faustian satire on God and the Devil, Heaven and Hell, beauty and the best-seller list.

THE STREET OF FOUR WINDS   ANDREW LAZARUS
Paris—just after World War II. On the Left Bank, Americans seek a way to express their dreams, delights and disappointments in a way very different from pre-war ex-patriots. Tom Cortell is a tough, intellectual journalist disarmed by three women-French, British and American. Along with him is a gallery of international characters who lead a merry and sometimes desperate chase between Pairs, Switzerland and Spain to a final, liberating and often tragic end of their European wanderings in search of themselves.

WHAT GOES AROUND   DON GOLDMAN
finalist in *ForeWord Magazine's* Fiction Book of the Year
Ten years ago, Ray Banno was vice president of a California bank when his boss, Andre Rhodes, framed him for bank fraud. Now, he has his new identity, a new face and a new life in medical research. He's on the verge of finding a cure for a deadly disease when he's chosen as a juror in the bank fraud trial of Andre Rhodes. Should he take revenge? Meanwhile, Rhodes is about to gain financial control of Banno's laboratory in order to destroy Banno's work

Nonfiction

FISH HEADS, RICE, RICE WINE & WAR: A VIETNAM PARADOX
LT. COL. THOMAS G. SMITH, RET.
This memoir set in the Central Highlands of Vietnam, 1966–1969, draws on the intensely human and humourous sides of the strangest and most misunderstood war in which American soldiers were ever committed. Lt. Col. Smith offers a powerful and poignant insider's view of American soldiers at their most heroic who in the midst of the blood and guts of war always find the means to laugh.

MIDDLE ESSENCE—WOMEN OF WONDER YEARS   LANDY REED
Here is a roadmap and a companion to what can be the most profoundly significant and richest years of a woman's life. For every woman approaching, at, or beyond midlife, this guide is rich with stories of real women in real circumstances who find they have a second chance-a time when women blossom rather than fade. Gain a new understanding of how to move beyond myths of aging; address midlife transitions head on; discover new power and potential; and emerge with a stronger sense of self

WHITE WITCHDOCTOR   DR. JOHN A.HUNT
Dr. Hunt's skillful blending of emotionally charged events with dispassionate storytelling makes this a truly compelling and powerful memoire of one white surgeon's fight to help save his beloved country of South Africa. The reader is drawn in the by South African culture, folkways and mores, the political upheaval and race relations. It is a memorable and fascinating look at a turbulent era during the time of Apartheid.

PROTOCOL   Mary Jane McCaffree, Pauline Innis & Katherine Daley Sand
For 25 years, the bible for public relations firms, corporations, embassies, governments and individuals seeking to do business with the Federal government.
This book contains a wealth of detail on every conceivable question, from titles and forms of address to ceremonies and flg etiquette. The authors are to be complimented for bringing us partially up to date in a final chapter on Women in Official and Public Life.
—Department of State Newsletter